A BURIED LIE

Roberta Isleib

BERKLEY PRIME CRIME, NEW YORK

A BURIED LIE

A Berkley Prime Crime Book / published by arrangement with the author

PRINTING HISTORY
Berkley Prime Crime mass-market edition / May 2003

ISBN: 0-425-18996-1

Berkley Prime Crime Books are published
by The Berkley Publishing Group,
a division of Penguin Group (USA) Inc.,
375 Hudson Street, New York, New York 10014.
The name BERKLEY PRIME CRIME and the
BERKLEY PRIME CRIME design are trademarks
belonging to Penguin Group (USA) Inc.

PRINTED IN THE UNITED STATES OF AMERICA

10 9 8 7 6 5 4 3 2 1

To the sweet family who made me—
Janet, Robert, Susan, Douglas, Martha

Many thanks to the people who helped with this project:

Lisa Hackney and Kate Golden, for a wonderful two-day experience and gracious answers to my questions about life on the LPGA Tour; my pro-am playing partners and the ShopRite LPGA volunteers.

Heather Brown for her expertise as tour guide and blackjack player; Drs. Dan Abrahamson and Michael Schwartzchild from the Connecticut Psychological Association for their input on psychology and ethics; my friendly drug company moles.

The Shoreline Writers' Group, Chris Falcone, Angelo Pompano, Liz Cippolina, Karen Olson, Cindy Warm, Jen Just, Susan Etkind; other friends and friendly readers, Sue Repko, Diane Burbank, Jane Novick, Steve Hamilton, Phyllis Kaletsky.

The mystery writers' community, including members of Murder Must Advertise, MWA, and DorothyL lists; my hometown, including the Scranton Library and RJ Julia's, for its incredible support.

My golfing buddies at Madison Country Club; Don Gliha, who did his best.

Paige Wheeler, Cindy Hwang, and the crackerjack staff at Berkley.

As always, to my family for their love and enthusiasm, especially John, life partner and caddie extraordinaire.

"A buried lie limits your options."

Amy Alcott's Guide to Women's Golf

Glossary

Approach Shot: a golf shot used to reach the green, generally demanding accuracy rather than distance

Back nine: second half of the eighteen-hole golf course; usually holes ten through eighteen

Birdie: a score of one stroke fewer than par for the hole

Bogey: a score of one stroke over par for the hole; double bogey is two over par; triple bogey is three over

Bump-and-run: chip shot for which the aim is to get the ball running quickly along the ground toward the green

Bunker: a depression containing sand; also called a sand trap or trap

Caddie: person designated or hired to carry the golfer's bag and advise him/her on golf course strategy, also called a looper

Card: status that allows the golfer to compete on the PGA or LPGA Tour

Chip: a short, lofted golf shot used to reach the green from a relatively close position

Chunk: to strike the ground inadvertently before hitting the ball; similar to chili-dipping, dubbing, and hitting it fat

Collar: the fringe of grass surrounding the perimeter of the green

Cup: the plastic cylinder lining the inside of the hole; the hole itself

Cut: the point halfway through a tournament at which the number of competitors is reduced based on their cumulative scores

Divot: a gouge in the turf resulting from a golf shot; also, the chunk of turf that was gouged out

Draw: a golf shot that starts out straight and turns slightly left as it lands (for a right-hander); a draw generally provides more distance than a straight shot or a slice

Drive: the shot used to begin the hole from the tee box, often using the longest club, the driver

Eagle: a score of two strokes under par for the hole

Exempt status: allows a golfer to play in official LPGA tournaments without qualifying in Monday rounds; exemptions are based on past performance (in Q-school, previous tournaments, or position on the money list)

Fade: shot that turns slightly from left to right at the end of its trajectory (right-handers)

Fairway: the expanse of short grass between each hole's tee and putting green, excluding the rough and hazards

Fat: a shot struck behind the ball that results in a short, high trajectory

Flag: the pennant attached to a pole used to mark the location of the cup on the green; also known as the pin

Front nine: the first nine holes of a golf course

Futures Tour: a less prestigious and lucrative tour that grooms golfers for the LPGA Tour

Gallery: a group of fans gathered to watch golfers play

Green: the part of the golf course where the grass is cut shortest; only a putter may be used to advance the ball to the hole

Green in regulation: reaching the green using the number of strokes considered par for the hole; one is regulation for a par three, two for a par four, three for a par five.

Hacker: an amateur player, generally one who lacks proficiency; also called a duffer

Hazard: an obstacle that can hinder the progress of the ball toward the green; includes bodies of water, bunkers, marshy areas, etc.

Hook: a shot that starts out straight, then curves strongly to the left (right-handers)

Irons: golf clubs used to hit shorter shots than woods; golfers generally carry long and short irons, one (longest) through nine (shortest)

Lag putt: a long putt hit with the intention of leaving the ball a short (tap-in) distance from the hole

Leaderboard: display board on which top scoring players in a tournament are listed

Lie: the position of the ball on the course; buried lie: ball hidden in rough or buried in sand, killer lie: extremely challenging position, fried egg lie: all but the top of the ball buried in a sand trap, plugged lie: ball sunk into the surface on which it lands

Looper: caddie

Money list: cumulative record of which golfers have earned money in the official tournaments and how much

Out of bounds: a ball hit outside of the legal boundary of the golf course, which results in a two-stroke penalty for the golfer; also called OB

Pairings sheet: sheet listing which golfers will be paired together for the round

Par: the number of strokes set as the standard for a hole or for an entire course

Pin: the flagstick

Pin high: the ball has come to rest on the green level with the flagstick

Pitch: a short, lofted shot most often taken with a wedge

Preshot routine: a set of thoughts and actions put into practice before each shot

Pull hook: a shot that turns abruptly left (for right-handers)

Putt: a stroke using a putter on the green intended to advance the ball toward the hole

Qualifying school (Q-school): a series of rounds of golf played in the fall, which produces a small number of top players who will be eligible to play on the LPGA Tour the following year

Rainmaker: an unusually high shot

Range: a practice area

Round: eighteen holes of golf

Rough: the area of the golf course along the sides of the fairway that is not closely mown; the grass in the rough

Scramble: team format in which each player hits a shot from the team's best ball after every stroke until the ball is holed out

Shank: a faulty golf shot hit off the shank or hosel of the club that generally travels sharply right

Short game: golf shots used when the golfer is within 100 yards or so of the green, including pitches, chips, bump-and-run shots, putts

Skull: a short swing that hits the top half of the ball and results in a line-drive trajectory

Slice: a golf shot that starts out straight and curves to the right (for right-handers)

Solheim Cup: competition pitting the best twelve U.S. golfers against an international team; occurs every two years; equivalent to the Ryder Cup for men

Swing thought: a simple thought used before hitting a shot intended to distract the golfer from mental chatter

Tee: the area of the golf hole designated as the starting point, delineated by tee markers, behind which the golfer must set up

Tour card: see **Card**

Top: to hit only the top portion of the golf ball, generally resulting in a ground ball

Trap: see **Bunker**

Two-putt: taking two shots to get the ball in the cup after hitting the green; a hole's par assumes two putts as the norm

Wedge: a short iron used to approach the green

Woods: golf clubs with long shafts and rounded heads used for longer distance than irons; the longest-shafted club with the largest head used on the tee is called the driver

Yips: a condition involving nervous hand movements that result in missed putts

Yardage book: a booklet put together by golfers, caddies, or golf course management describing topography and distances on the course

Chapter 1

Last October, luck finally became a lady. When my birdie putt dropped on the seventy-second hole at qualifying school, I wanted to pump the hand of everyone I saw. I wanted to dance the rookie rumba. I wanted to pass out cigars with pink bands circling them that read "It's a golfer!"

That putt earned me partially exempt status on the LPGA Tour. Which translated into seven or eight sure entries into tournaments, with possibilities the rest of the season for last-minute openings or success in the crapshoot called the Monday qualifying rounds.

But fewer spots opened up this summer than I'd expected. So just recently, I caught myself hoping a couple of the regular players would fall ill. Not fatally ill, maybe a light case of chicken pox or measles or even poison ivy. Something where they'd be contagious to the other girls and scratching too hard to swing their golf clubs anyway.

Needless to say, when the stomach flu laid out seven of the top twenty money winners the week of the ShopRite LPGA Classic, and they called me to fill in at the professional-amateur tournament, I jumped on the opportunity. My dance card was not full.

A full week's gig situated twenty miles from Atlantic City—oh baby. I could feel Lady Luck's hot breath on my dice again. Even though the pro-am involved two long days of coddling anxious hackers through thirty-six holes of golf, it also translated into exposure, extra practice, and goodwill with my bag sponsor, Birdie Girl. The goodwill was critical, since I hadn't made a dime in my six outings on the Tour so far. Which meant that the Birdie Girl embroidered in fancy script down the side of my golf bag was not an outstanding advertisement for their product. From their perspective, so far the money had flowed in one direction only—to me. Here was my chance to reverse that trend.

I swore I would not bitch about the oppressive heat or the bumper crop of greenhead flies—flying teeth, one of the girls called them. Even if the blood ran down my legs and soaked my white FootJoys to maroon, I would not complain. The first day's outing would give me another look at the golf course where the official tournament would be held. The second day, although not on the tournament course, would put enough cash in my pocket to pay my friend Laura's caddie fees and buy dinner someplace other than Mickey D's.

Drawing Erica LeBoutillier's name as a playing partner—that seemed lucky, too. Not that I had anything against men. But they did tend to wear on me, with their macho need to outhit me on every tee, their constant underclubbing based on overestimation of their own abilities, and then their outraged disappointment with the results. Plus, in my previous incarnation as a PGA Tour caddie, I'd lived through a lifetime's worth of boasting, temper tantrums, and worst of all, pinched rumps, from the amateur men.

On the first tee, the pro-am photographer arranged my teammates in a group shot, juggling their placement so the potentially embarrassing height differences were minimized. He put the tall, skinny guy on one end, the medium-sized older man in the middle, and then the roly-poly fellow beside Erica. I noticed right away how he leaned in toward her, and then how she finessed pulling away. She was subtle—tucking in her white Lizgolf shirt with one hand and smoothing her auburn pageboy with the other. But in the end, she'd created a comfortable space between them.

Then I introduced myself and posed for individual photographs with all four—Erica, plus the two physicians and a Ph.D.—all employees of Meditron Pharmaceuticals, I was informed. Clutching enormous drivers, with their free hands draped around me, the men insisted I call them Hugh, Travis, and Roger. I didn't need an advanced degree to understand that this afternoon's informality was a special exception. Besides, I'd never met a doctor who didn't have the confidence of Magellan; I hated to see how that inflated conviction of their own importance would translate into choosing shots in our team event.

A woman, I thought, might be different. Maybe a little less arrogant, a bit more flexible, and a lot less trouble.

The problems started early, on the first hole of the Bay Course at the Seaview Marriott. We were playing a scramble; all the teammates hit their shots, then proceeded as a group to the one we identified as the best. We repeated the same process from that point, until we holed the putt. Amateurs often groused that for the amount they'd paid for this outing, they should be allowed to play their own balls. We players thanked God and the tournament officials for the truncated format.

"On the tee, Dr. Hugh Gladstone," bellowed the starter.

The silver-haired, medium-sized man stepped onto the tee box. He wore a silver straw cowboy hat and coordinated Bobby Jones golf clothes that had to have cost more than I'd make this whole week. Barring some miracle in which I won the damn tournament. Hugh Gladstone waggled a driver with a head the size of a car muffler. Then he looped the club back, lurched at the ball, and sent it skittering across the access road that lined the right side of the fairway.

"Nice shot, Doctor," hooted Dr. Travis Smith, the short, round man whose face glistened with perspiration just from mounting the steps to the tee box. His own drive bounded into the knee-high rough in front of the left fairway bunker. Finally, Roger Ranz, Ph.D., the beanpole in canary yellow trousers, came as close as he could to missing the ball altogether.

"Just some first tee jitters," I said, in what I hoped was a reassuring but not condescending tone. "We'll settle down."

"Your professional today, from Myrtle Beach, South Carolina, Cassandra Burdette," hollered the starter. That intro still gave me a thrill. I belted a textbook drive 240 yards straight out.

"Looks like you'll be using that one," cracked Diana Adams, a Tour veteran who'd be playing with the group behind us. Erica hit her drive without incident from the red tees, and we marched to my ball. The next shot should have been, at least for me, a bread-and-butter nine-iron approach into the green, even with a stiff breeze picking up off the bay.

"What are you hitting?" asked Dr. Gladstone.

"Nine iron."

"Give me the wedge," he told his caddie in an imperious tone.

"Pompous ass," muttered my caddie for the day.

I was not surprised when Hugh's ball landed well short

of the green. Then the rest of us hit in what Travis had determined was our lucky order. Still no balls on the putting surface, including mine. Now I had my money on a simple pitch shot from the right rough. Chip up close, sink the putt, and slink off grateful for a par. Instead, both the doctors insisted we attack the green from the ball in the left front bunker.

"It's an uphill lie, pin high, and a lot closer," said Hugh.

"Lie, schmie," said Travis. "We get to place it any way we like. But I agree with you. We can get a lot closer to the pin from a bunker than from the rough."

I assumed they'd heard TV announcers talk about how much professional golfers liked hitting out of a sand trap. Why not them, too? Why not? Because the professionals had spent hours practicing in bunkers and the amateurs, next to none. But I kept my mouth shut. We Tour rookies had had a little seminar on handling the amateurs at the beginning of the season.

"It's their day," said the official in charge. "Don't argue, don't criticize, and don't protest if they don't take your suggestions."

"I like to tell them: I can putt from anywhere," said Diana Adams, who was helping run the seminar. "Fact is, we don't know where the pin placements will be during tournament, so what difference does it make which putt you choose? Lighten it up out there, and try to help them have some fun. My worst experiences have been with teams who are bent on winning."

Hugh Gladstone took an enormous backswing and picked his ball clean. The shot screamed over the green and whistled past Dottie Pepper, waggling her driver on the second tee. He scowled and slammed his club against his bag. Then Travis shanked his ball dead right into the twin trap on the opposite side of the fairway. Finally, Roger Ranz, Ph.D., buried his wedge so deep in the trap, the ball failed to advance at all.

"Come back next spring," said Travis. "That ball might make an appearance after the frosts heave it out." Roger curled his lips into a chilly smile.

Having fun with this crew was not going to be easy.

Erica snickered behind me. "Dodos," she said. "It's a miracle Meditron hasn't sunk under the combined weight of them. Doesn't it make you wonder which year in medical school they teach them the doctrine of infallibility?"

I fought not to laugh out loud.

Erica rehearsed her shot outside the sand trap: weight positioned forward, steep backswing, good follow-through. In her practice swing, she looked like the polished amateur golfer she'd told me she was. Then she dug her feet shoelace deep into the bunker, ready to splash her ball out onto the green. But now she was tense, man, forearms like concrete and mind obviously reeling. Watching her freeze up was enough to get my mind off my own problems, of which there were plenty. Problem one being this, my rookie year on the LPGA Tour, and I hadn't made a damned cut yet.

"You can do it," I called out to Erica. "Take some sand and follow through." You could almost never go wrong telling someone to follow through. In life, as well as the golf swing. At last she swung, producing an ugly chunk that sank deep in the bunker lip.

I marveled at the difference between her practice shot and the real thing. Joe Lancaster, my friend and psychological consultant, would have said Erica did not have her mind on golf. She lost her focus. And silly as it might sound, you simply cannot play a decent round of golf with your brain wound up about something else. You'd have thought she'd be there one hundred percent, her company having spent in the neighborhood of four thousand big ones for her pro-am spot. A fact my own mother found incomprehensible.

"People are spending four thousand dollars to play with

you?" Mom had asked. Good old Mom, the human weed-
whacker. She could spot and lop off a fledgling shoot of
self-esteem without even blinking. "How much of that do
you get?"

"None, Mom. It's to give something back to the Tour."

"When does the part come where you get paid? I've
never heard of a job where you don't earn anything. You
might as well come home and work with me at Littles'.
You'd have to start out busing tables, but waitress shifts
always open up. And you wouldn't have all those hotel
bills to pay, living here at home."

I glanced over at Erica, who remained frozen in the
bunker. Her coworkers paced in annoyance around the
flagstick. Back down the fairway, I saw Diana Adams's
foursome stumping vigorously in our direction.

"My turn," I called out in a cheery voice and offered
her a hand out of the trap. I took a quick swing and
plopped the ball onto the green, twenty feet from the hole.
With that result, I'd be spending some extra time in the
practice bunker later this afternoon. We putted out for
bogey and set off for the second hole.

"One stroke over par already," said Hugh. "A team with
a bogey on their card doesn't have a prayer of winning."

"Two thirds of the teams that have come through so far
made birdie," announced the eager volunteer stationed
next to the green. Hugh glared in his direction.

"You should have just picked your ball up," said Travis
to Erica. "We're falling behind. We're playing a damn
scramble."

"You should have never insisted we play out of the
damn trap," she answered. "There's only one professional
in this foursome, and it isn't you."

I had to agree with her assessment, but I kept my
thoughts to myself. My confidence that my luck had
changed was draining away. I could almost hear my father's voice. Not the tight voice he used on the bimonthly

phone conversations we'd had over the last fifteen years. The voice I remembered as a kid, deep and warm, and always teaching.

"Don't make assumptions about luck," he told me when I was thirteen. "Lots of times I thought I got lucky because something happened. Then it turned out I would have been luckier if it never occurred. Or the other way around."

Looking back, I didn't know how to take that. Things were real bad with him and Mom around the time he passed out this advice. So I had to assume he *thought* he'd been lucky to marry her, and then later he found out different. In which case, as the product of their unhappy union, I was part of the bad luck. Or maybe he meant the head pro job he didn't get hired for, which seemed unlucky as hell that summer. But his rejection paved the way for him blowing town, leaving Mom and me and their miserable marriage behind him.

Roger's scolding brought me back into the present. "Cut the squabbling, children," he said to Erica and Travis.

"All four of you work for Meditron?" I asked, hoping to divert the conversation onto a less contentious topic.

"I work, Roger crunches numbers, and Travis surfs for new porn sites and cures for hemorrhoids," Erica said, sidestepping to avoid the stab of Travis's sand wedge. I noticed she'd left Hugh Gladstone out of her description altogether.

"It's a drug company?" I asked. "Which drugs do you sell?"

"The usual, antidiarrhea, antidepressant, antiemetic, antibiotic. You name it, we eliminate it," said Travis. "Hugh here, though it's hard to imagine with him wearing a silver cowboy hat, is our honcho. Neuroscience Division vice president."

Hugh gave a regal nod. "I'm the project director,"

Travis continued. "And Roger's our biostatistician. We'd be lost without him." Now Roger smiled, too.

The three men and I hit from the back tees and moved ahead to where Erica waited. I didn't think the tension in her forearms and shoulders was purely a function of playing in the tournament. Maybe related to the pressures of a big job? Clinical scientist, she'd called herself.

"These guys tell other people how to collect the data, then I tell them what it means," she'd said. They had laughed, but without any warmth. Maybe they'd heard that joke one too many times.

As I'd seen in the sand trap, Erica's practice swing was fluid and flawless. Then she yanked the real drive deep into the tall rough growing on mounds along the left side of the hole. She cursed under her breath.

"What's your company working on now?" I asked as we walked down the fairway.

"There's a whole formulary," said Hugh. "But this team," he waved to include the other three, "has been developing a treatment for Alzheimer's disease."

"Wow. That sounds important."

"It will be huge," said Travis. "If you don't own Meditron stock, you might want to look into it."

Hugh turned toward him and frowned furiously.

"Hey, just a tip from a friendly caddie," said Travis, holding his palms up in an *I didn't do anything wrong* gesture.

Damn, every conversational avenue in this group felt like a minefield. We stopped beside my drive and waited for the players ahead of us to clear the green.

Hugh pulled a cell phone out of his back pocket. "I'm going to call Regulatory. Maybe there's some news."

He listened to a series of messages, his face reflecting their content: annoying, silly, routine, and suddenly, riveting. "The report should be back by next week," he called to the others. "It looks great!"

Erica turned her back to the doctors and with a beautiful, smooth swing, her ball arched up toward the green. As she handed her club back to her caddie, she wiped a tear away.

An unusual reaction to an opportunity for a birdie putt, I thought.

Chapter 2

We finished the round at thirteen under par—a damn good outcome, we all agreed. After the rough beginning, the team had really begun to click. Every one of the men contributed good shots, and Erica and I knocked in putts from all over the green. If they worked the way they played, I could see the whole gamut of possibilities with this foursome—from angry backstabbing when mistakes were made to an enormous surge of energy and enthusiasm when things went well. Like making twelve birdies and an eagle. Or discovering the cure for Alzheimer's.

Now they stood around the leaderboard studying the scores, reviewing high points of the round, and trying to talk me into joining them for a victory dinner at the Showboat Casino. I waved them off with a "Maybe I'll catch up with you later" and went to work on putting and then sand shots at the practice green.

When it got too dark to see the holes, I left my golf

bag at the bag drop next to my team's stack of equipment.
I coughed up ten bucks to make sure the bag boy gave
our stuff priority treatment. A flash of my LPGA money
clip ID got me past the volunteer guarding the locker
room. I could see her mind churning as she waved me by.
*Is this someone famous? Someone I've even heard of?
Someone about to break through?* Probably all answered
in the negative.

Given my group's late starting time and my extra practice, the locker room was deserted. The brass plates on
the lockers were covered with cardboard name tags written in fancy calligraphy. I found mine between Pat Bradley, proud owner of thirty-one career victories and a spot
in the LPGA Hall of Fame, and Brandie Burton, five-time
Tour winner. Sheesh, what the hell was I doing here?
Maybe some of their magic would rub off on me this
week.

I dawdled in the shower. Should I join the Meditron
crowd for dinner or grab a pizza and retreat to my low-
budget motel? I wasn't quite comfortable with the amateurs' hunger to crawl into my professional golfer's skin.
On the other hand, even if they considered me their mas-
cot of the week, a free meal was a free meal. And it would
be lonely here until Thursday night when my caddie/
friend, Laura, and Joe Lancaster arrived in town.

In front of the mirror next to a barber chair, I made a
halfhearted attempt to blow-dry my curls into submission.
I considered signing up for the Tour stylist at the next
tournament stop, but thirty-five dollars for a trim would
strain the budget. There were definitely higher priorities,
like food and Budweiser. I kicked at the clumps of hair
lying around the chair. Some of it was dark brown, wavy,
and streaked with gray—Nancy Lopez? And some stick-
straight and blond—Annika Sorenstam? Maybe if I kept
a few strands tucked away in a locket, my fairways and
greens in regulation statistics would shoot up.

I paid two bucks to park in the back lot of the Showboat Casino. Where the Music Is Jumping, the Slots are Pumping, and the Party Has Just Begun, read the sign at the entrance. Not so for half the senior citizen population of New Jersey, who appeared to be leaving the party as I walked in. Old people of every description tottered out on canes, including one that appeared to be a well-used field hockey stick. Then came the less mobile: people in walkers, people in wheelchairs, people dragging their oxygen tanks behind them like canister vacuum cleaners. Some stood in line to purchase Coke and potato chips at the vending machines that crowded the corridor to the casino exit. Others waited for the tour buses that would return them to what I pictured as dreary apartments, made drearier by tonight's depletion of their Social Security checks.

My pro-am buddies waved me down as soon as I stepped into the restaurant. In sharp contrast to the seniors I'd seen leaving the casino, they were pumped high by having coalesced into a leaderboard-quality team by the end of the day's round. And probably by their expected coup in the pharmaceutical market, too. Hugh leaped to his feet and pulled out a chair for me. He looked a lot less silly in a navy blazer and chinos than he had in his silver golf duds.

"What are you drinking, Cassandra?" he asked.

"A Bud Light will be fine." Another suggestion by the LPGA powers that be: we were now representing the most prestigious women's golf organization in the world. Inebriation and other sloppy conduct around the amateurs and sponsors were heavily frowned upon. My compromise: I vowed to skip the hard stuff and order only light beer instead of high-test.

"Cassie, now that you've studied it all day, do you have any tips about straightening out my cut?" asked Roger, as soon as I'd taken my seat.

I kept my face straight. A ball flight curving right was

called a slice or fade, a cut only if you'd hit it that way intentionally. Roger's shots bore a close resemblance to a boomerang. His caddie had spent most of the day in the woods searching for Titleist Pro VIs, one of the most expensive balls in golf in the neighborhood of five bucks a pop. Hard to imagine he planned on that. Some teaching professional could have his lifetime annuity assured if he took Roger on.

"For God's sake, don't bore her with your miserable game," said Travis. "She's not billing us by the hour, she's our guest tonight." Roger's hopeful smile stiffened.

"Maybe we could take a look on the range after your round tomorrow," I said. "Who are you guys playing with in the morning?"

"Annie Strauss," said Erica.

"You'll have a lot of fun with her," I said. "She's a sweetheart. And a solid player, too."

"You were more than solid, you were incredible out there on the back nine," said Travis, as the waiter set my beer down on the table. "You're going to be great this week. I wouldn't be surprised if you won the whole GD thing." I *had* sunk four or five long putts, but I attributed the lion's share of his praise to the effect of his previous cocktails.

"Easy does it," said Erica. "It won't help her to get that far ahead of herself." I nodded my thanks.

"Let's have a toast to a great day!" said Travis. We drank.

"And to a great American golfer with a bright future," said Hugh, raising his glass of Glenlivet. The guy was beginning to grow on me.

"Let's drink to Cassie, too," said Travis.

"Thanks a lot, pal," I said. The others laughed, and Roger flagged down the waiter to order more drinks and an assortment of Cajun-style appetizers.

"On a serious note, let's raise a glass to the end of the

agony of Alzheimer's disease," said Hugh. He held up his scotch again. "To seeing the light at the end of the tunnel."

"And a toast to fat stock portfolios," said Travis, his words slurring slightly.

Hugh frowned. "We've been over this, Dr. Smith. I asked you not to discuss the finances."

"It's only Cassie," said Travis. He smiled in my direction. "We'll swear her to secrecy."

"I don't have a big-line item in my budget for stocks right now anyway," I added.

"She knows we'd have to kill her if she talked," said Travis. I nodded and laughed again.

Erica looked up from her plate. "I'm aware that you guys are tired of hearing this, but I think we should ask our FDA reviewer to take another look at the liver function test data. I'm still worried about hepatotoxicity."

"We did that. The data look fine. You're out of line here." Hugh's sharp response brought tears to her eyes.

"Erica," said Travis, reaching around me to pat her on the shoulder. "Listen, sweetheart. If we draw their attention to the safety profile, they're liable to ask for more studies. It could be two or three years before we get enough data to satisfy them. And probably with the same outcome."

She shrank away from his touch. "What's two or three years to make sure our product doesn't hurt someone?"

"Boy Scouts' honor." Travis grinned and held up the three fingers of the scout pledge. "I'd have never let the application go out if I had concerns about the safety of the compound. You know that."

"The liver experts were satisfied, for Christ's sake," said Hugh.

"And who paid the liver experts?" Erica demanded. "What do you think they're going to say?"

"This drug is a big deal, huh?" I asked. *Duh*. But growing up with screaming parents, I'd spent a lot of time trying to be the peacemaker.

"This is huge," said Roger. "Every baby boomer who's forgotten where they put their car keys will be rushing to the pharmacy. It'll be like ginkgo biloba, only without the herbal voodoo."

"That's not the point," said Travis. "The point is millions of people suffer from a tragic disease. We have a chance to change that."

"The point is, we've done everything by the book, and you're not going to screw this up now," said Hugh. "Case closed."

The waiter delivered our meals, and we began to eat in silence. "How often do you guys get to play when you're back home?" I asked. As I'd hoped, steering the conversation toward golf lightened the tense mood at the table. Now I could only pray for a quick escape. The emotional price of my free meal had begun to shoot up.

"I need to call Lila Rose," said Erica, pushing her plate away. "She has trouble falling asleep if we don't talk." She pulled her wallet out of her purse, extracted several photographs, and offered them to me. "This is her fifth-grade school picture. And here," she tapped on a snapshot of a blurry figure, "she was the star in the spring play. She didn't forget a single one of her lines. And this is when we went to Steamboat Springs for February school vacation. She'd never been on skis before, but the instructor said she picked it up faster than any kid he'd seen."

I leafed politely through the pictures. "She's adorable."

"Even cuter in person," said Erica, beaming. "She's still got a little of her baby fat, but you can start to see the woman she'll become. I'll be right back."

"Jesus, she acts like she's the only parent in the world," Roger grumbled.

"Give her a break," said Travis. "She doesn't get to see her kid that often."

"Even so, preadolescents are hardly photogenic. You can quote me on that."

I could see that more ruffled feather smoothing was in order. "Do you have children?" I asked Roger.

Travis rolled his eyes. "Here we go."

"A boy," said Roger, ignoring Travis's jab. "He's a good kid. Eighth grade." A small, proud smile broke through his grumpiness. "His mother spoils him, but what can you do?"

"How about you guys?" I asked the other two.

"None that I know of," said Travis with a smirk.

"Grown and gone," said Hugh. He lifted his glass in a mock toast.

"What kind of work do they do?" I asked graciously.

"We're not close. My ex made sure of that."

Okay. Another conversational gambit torpedoed. I was relieved to spot Erica weaving her way back through the nearby tables. She wore fresh lipstick, a puff of sophisticated perfume, and a hard frown that softened slightly once she reached us.

"Let's play a couple of hands of blackjack as long as we're here."

"It's all fixed," protested Roger. "They have it fixed so you can't win."

"That's the slots. Blackjack's different. Come on. I'll show you." Erica herded her reluctant coworkers and me out of the restaurant and into the clatter of the casino. "My friend Lucia should be here tonight. We'll see if she has room at her table." She led us to a secluded room off to one side of the casino and saluted a small Latino woman dressed in a tuxedo shirt with a red bow tie and cummerbund.

"Lucia! How are the cards lying tonight?"

Lucia's laugh was light and musical. "Lucky tonight, my friend. Always lucky for you. Have a seat. How's that beautiful daughter of yours?"

"She's great." Erica squeezed in between an obese man in a Hawaiian shirt and two businessmen. "I took her out to the range for the first time last week. You should see how far she can hit a golf ball." She motioned me to take the seat at the opposite end of the table. "My friends here would like to experience the results of your dealing expertise."

Lucia laughed again. She dealt one card facedown in front of her, then a card to each of the players at the table. "Good luck, Erica's friends."

Erica looked at me across the gaming table. "It's not like playing blackjack at home with the guys. You're not trying to get closest to twenty-one here. Your object is to beat the dealer. No offense, Lucia."

Lucia laughed. "None taken." She dealt second cards faceup to each of us, beginning with an ace of hearts to herself. "Anyone want insurance?" Erica mouthed *no* to me across the table. Lucia dealt Erica an ace on top of her jack and knocked her fist on the table. She began to sweep in the cards and the losing chips, as Erica explained her gambling philosophy.

"You always begin by categorizing your hand and hers, and then parcel out hits and stays accordingly. A basic hand, that's between two and eleven points, is hard to screw up. A small hand is twelve to sixteen; obviously, if you take a hit and get a face card, you lose. You always stay with a big hand, that's seventeen plus."

"And always split aces and eights," said the fat tourist.

"No offense again, but that's bullshit," said Erica. After fifteen minutes of losing hands, the tourist and the businessmen left the table, emptying places for Travis, Roger, and Hugh.

"This is ridiculous. Fifty dollars is my limit," said Roger. "After that, I'm out of here."

"Lighten up," said Travis. "Where's that pretty girl with our drinks?" He waved to a woman carrying a tray of

glasses, dressed in something my mother might have had
me wear to a tap dance recital twenty years ago. But in
this case, two thirds of the square footage of her breasts
was exposed. Designed, I supposed, to encourage tips for
the waitress and gambling risks for the house's benefit.

"Give me a light one," said Erica to Lucia. "A five
would be nice. No one else in my life pays any attention
to my requests."

Hugh glared at her. "Hit me." He scraped the table in
front of Lucia with his index finger and waved over the
scantily clothed waitress. "Could we get some drinks here,
please?"

Lucia dealt another round of cards.

"I'll stay," said Roger.

"Mr. Conservative," said Travis. "I'd hate to see your
retirement portfolio."

Roger's face darkened. "That's not amusing, asshole."

"*Mr.* Asshole to you," Travis replied.

I saw him reach under the table to stroke Erica's thigh.

"Twenty-one," Lucia announced, knocking on the table.

"I'm broke. I'm out of here," said Roger, pushing his
cards toward the dealer and standing up.

"It's not a bad idea to turn in early," I chirped. "You
have another big day coming up. You don't want to let
Annie down. I told her she could expect some great shots
from you all." Truth was, I couldn't wait to turn them
over to her. The road not taken—cold pizza alone in my
motel room—was looking better and better.

"I'm going to play a little longer. I'll see you guys
tomorrow," said Erica. "Cassie, stay for a half hour to
bring me luck?"

"I'll stay with you, babe," Travis said.

"Girl talk," said Erica firmly. "Only Cassie will do."
She winked at me and offered Travis a cheerful smile.

I wanted out, now, but I knew I'd feel bad later about
leaving Erica with Travis. She appeared desperate to

shield herself from his unwelcome attention. So I shifted down to the seat beside her. "Just half an hour then."

"Thanks."

Without returning Erica's smile, Travis scraped his chair away from the table and offered me his hand. "If you get out our way, stop by Meditron, and we'll give you the five-dollar tour." Hugh and Roger nodded without visible enthusiasm. Then the three men left the table and headed out of the casino.

I couldn't see any good coming out of delving further into Meditron business, so I went directly to my fallback topic. "You played really well today after you got warmed up," I told Erica.

"Thanks again. Right now, my game is all potential. I just don't have the time to follow up on it. Hell, I'm supposed to play in the New Jersey Women's Golf Association championship next week, and I've barely swung a club all summer."

"You looked good. You'll be fine." I didn't want to get into counseling her about her game; I'd used all my energy on Roger. "Tell me about your daughter. She's a golfer, too?"

Erica looked sad. "She's ten. She's beautiful. I miss her a lot."

"Where is she?"

"Living with my soon-to-be ex. And it can't be soon enough. That arrogant imbecile wouldn't even let me speak with her tonight. It's not fair, what's going on." She frowned and motioned to Lucia that she would stay with her cards. "I admit I made some serious mistakes. But that rotten son of a bitch managed to hire the slimiest lawyer in the state. Then we ran into an antifeminist buzz saw in the courtroom—drew a judge who gets his rocks off putting women in their place. The result? That bastard has temporary custody of Lila Rose, and I have to ask his permission to see her."

"Sounds tough," I said, now wishing I'd offered tips on her swing. "Anyway, it's really nice that Meditron bought the pro-am spots for you. Nothing like a golf tournament to get your mind off your problems."

"Right," said Erica, her voice hard and flat. "They think they can buy your allegiance with two days on the golf course with the Three Stooges." Then she smiled. "You were the high point, Cassie. I really admire what you're doing."

"Thanks." I grinned back at her. "Obviously you guys work hard, but it looks like you have some fun together, too." Always the optimist.

"You don't know the half of how hard it's been, with the hours we've had to put in lately. I get every other weekend with Lila Rose and dinners on Wednesday. And what am I supposed to tell Hugh? I know I'm the team leader, but may I please leave at five so I can eat supper with my daughter? Not likely." She slugged down the rest of her scotch and knocked on the table. "Let's get out of here." She raked in her chips, threw down a tip for the dealer, and stalked off to the cashier. I followed her down the dim hallway leading to the back parking lot.

"Excuse me." A teenager in an orange halter top and tight jeans stepped in front of us out of the shadows. "Excuse me." She began to cry with a startling intensity.

"What is it? What's wrong?" asked Erica.

"I'm in so much trouble. I don't have any money. I don't know where to go for help. Can you help me?" She sank down at our feet, sobbing.

Erica touched her hair. "Is your family here?" The girl shook her head and continued to sob. Erica took her arm. "Come on. Let's find a place where we can talk."

As we moved down the hallway toward the bathroom, a wedding party blocked our path. The bride wore skintight white satin Capri pants, with only a band of white spandex protecting her boobs from full view of the casino guests. The ample flesh of her belly was left entirely exposed. A floor-length beaded veil and white platform sandals completed her attire. She carried an enormous bouquet of carnations, playing cards glued to flower stems, and large Styrofoam dice.

"Good God," Erica muttered.

"Photo op!" called out the bride. She took a sloppy swig from the champagne bottle her new husband handed to her. "Here's where my sweetie proposed." Using the champagne bottle as a pointer, she posed in front of the Coke machine where we hunched with the distraught teenager. Lightbulbs flashed. The bridal party swept down the hall and into the main casino.

Erica renewed her grip on the girl's arm and ushered her into the bathroom. She sat down next to her on a bench in front of the mirror and stroked her hair until the crying subsided.

"Now, who are you, and what's wrong?"

"I'm Aimee."

"Aimee who?"

"Aimee Joy. Mr. Horton brought me here."

"And who is Mr. Horton?" Aimee burst into another round of hysterical weeping. Erica patted her to calmness a second time.

"He's my English teacher back home in Rye." She gulped and smeared mucus across her cheek with the back of her hand. "He said he'd take me to the boardwalk if I came down here with him." More tears. "He said we'd win the biggest teddy bear I'd ever seen. Instead, we spent the night in a hotel room. . . ." She left the rest to our horrified imaginations.

"How old are you?" asked Erica, her voice shaking with indignation.

"Fifteen." Another flood of tears.

"Where is Mr. Horton now?"

"He went to the men's room. I thought it would be my

chance to get help, but only guys came by. I was afraid to ask one of them. Then I saw you," she looked at Erica through her long, dark lashes, "and I thought maybe you would understand."

"We should call the police," I said.

"No police!" Aimee began to cry again. "I swear he'll kill me if I call the cops. He warned me he would."

"Let's go to my hotel room," said Erica. "I'm staying at Caesar's, just down the block. You go to the bathroom and wash your face. Then we'll go where we can hear ourselves think."

"This doesn't seem like a great idea," I whispered, once the girl had disappeared into a stall. "I really think you should turn this over to the cops. Let them handle it."

"I'm sure I can talk her into phoning her parents once we get out of here."

"The whole thing sounds fishy," I said.

"If this was my daughter, I'd want someone to help her if she needed it. You go on; I'll be fine."

I stood slowly. Maybe she knew better than I. On the other hand, she seemed to feel powerless in every part of her life. I had a hunch that rescuing Aimee was connected to grasping some badly needed control.

"Be careful?"

She nodded. "I'll look for you tomorrow. Good luck with the new team. They can't possibly be as fascinating as we were." She grimaced and turned back to wait for Aimee Joy.

Chapter 3

🚩 **Wednesday** flew by without noticeable incident. Unless you count being snubbed by four men amateurs who made it clear their ideal bonus corporate outing did not consist of playing with a floundering rookie. So I concentrated on staying positive—always good practice for talking yourself through a less than stellar round. "Good swing," "You made a good run at it," "It's okay," I told their impassive faces, even when they shanked their balls into the woods. I tried to ignore their rudeness and just focus on small improvements to my swing tempo.

Sometimes, small improvements can backfire. In this case, the straight drives I'd produced yesterday morphed into pull hooks. And pull hooks meant double time tromping through the tall grass looking for lost balls. We were all relieved when the round ended. I headed over to the practice range to address the case of my missing tee shot and to wait for Roger Ranz and his free golf lesson.

Roger showed around three-thirty, looking as deflated as I felt. Yesterday's yellow slacks had been replaced by lime green. His wavy hair had dissolved into fuzz, and the sun had burned a red slash across the back of his neck.

"How'd it go?" I asked.

"Not too well. We didn't have yesterday's magic. Besides, without Erica, we were at a real disadvantage. She was our best putter—showed everybody the line and the speed. You gals must have had one hell of a winning streak last night."

"Erica didn't show?"

Roger shook his head.

"But we only stayed about forty-five minutes after you left."

Roger shrugged. "Maybe she forgot she had an appointment in divorce court or something. She's been more than a little flaky lately, that's for sure. So, about my cut." He grinned. "I bet you've been thinking about it all day."

I had been thinking about his problem, though probably not in the terms he would have wished. I'd spent enough time watching my friend Laura teach golfers to know that a one-shot lesson rarely hit the mark. The only hope was to offer a simple, small change that couldn't easily become distorted over time in the pupil's mind and body. But first, I'd take one stab at passing him off to someone else.

"You won't like this, but my best advice would be to find a teacher you could work with over a period of time. Then you could go back for help when your game starts to slide. No offense, it happens to everybody, even the professionals. Even me." I laughed. *Ha-ha*.

"I don't have time for that," said Roger firmly. "With things breaking open at Meditron, no one's going to be clocking many leisure hours. I've done some reading about this though. I've been working on a steeper swing plane and a late wrist cock so I'm sure to turn it over on the follow-through."

Oh baby. I was going to need hip boots to wade through this crock. "Why don't you hit a couple for me. Maybe I'll spot something that'll help."

I watched him slash at five balls. "Part of the problem seems to be your tendency to overswing," I told him. "Let's not worry about all the stuff you've been reading, just try this."

I arranged him in his normal stance and had him swing the club with his right foot balanced only on his toes. "If you practice the way this feels now, you'll shorten the swing and improve your timing." I watched him take a fast swipe. "Slow down, for crying out loud. You're not trying to catch a plane." He laughed and swung again.

"Didn't Erica call to let you know she wasn't coming?"

"No," he said. "Am I doing this right? It feels incredibly awkward."

"It'll feel odd until you practice it over and over. Did you guys knock on her door this morning?"

"Our rooms are here at the Marriott," Roger said. "She insisted on staying at Caesar's. She said she loves coming downstairs and seeing who's playing the slots at all hours of the day and night." He shook his head. "I find those people pathetic, but I guess that shows I'm not a gambler. Are you going to the Taste of the LPGA party tonight?"

"Am I going? I'm cooking. Well, I'm a figurehead chef, anyway."

Part of the charitable fund-raising this week involved a huge party at Caesar's: thirty high-powered chefs from across the country offering their prize dishes to patrons who'd paid major bucks to see and be seen. We golfers had been encouraged to show our support in whatever way possible. In my case, since hot dog casserole was the only main dish in my repertoire, I doubted I'd be allowed near any serious food prep.

I glanced at my watch. "In fact, I have to hustle, or I'll be late. Good luck with the swing. I'll look for you at the party."

I hesitated halfway across the range and called back to him. "Do you know Erica's room number?"

"Fifteen-twelve, I think she said."

I stopped at the Fairview Inn to shower and change into a jean skirt and Hawaiian shirt, then drove back into the city. I'd called Erica's room twice without results. The more time I had to think about her skipping the tournament today, the more worried I got. Even if she was unhappy with some of the decisions made by her bosses at Meditron, she struck me as a team player. Not to mention an avid golfer who'd trade her next big promotion for the chance to play with a real up-and-coming LPGA star like Annie Strauss. Add this to my uneasiness last night with Erica's decision to take Aimee Joy back to her room, and I was beginning to wish I'd made a serious stink.

At the hotel reception desk, a snooty clerk dressed in a Roman toga informed me that only guests of the hotel were allowed on the higher floors. So I insinuated myself into a rowdy group of casino refugees and snuck past the security guard and onto the elevator. I hurried down the plushly carpeted hallway of the fifteenth floor and took a right turn at the waterfall dripping over a bust of Caesar's head, as one of the hotel guests had instructed me. Ignoring the Do Not Disturb sign hanging from the knob, I knocked on Erica's door. No response. After several more tries and a final unanswered call from my cell phone to the room, I returned to the reception desk.

"I think my friend's in trouble," I said. "Can you send someone up with me to unlock her door?"

"It's not our policy to interfere with the privacy of our guests," said the clerk, who took his job a little more seriously than his toga seemed to warrant.

"Is it your policy to allow guests who are ill or seriously injured to fend for themselves?"

The clerk fidgeted with his pinky ring and frowned. "I'd better call my supervisor." Ten minutes later, three of us trooped back up the fifteen floors and down the maze of hallways to Erica's room.

"Ms. LeBoutillier, hello! It's the hotel management. Ms. LeBoutillier? Are you feeling all right?" After a period of knocking and calling, the manager gave the clerk his grim approval to unlock the door. The small foyer leading to the room was cold, tundra cold, and quiet except for the smooth hum of the air conditioner. I moved further inside.

"I'll just take a quick look. If she isn't here, we'll go."

Three giant steps into the vestibule, I saw her limp form on the bed.

"Erica! It's Cassie. Are you okay?" The instant I picked up her hand, I knew that she was not. Her skin had the chill and texture of a beached jellyfish.

"What's the matter with her?" asked the reception clerk. I swallowed the wash of bile that had rolled up my throat and managed to shrug.

"We need to call an ambulance." I didn't mention my sick feeling that any help we might offer was way too late.

"Does she have a pulse?" asked the manager. I picked up her wrist a second time and felt for a beat. Nothing. And the hand was ice cold.

"Do you know CPR?" The manager's voice had risen to a frantic screech.

I took a deep breath and stepped closer to Erica's body, stumbling over the clothes she'd had on at the casino last night: a white silk blouse, navy pants, and silver sandals. She appeared to be naked beneath the bedclothes except for a gold pendant that had slid behind her neck. Despite the remaining vestiges of her expertly applied makeup, her face had a waxy blue tone.

"I took the class in high school, but I don't remember anything. I'd do more harm than good." I backed away across the room. I couldn't admit out loud that I lacked the courage to touch Erica's body again, especially lips to clammy lips.

Scowling, the manager pushed the clerk toward Erica and instructed him to pinch her nostrils shut and begin breathing into her mouth. "Call 911, for Christ's sake," he snapped at me.

Within minutes, the room swarmed with the casino security staff, then EMTs, and finally, the police. The desk clerk was relieved of his tepid efforts at CPR. After giving my vital statistics, I was relegated to a stool beside the opulent bathtub and told to wait until I could be questioned.

The blank look in Erica's eyes kept swimming to the front of my mind, bringing waves of nausea with it. I paced. I did yoga breathing. I recited an abridged version of "The Cremation of Sam McGee," my father's favorite poem. Anything to distract myself from the scene in the next room.

After fifteen minutes passed, I'd exhausted my arsenal of mental techniques. I removed a loose towel bar that hung next to the tub and began to practice my golf swing in front of the wall of mirrors. Focus, Cassandra, focus. If I kept my elbow tucked in firmly, I thought I could nip the case of pull hooks in the bud.

The bathroom door swung open with a crash. "Cassandra Burdette?" A middle-aged woman with graying curls, khaki pants, and a winter-weight, blue wool blazer that had to keep her sweating like a pig appeared next to the reflection of me posed in full backswing. "Could I have a minute of your time?"

"Of course," I said, fumbling to replace the towel bar into its slot on the wall. "I'm sorry."

"I'm Detective Caroline Rumson from the Atlantic City Police Department. I understand you found the deceased. You were a friend of hers?"

"A new friend. We actually only met yesterday in the pro-am tournament." With the detective's prodding, I walked through the events of the two days, beginning with the golf outing and ending with my decision to check on Erica this evening.

"Who do you think killed her?" I asked. Having stumbled across two murdered corpses in the last year, I no longer assumed any death to be from natural causes.

Detective Rumson's eyes narrowed. "What makes you think she was murdered?"

I described the tension I'd noticed between the Meditron players, Erica's trouble with her husband and their angry divorce proceedings, and the appearance of Aimee Joy. "Will there be an autopsy?"

She ignored my question. "So you'd never seen this Aimee Joy before?"

I shook my head no.

"How old would you say she was?"

"She told us she was fifteen. I remembered thinking she looked older. But she had on a lot of makeup. The way girls dress today, it gets hard to tell. They leave hardly anything to the imagination." I knew I was babbling, but I couldn't stop.

"Did Erica say anything to you about any medicine she was taking?"

Apparently Detective Rumson was not interested in my treatise on the deterioration of teenage values.

"No, but again, we barely knew each other. Did you find something in the room?"

The detective brushed a clump of curls off her face and shoved her notebook into the pocket of her blazer. "Look.

We don't have a definitive answer yet. But off the top of my head, it appears to be a straightforward suicide. We found an empty bottle of pills on the floor beside the bed and no signs of foul play."

"But what about the girl?"

"We'll look into all of it. In the meanwhile, you're free to go." She scribbled my cell phone number on her pad and passed me one of her cards. "We'll call you if we have more questions. Thanks for your help."

She put a firm hand on the small of my back and guided me through the entranceway and into the hall. The sharp click of Erica's door closing echoed down the empty corridor.

Chapter 4

◁Ò **The** spacious vestibule outside the ballroom was crammed with partygoers, most in extravagant formal attire. Feeling dowdy and underdressed did not enhance my enthusiasm for the night's event. I skulked around the hors d'oeuvres table, stunned by the discovery of Erica's dead body. And somehow, ravenous. I found only empty shrimp tails and a few limp stalks of celery.

The main ballroom was even more crowded, with the clientele serenaded by an ear-splitting, easy listening band. They were crooning a smaltzy rendition of "Feelings" at top volume as I walked in. I located my evening's assignment, a booth sponsored by an Italian restaurant from New York City called Mama Roseata's. Which sounded more like a disease than a gourmet hot spot. I pinned on a golf ball–shaped name tag, donned a tissue paper chef's hat, an apron, and a frozen smile, and took my place behind their table. The chef's signature dish, macaroni in a rich white sauce, studded with lobster chunks the size of small plums, was to be presented in martini glasses. A large, sweating man in a white uniform explained my job: stab a star-shaped Parmesan cheese wafer into the pasta, describe the dish ("Penne please, *not* macaroni"), and offer it to the patrons.

"Creamy lobster penne with a homemade parmesan crisp," I said, handing a glass to every customer who passed by and smiling, smiling, smiling. I tried to push Erica's cloudy eyes and the dead jellyfish feel of her hand out of my mind. It did not compute, her taking all those pills. She had too much to live for, with her daughter, Lila Rose, at the top of the list. I must have looked at my watch a hundred times, but still only half an hour groaned by.

"Cassie! Look at you. You're so cute in that toque," said Travis, leading the remainder of the Meditron foursome in line to snag a glass of pasta. He peered at it suspiciously. "What is this stuff? Some kind of gourmet macaroni?" Considering his stout shape, he did not look like a man who turned down anything edible.

"Creamy lobster penne with a homemade parmesan crisp," I said. "And don't call it macaroni."

"I think the baseball cap is more you," said Roger. "Have you tried the beef Wellington across the room? It's wrapped in this unbelievable pastry crust. And the meat is rare—something a man can really sink his teeth into." He lifted his lips and growled as he reached for a snifter of lobster pasta.

Hugh rolled his eyes. "I'm allergic to shellfish. I'm going to get a glass of wine. I'll find you later."

"What's the deal with these celebrity chefs?" asked Travis, wiping white sauce off his chin with the back of his hand. "It seems the bigger the name, the more raw fish they feel obligated to serve. Who the hell ever heard of gazpacho with ceviche floating in it? Half the food here is disgusting."

"Erica's dead." I blurted it out without preamble. How do you casually work a suicide into a conversation about rare beef and raw fish?

"You're joking," said Roger, the color draining from his face.

"I wish I was." The whole story fell out in a whispered rush: how I'd gotten worried, how I'd gone to her room, how the hotel management had opened her door, and how we'd found her body. A crowd had begun to back up at my station, clamoring for lobster pasta. I went back to work, but my hands shook so hard that I missed the martini glass I was holding and stabbed Chef Roseata's hand with a Parmesan star. He glared at me.

"May I take a five-minute break?"

He motioned for me to leave.

"How could this be?" asked Travis, when I'd made my way out from behind the booth. He folded me into a sudden and sweaty hug. "How the hell could she be dead?"

"The detective told me she overdosed."

"What the hell are they basing that bullshit theory on?" Travis's voice screeched above the chatter of the crowd. "She was a rock. She would no more kill herself than Mother Teresa."

"Calm down," said Roger. "Cassie's upset enough without you yelling at her." I stepped away from the booth and rubbed my arms. Though the crush of partygoers had raised the temperature in the ballroom to near sauna, I couldn't get rid of the crop of goose bumps that had erupted in the cold shock of Erica's hotel room.

"Has her husband been notified?" Roger asked.

"That fucking bastard . . ." said Travis, raising his clenched fists.

"The cops were calling him when I left the room," I said.

Just then, Hugh returned carrying a large goblet of red wine. He scanned our faces. "What's wrong?"

"Cassie says Erica overdosed on something. She's dead." Roger's voice reflected concern and something else. Anger? Disgust? "Cassie found her."

Hard as I tried to hold it back, I felt a tear run down the length of my cheek and chin. It dropped to my chest and blurred the ANDRA part of my name tag to a fuzzy blue.

"Here." Hugh held out his drink. "It looks like you need this more than I do." He grabbed my elbow and guided me toward a less-crowded corner of the room. The other two men trailed along behind. "Tell me exactly what happened."

I drained the glass of wine, then repeated the story, this time with more details about Detective Rumson's line of questioning.

"You're sure they think it was suicide?" he asked.

I nodded. "That's what the detective said. No signs of foul play, and with the empty pill bottle and all—"

"I knew she had to be taking something. She's been a bitch on wheels for months." Hugh turned toward the other men. "What the hell was she on?"

Travis's eyes shone with tears. "Prozac," he admitted.

Something I doubted had ever crossed the lips of Mother Teresa.

"I'm not completely surprised," said Roger. "That woman was a powder keg waiting to blow."

"You're an asshole," Travis snarled.

"Maybe she finally had enough of your disgusting come-ons," Roger answered.

It shocked me that the men had chosen this moment to brawl. "I didn't know her well, but I can't believe she'd leave her daughter like this," I said. "She adored that girl. She had so many plans for her."

"When people are mentally unstable, they don't think things through the way a normal human being would," Roger explained.

"Was she taking anything else?" Hugh asked Travis, his voice shaking with barely controlled anger.

"She only took the Valium when she really needed it."

"Why didn't you keep me informed about this? I can't believe this. You know how sensitive our data are—"

"She asked me to keep things quiet. It was a short-term thing, while she got through the divorce."

"Did she ever threaten to kill herself?"

"No," said Travis.

"Not in so many words," said Roger at the same time.

"This better not screw up the fucking project," said Hugh. He turned and stomped off in the direction of the raw fish soup.

"Mr. Sensitivity," said Roger. "Let's tender your resignation over at Mama Cacciatore and we'll get you some dinner."

"Thanks anyway," I said. "I think I need to just go home." I wasn't all that eager to go back alone to a strange motel room, but spending the evening with Erica's squabbling coworkers appealed to me even less. I folded up my apron and returned it to the chef with apologies. With my luck, he'd report me to the LPGA office as a public relations nightmare. I watched Roger and Travis argue as they moved to the next station, where Se Ri Pak was serving miniature crab cakes doused with a jicama-cilantro salsa. Despite their initial shock and Travis's visible distress, neither of the men seemed to have had his appetite diminished by the news of Erica's death.

On my way out, I bought a Budweiser at the bar in the main casino and sat down at a quarter slot machine. An older, heavyset woman in a polyester short set nodded at me without losing a beat in the rhythm she used to feed her machine. She was methodical: insert three quarters at a time, press the button, three more quarters, press the button. No wasted motion, no casino carpal tunnel syndrome for her. After several minutes, the machine flashed and whistled, and coins began to slop noisily into her tray. She scooped them up into a plastic cup and started her routine again. I fed the last quarter in my pocket into my own machine and pulled the arm. The display board ground to a halt, revealing a diamond, a bar, and a lemon. Shit, wasn't that just the way the day had gone.

"Just keep at it, honey," the big woman said. "If you feed them, they will come. That's my motto." She laughed, cigarette smoke streaming from her nostrils, and pressed her button.

I wondered if the casino owners had planted her here. I drained the rest of my beer and headed for the outdoor bar overlooking the Atlantic Ocean. I needed fresh air and another ice-cold beer. Just one more, I told myself. It had been a lousy, stressful, miserable day, and I deserved to unwind.

Seated out on the boardwalk, I mulled over the conversation I'd had with the Meditron men about Erica's death. I hadn't mentioned Aimee Joy. I hadn't pushed my own feeling that this death was not self-inflicted in nature. Only Travis seriously questioned whether Erica was capable of killing herself. I wondered how intimate they actually were. He appeared to have had the closest connection to her, with Roger friendly enough, and Hugh most distant in his role of big boss. But also most critical and angry.

A small group of chattering teenagers passed the bar, heading in the direction of the amusement park. Their hair swung in the ocean breeze, straight, long, and shiny. Like Aimee Joy, their clothes hugged their adolescent curves with no room to spare. Who was Aimee Joy? Had she been involved in Erica's death? Detective Rumson had seemed only moderately interested in that angle of my story.

I promised myself that tomorrow, after a solid morning's practice, I would make some calls to Rye, New York. I wished I could leave the whole mess alone. But Erica, and her daughter, deserved at least that much.

Chapter 5

I reached the practice range by eight A.M., congratulating myself for last night's three-drink limit and this morning's absence of hangover symptoms. Pushing away a pervasive gloominess left over from the grim scene in Erica's hotel room, I hauled my clubs to a station near the end of the practice area. Today I needed minimal distractions from other golfers or spectators. I nodded hello to a tall, redheaded woman who worked next to me with her caddie/husband. He steadied the butt of her driver against her left hip as she pitched shots out into the range. From the looks of it, she must have inserted a little too much movement in her swing lately.

As I ran through my stretching exercises, they bickered about whether their son should accompany them on today's practice round. Her side: the kid would be overheated, tortured by the greenhead flies, and distracting to her practice. His side: what the hell else did she suggest?

Could she carry her own bag? Leave the kid alone in the hotel room?

I rolled a ball off the pyramid of new Titleists next to me. Times when I felt lousy traveling by myself, chats like this one reminded me how difficult it was to have a family, or even a steady relationship, out here on the Tour. Yet I knew seeing the friendly faces of Laura and Joe would cut through the shroud of loneliness that had settled in since finding Erica's body. Laura would hug me and cheer me up with some silly saying about how life is a treacherous journey, but buddies and Budweiser smooth the way. And she would be right about both.

With Joe, things were a little more complicated. He tried to walk the fine line between working on the mental side of my game and remaining friends. So far, he'd refused my offers to pay him for his advice.

"We're friends," he told me. "I'm happy to help. When you break through big time and the other players hear I was behind it, I'll get more business than I can handle."

I couldn't wait to talk to him about Erica; Joe was a whiz at figuring out people and their problems. He swore he couldn't read *my* mind, even if it felt like it sometimes. How embarrassing would that be! Then I'd be caught admitting that between the dimples, the flyaway hair, and the outdated tortoiseshell glasses, he was the kind of guy I could see myself falling for. Except I'd come up with a thousand excuses why it wouldn't work whenever we were close enough to try it out—a pattern my own shrink, Dr. Baxter, had called "intimacy issues." A label I told him was psychobabble horseshit.

I began to hit half-wedge shots out to the red flag in front of me. The heat already felt smothering. By the time I'd worked through my irons, sweat soaked my golf glove to a slimy mass. I unzipped the back pocket of my golf bag to get a new one before tackling the woods.

In the bottom of the pocket, I found an unfamiliar plaid

cosmetics kit. Weird. The back side of the kit was embroidered with the initials EJL. I pulled open the zipper.
A complete set of Bobbie Brown makeup was stored
neatly in the bag—not my usual gig. Other than lip gloss,
and despite my mother's lamentations about my ghoulish
complexion, I only wore makeup for costume parties or
stage appearances, neither of which had come up in over
ten years.

Underneath the peach blush, I found a small gold case,
also monogrammed, which contained Erica LeBoutillier's
business cards, listing a Meditron address and a home
location in Edgewater Estates. I figured her caddie or the
bag boy had stuffed the makeup kit into my bag Tuesday
by mistake. And on Tuesday, she would have been alive
to put that makeup on.

Before I could spiral off into more morbid thinking, I
forced myself to replace the kit in my bag and fish out a
new glove. Then I began hitting woods: twenty nine
woods, then twenty seven, five, and three woods, and
thirty drivers. Halfway through, I recovered the rhythm
that had escaped me the day before and was rewarded
with a steady stream of straight shots.

As I began to wipe down my clubs and pack them back
into the bag, I took a second look at Erica's makeup kit.
The home address on her card read: 264 Edgewater Circle
in Edgewater Estates. It had a familiar ring; I thought I'd
passed a ritzy development with a similar name on my
way to the casino the night before. Returning the kit
would give me the perfect excuse to drop by and meet
Erica's husband. If I was lucky, he might shed some light
on my growing discomfort with the police conclusion that
Erica had overdosed. At the very least, I would feel I'd
done everything possible to help my new friend. Closure—that's what my shrink called it. He loved closure.
And he always seemed anxious for me to have it, too.

I rummaged through the large pocket of my bag one

last time. At the bottom, I found a single key taped to a card containing an address in Manahawkin. Erica's temporary apartment? Without any definite plan in mind, I removed the key from the bag, slipped it into my shorts pocket, and headed to my car.

An elaborate stone arch and a carefully tended arrangement of lilies and beach grasses guarded the entrance to Edgewater Estates. This was light-years from the slums of Atlantic City or even the faded farmhouses in the small towns surrounding the property. These houses were enormous: architectural playgrounds with multiple pillars, turrets, and chimneys, and expansive lawns and perennial gardens. I found number 264 in a cul-de-sac at the back of the development. It had whitewashed wood shingle siding and cedar shutters. The curves above the four-car garage lent an incongruous Moorish flavor. Large white hydrangeas set off the cobblestone path leading to the front door. Welcome to big bucks territory.

I parked at the end of a long line of cars that swept around the bend and hiked up the oyster shell driveway. A soft hum of conversation wafted out from behind the house. As I drew closer, I saw a cluster of people around the pool, being served by waiters in formal attire. My stomach growled reflexively. With the lady of the house dead, it could not have been a cocktail party or women's luncheon—maybe relatives who had gathered at the news of Erica's death. As if a catered lunch or a wall of casseroles could numb the grief of unexpected loss.

The doorbell echoed deep into the recesses of the house, but no one answered. I peered into the slender window flanking the mahogany door. The dark hardwood of the hallway was laid out in a geometric pattern, then overlaid with a lush turquoise rug. On the walls, I recognized watercolors of the seventeenth hole at Saint Andrew's and the seventh at Pebble Beach. Two antique putters leaned against an umbrella stand just inside the window. I pressed the doorbell a second time and clanked the brass clamshell door knocker for good measure. As I turned to leave, the door swung open.

"Can I help you?"

I recognized the girl who spoke from Erica's wallet pictures. She was blond and chubby, with the nubs of preadolescent breasts and a rounded stomach defining the landscape of her tank top. She had her mother's soft brown eyes.

"You must be Lila Rose."

She nodded.

"I was a friend of your mother's. I'm so sorry to hear about her death."

The girl nodded again, two huge tears squeezing from her eyes and beginning to make their way down her cheeks. In the face of her raw sorrow, I had desperately begun to wish I hadn't come.

"I played golf with your mom yesterday," I stammered. "She left her makeup kit in my bag by mistake. I brought it for you." She accepted the bag that I offered and traced over the initials, EJL, with her index finger.

"Are you one of the famous golfers?"

"Cassie Burdette." I stuck my hand out and squeezed her small one in mine. "I'm just a rookie."

"Mommy said I could come and watch her play with you this week." A deep flush darkened her cheeks. "Then Daddy said it wasn't her day to see me."

"Do you play golf, too?"

She flashed a shaky smile. "Not yet. We went out once. Mom said she was going to get me lessons so we could play together." She set the bag down on a small table.

"Lila Rose? Who is it?" A swarthy man in sharply pressed khakis, a striped polo shirt, and sockless loafers flung the door open and stepped in front of the girl.

"It's a lady golfer, one of Mommy's friends," she said from behind him.

"Go help Grandma with the cake, honey." He shoved her gently down the hallway. "Who are you?" His flared nostrils and tight lips told me unfamiliar visitors were definitely not welcome.

"Nice to meet you Lila," I called after her. "Good luck with your golf lessons."

"Who are you?" he demanded again. "What do you want?"

"I'm Cassie Burdette. You must be Mr. LeBoutillier. I'm terribly sorry for your loss." I pointed to the plaid makeup case. "Erica's makeup kit was put in my golf bag by mistake."

"Thanks for dropping it off." He began to close the door in my face.

"Please! I was hoping I might be able to talk to you for a couple minutes."

His eyes narrowed. "This is a very bad time for us. I'm sure you can understand that."

"I found her," I said.

He opened the door again, his eyebrows now crinkled into one extravagant and furry curve.

"Come in. I apologize for sounding abrupt. This situation has been a nightmare. And now I'm expected to entertain a house full of guests." He ran his hands across his face and through his bushy hair, then led me across the turquoise carpet to a formal living room decorated in shades of white. The same color scheme my own mother had chosen, only their budget allowed for high-grade leather instead of cheap velveteen. Mr. LeBoutillier glanced at his watch. "So . . . ?"

"So, I know the police think it was a suicide. But I spent the day with her on Tuesday. She had so many plans, and she talked so much about your daughter. I just can't believe she killed herself."

"This is what made life with Erica so very painful." He

gazed at me for what felt like a long time. "She had more than one woman's share of charm."

"But . . . ?"

"It took me years to understand that my smart and talented wife was a self-destructive time bomb. She had made a terrible mess of her life, and mine along with it. When I think of all that's happened this past year, I have no doubt that she killed herself. She probably saw no other way out of the stinking shithole she'd dug. Excuse my French. Did she tell you about the divorce?"

"She mentioned that you two were having some difficulty sorting things out."

"Difficulty sorting things out, is that what she said?" He threw his head back and laughed until the stripes running across the hard lump of his belly quivered. "She did everything she could to run our family into bankruptcy. I begged her to get help. I was prepared to pay for the finest psychiatric consultant available. Did she by any chance gamble when you were with her?"

"She showed us how to play blackjack," I admitted.

"Her favorite," he said, lifting his lips into a stiff smile. "Look. Erica could be a delightful companion. After all, I married her, right? From what I understand, she was also a dynamo at work. But bottom line, over the past few years, she became a lousy wife, and a lousy mother." He leaned forward with an earnest look on his face. "I know I sound bitter. I tried to work with her, but in the end, with the drugs and gambling, I was afraid for Lila Rose. Our life had deteriorated to the point where I had to get my little girl away from her. And much as I hate to admit it," he smiled again, "I was afraid for myself."

"I'm sorry," I said. I had no clue what else to say.

"How are you playing?" The intense rage and hurt in his face was suddenly smoothed aside.

"Excuse me?"

"How's your game look this week? You are playing in the tournament?"

I laughed. "Yes, I'm playing. The long game looked pretty good at the driving range this morning. But you never know what'll happen when you get out there. I need to get back and sink a few putts." I smiled. "Thanks for asking."

"I don't play much myself anymore. The business and Lila Rose keep me running. But putting is definitely the key." He winked. "I'll look for you on the leaderboard."

Just then, a tall, bald man in a gray business suit stuck his head into the living room. "Pierre? Marilyn and I are leaving. You'll call us if you need anything?"

"Thanks for everything. I promise I'll call." Pierre stood and received the bald man's clumsy hug. Then he turned to the woman behind him. Every detail of her country club wake attire was in perfect order: freshwater pearls, low-heeled pumps, a black linen pantsuit. But her face was an angry red and puffy.

Pierre reached for her hand. "Thanks for coming, Marilyn. Erica was so fond of you."

This comment precipitated a surge of tears. Marilyn snapped her hand away from Pierre's grasp and stomped out the front door. Through the wavy glass of the window, we watched her disappear across the lawn and into the three-story colonial next door.

He shrugged. "Where are my manners? Cassie, this is Paul Porter, our neighbor. Cassie played golf with Erica on Tuesday."

"You're playing in the Classic?"

I nodded.

"Good luck this weekend, then." Paul tipped his head in the direction of his missing wife. "Please excuse me. I'd better go after her."

Pierre ushered both of us through the vestibule, shook my hand, and closed the door firmly behind us. I stood staring at the house where Erica had lived. The gorgeous home, the adorable daughter, the Onassis lookalike husband. If I didn't know better, I'd have described it as a dead ringer for Shangri-la. What could have gone so wrong that she chose to walk out?

Chapter 6

I sat in the car with the air-conditioning running and dialed directory assistance for Rye, New York. The operator assured me in clipped tones that there were no listings in the city for Joy, Joye, Joie, or in desperation, Joey. Then she connected me with the Rye High School guidance office. While the phone rang, it occurred to me that the school would not release information about one of their students to a stranger. I did some fast thinking.

"This is Cassandra Burdette from Harvard University. I need to speak with Mr. Horton, who teaches in your English department. I understand he will be the contact for our summer gifted intern program."

"We don't have a teacher here named Horton."

"Are you certain?"

She was certain.

"Maybe he's a substitute teacher? Maybe he's new?"

I could almost hear her dismissive sniff over the line.

As far as the secretary was concerned, Mr. Horton did not exist.

"Hmm. There must be a misprint in my bulletin. Can I leave a message for Aimee Joy, in that case? She's mentioned as your student contact."

The secretary's officiousness overcame her commitment to confidentiality. Harvard had made another bone-headed administrative error. Aimee Joy did not attend Rye High School. I called Detective Rumson and reported what I'd learned.

"Thanks for the heads up, Ms. Burdette. I must ask you not to get any more involved in this than you have already."

With the detective's voice verging on scolding, I chose not to tell her I was sitting outside the LeBoutillier home and had already talked to Pierre and Lila Rose.

"The preliminary tox screen came back, and it confirms what we suspected: overdose by antidepressant medication. Off the record, we anticipate finding other substances, too." Her tone softened. "I know it's not what you were hoping to hear. It's hard to lose a friend this way. But please, do all of us a favor and spend your free time on the practice range. We'd love to see you win this tournament." She chuckled. "I plan to be on the eighteenth green Sunday when you hold up that trophy."

I thanked her and switched off the cell phone. She was right. I'd turned up nothing in my amateur investigation that cried out for further attention. At least from me. I still had no idea who Aimee Joy really was, nor was I likely to find out. I had nothing to go on except my own gut feeling that Erica had not killed herself. And this was not enough to send me off on tangents that would only hurt my chances of a strong performance at the tournament. I drove back to the Seaview Marriott, planning to grab some free lunch and hit the putting green.

I flashed my ID to the volunteer manning the meal

voucher table. It was almost two o'clock, which meant most of the tables were empty, though the trays of food had been picked over. I snagged a withered-looking hamburger and some potato salad. Then I spotted Annie Strauss across the room. I snaked my way through a maze of folding chairs to sit next to her.

"All set for the junior clinic?" she asked. "I'm really, really looking forward to working with the kids."

"I wasn't tapped this year," I said. "Maybe when I crawl a little higher on the money list."

Annie had started on Tour just two years ahead of me. But in contrast to my struggle, the trajectory of her first season peaked with Rolex Rookie of the Year honors.

"I can't wait to get home this week," she said. "My older sister just had a new baby, and they named her after me. Anna Maria Shaw. Isn't that pretty? According to Maria, she has a miniature widow's peak just like mine. It'll be so great to see them. And little Frankie, too."

For several minutes, I listened to her chatter, just nodding or inserting uh-huhs as seemed necessary. Not half an hour ago, I'd promised myself to mind my own business. But now the coincidence of finding Annie alone was too great a temptation to resist.

"How did you like playing with the Meditron gang?" I asked when she finally drew a breath.

"They were super guys. By the time we finished, my stomach hurt from laughing. Plus, I got some great practice in."

Had she played with the same group I had? My gut hurt after the Meditron round, too, but it sure wasn't from laughing.

In the past, Annie had never struck me as what Joe Lancaster would call "psychologically minded." What you saw was what you got: a sunny personality baked until done in the hot oven of Texas for over twenty-three years. As a kid, she'd taken a couple of lessons from the great golf guru Harvey Penick, and she lived life by his positive and homey aphorisms.

"Take dead aim," she'd have told Roger about his vicious slice. If I'd confided in her that I felt down in the dumps about my game or my love life or you name it, I could imagine her advice would go something like: "Never say never, and don't say don't." Beyond annoying, these truisms worked for her like a damned charm. She'd moved steadily up the money list since her rookie season two years ago. And I guessed that her tendency to avoid ruminating was part of the secret to her success. Even so, I thought I'd try to eke out a little insight from her on Erica's coworkers.

"Did you hear the woman who was supposed to be your fifth was found dead yesterday? Overdosed, the cops think."

"I heard that. I'm mighty sorry. I would have liked to have known her." She crossed herself quickly.

That took me aback. I would have picked her for a don't-ask-too-many-questions-just-count-on-God-will-come-through-in-the-end Protestant.

"Were her partners surprised she didn't show?"

"Surprised is hardly how I'd describe it. They were pissed. I guess she sank a lot of putts for y'all yesterday."

I laughed. "I could use some of her magic tomorrow." I tried to phrase the next question carefully. How do you ask someone who takes everything at face value and interprets all news as good, which of her playing partners made a good murder suspect? Assuming that a certain someone had in fact been murdered.

"How did the three guys get along?"

"Get along in what way?"

"Did they seem tense?"

She shrugged. "They seemed okay, I guess."

"Did they say anything else about Erica?"

"Like I told you, they were just mad she didn't show."

"But can you remember exactly what anyone said?"

Annie had begun to look bored and annoyed.

"It's important. Erica has a little girl who's going to want to know why her mom killed herself."

Annie took a bite of her sausage and chewed it slowly. "Hugh's the boss, right?"

I nodded.

"He told Travis to get his butt to the personnel department as soon as they got back to the office. He wanted all her records pulled—references, sick days, comp time— he wanted to see it all."

"Why?"

Annie shrugged. "I have no idea."

"Was he trying to can her?"

Annie only shrugged again.

"What did Travis say?"

"Not much. He certainly didn't argue. Then Hugh said something about this is what happens when someone is wound as tight as she is. Once you loosen up the cork, the whole thing blows sky high." Annie blushed.

"What?" I prodded.

"He mentioned you, too."

What could he possibly have to say about me? I thought I'd been as helpful to him and pleasant to the whole group as possible, even spending time with Roger at the driving range when I should have been practicing my own shots. Did some part of my golf game strike him as substandard? I plastered on an encouraging smile. "Go on."

"He said you and Erica made a good pair."

That wasn't so awful. I glanced at the chagrined smile on Annie's lips. He couldn't have left it there. "And what else?"

Annie rubbed her chin on her shoulder, still smiling. "Nothing really. Just that you were both big party girls."

Now that hurt. He was the one who'd pressed the glass of wine on me at the party last night, and he was also the main force behind the multiple rounds ordered when we'd gone to dinner on Tuesday. Other than that, what the hell did he know about what I did or didn't do off the golf course? Keeping in mind a few disastrous and too-public instances of hard partying while I caddied for Mike Callahan on the PGA Tour, I'd gone all out to keep my indulgences moderate lately.

"I'm sorry to bring that up." Annie leaned over to pat my hand, then hurried past our mutual embarrassment. "Travis seemed the most upset that Erica wasn't there." She furrowed the thin lines of her overplucked brows. "It was almost like he felt jilted." Little Miss Oblivious turned out to have picked up a lot.

"And Roger?"

"He didn't have all that much reaction. Well, he did make fun of Travis, and he joked about how the team was sunk without Erica. Even though he was laughing, I could tell he wanted to win. So he was a little annoyed that she wasn't on the tee. Listen, I gotta go. I told my caddie I'd meet him at the range at three." She patted my hand again, her face creased with unspoken apology. "Good luck tomorrow. Take dead aim!"

I dumped the remains of my lunch in the trash and walked over to the practice putting green. After the obligatory exchange of greetings with the other women practicing, I emptied my shag bag onto the short grass next to the green and began to chip. The tempo I'd recovered on the range this morning was gone.

No doubt about it, the conversation with Annie had crawled under my skin and stuck there. In the final weeks before I headed out on the Tour, Dr. Baxter had made an irritating habit of mentioning that alcohol looked like my Achilles' heel. Sure, I'd told him about reaching for a few pops in circumstances when some other girl might have called her mom to talk things over. But as I explained to him later, with my particular mother, sharing my deepest secrets just wasn't an option. Then Baxter pointed out that the gin seemed to flow pretty freely for old Mom, too, and suggested I needed to develop some other methods for relieving tension.

Bad enough that I had to think about this stuff myself. Worse that my couple of wild nights out on the town several years ago might have become the topic of casual amateur gossip.

Now the last session I'd had with Baxter hovered in my mind.

"At the professional level you're reaching for," he'd said, "it's not enough to be good. You can't have something blocking you from success. With some athletes, it's a physical thing, others, emotional. My opinion? You still have some work to do here."

So now he was an expert on the professional golf world, a guy who probably couldn't break eighty for nine holes.

"What would you suggest? That I take a checkout clerk position at Wal-Mart so I can stay home and see my shrink? The LPGA Tour doesn't make too many stops in Myrtle Beach."

We'd ended on a draw. He wouldn't close out my case file, in the event I changed my tune and returned to therapy. And I wouldn't close my mind.

I tried to refocus on chipping. After six short jabs had not even reached the putting surface, I went for a longer bump-and-run shot out to the farthest hole. The ball skidded across the green, hopped the cobblestone curb and blacktop walkway, and came to rest in a bed of purple petunias. I walked over to fish the ball out of the flowerbed.

"Looks like your game is starting to blossom!"

I turned around in time to be squeezed into Laura's solid form. "This pretty much sums it up," I said, laughing. "I sure am glad the cavalry has arrived." I reached around her to hug Joe.

"I need to take a ride around the golf course, roll some balls on the greens, and map out the shady spots where a weary caddie could rest," Laura said. "When's our tee time? What's for supper?"

"We tee off at eight-fourteen. Say we meet back here in a couple hours, and I'll take you guys into the city for dinner?"

"Let me see you hit a couple," said Joe after Laura left. I chunked three balls onto the green.

"What's the diagnosis, Doc?"

"Looks to me like your mind's somewhere else."

The guy was uncanny. "It's been a crazy week."

"I want to hear all about it. Right now, let's concentrate on your short game."

Chapter 7

I watched Laura empty the contents of her duffel bag into the hotel dresser.

"You seem tense," she said.

"This woman I played with in the pro-am on Tuesday, I found her dead last night. The cops think she overdosed."

Laura whistled. "No shit. Finding bodies is getting to be a regular gig with you. No wonder you're a basket case."

"Who says I'm a basket case?"

She leaned toward the mirror and tucked her hair behind her ears. "I know you, pal." She applied Chap Stick and smacked her lips together. "I'm ready to roll. Sounds like you could use a couple of pops and some conversation with your best buds."

I laughed. "On the money, as usual."

As we followed Route 9 around the bay and into Atlantic City, I described how I'd found Erica's body in her room. I glanced at Joe as he parked the car behind the Showboat Casino.

"I'm having trouble letting the whole thing go. Her kid haunts me. And she just didn't seem like the type who'd do herself in. She had a lot of fight in her."

"Let's get settled, and you can tell us the whole story," he said.

"Can't they make these people puff their poison out-side?" said Laura, as we maneuvered down the hall through a haze of cigarette smoke. "They need to take a page from California. Even the bars are nonsmoking there."

"Now start at the beginning," said Joe, once we'd ordered dinner.

"I'll try to be methodical," I said. "I'll lay it out, and then you guys tell me what it sounds like. I've gotten too close in the last two days. Nothing makes sense to me anymore." I took a swig of my Budweiser. "Her name was Erica LeBoutillier. She and the other three guys on our team all worked for Meditron."

"The big pharmaceutical company up in Manahawkin," said Joe.

I nodded. "Their group was working on a major proj-ect—some medicine they claimed was going to cure Al-zheimer's."

"What was the drug?"

"I don't know the details. I was just trying to get through the round without any of them killing each other. Or me."

"Your score didn't look half bad. You won second prize for the day, didn't you?"

"I hit the ball pretty good. Hugh—he's the big cheese—was steady, once he settled down, and Erica had a fabu-lous short game. She sank a couple of no-brainers that put us out ahead."

"So you think one of them did her in at the nineteenth hole?" asked Laura.

"You're getting ahead of me." I drank another couple inches of beer. "They asked me to a celebration dinner, but then they fought all the way through the meal. Erica wanted them to run more tests before the drug goes to market. Liver function tests, I think she said. The other guys were pissed that she would even bring that up." I turned to face Joe. "Why would they be so upset about the possibility of a delay? What's the worst that could happen? It seems to me that they'd prefer to take their time rather than risk a negative outcome."

"If I'm remembering right, Meditron's been in the news more than they would want lately. Troubles with other products, I think. They may be counting on this drug to vault them past those other problems."

The waiter delivered a second round of drinks.

"We went to the blackjack tables afterward, and I stayed a while with Erica after the men left. She was under a lot of pressure: a messy divorce, deadlines at work, no time to get ready for a huge amateur tournament she'd entered. And most important of all, the reduced contact with her daughter. But I never got any feeling she'd bail out." Then I described our interaction with Aimee Joy.

"Sounds like she got more involved than she should have," said Joe. "Maybe because of the forced distance from her own daughter."

I nodded. "My gut told me this girl was running some kind of scam, but Erica insisted she could get the kid to call her parents once they got up to her room. So I left. And next time I saw her, she was dead." I felt tears well up and threaten to crack my composure.

"You think it's your fault." Laura's voice was accusing. "You go out of your way to shoulder blame for other people's screwups."

I no longer took it personally when she used that tone; by now I knew it meant she was worried I'd blunder into something dumb.

"It's not that. I don't think the police gave her a fair hearing. I don't believe she'd go home and swallow a bunch of pills."

"So what's your theory?"

"I think she was murdered."

"Who did it?" said Laura.

"And why?" asked Joe.

"It could have been any number of people. Aimee Joy, certainly, whoever the hell she is. Who by the way, does not exist, according to official records at Rye High School. And the Meditron guys, who want the Alzheimer's drug to blitz the market without any hitches. That would probably put them in line for big promotions and big bucks from their company stock holdings."

"Tell us a little more about her coworkers," said Joe.

"Roger's the biostatistician on the project. As you could imagine, he likes things predictable. He quit at blackjack when he couldn't win according to his analysis of the mathematical odds. I spent a little time working with him at the range yesterday. He wanted to know the mechanical details of every inch of the swing."

"One of those guys," Laura said with a groan. "When I get a student like that, I know progress is gonna be slow, and I'll be working twice as hard for my money. Were they all like that?"

"Not exactly. Hugh, the vice president of neuroscience, he's a stuffed shirt par excellence. He's got the million-dollar golf wardrobe and the million-dollar golf swing to match—big investment in making whatever he does look good. Everything about the company and this drug seems to mean a lot to him. According to Annie Strauss, he was furious when Erica didn't show up for the second pro-am round. He threatened to pull out her records and go over them with a magnifying glass when they got back to the office."

"What about when he heard she was dead?" Joe asked.

"Angry again," I said. "He pegged her immediately as a drug-dependent loser."

I was quiet for a minute, wondering whether to mention his rude comment to Annie regarding my reputation as a hard drinker. If it had been only Laura, I knew we could have laughed it off. But I didn't want to see the subtle wave of concern that would wash across Joe's face before he hid it away. So I hurried past the temptation to confess.

"Travis was the third man—the medical director. Hugh kept getting mad at him for suggesting I invest in Meditron. I thought maybe Travis had something going with Erica. He certainly came on to her, but I couldn't tell for sure whether it was only his wishful thinking."

"What did you notice?" asked Joe.

"He was by far the most upset when I told them she was dead. I wouldn't swear he was in love with her, but he had the hots for her, anyway. He seemed to want things easy and warm between them, but there always ended up being an edge. Same with him and Roger—an edge." I drank the last bit of my beer. "None of them an obvious standout in the murder suspect department."

"What about Erica's husband?"

"From what she had described, I didn't expect to like him as much as I did. He claimed Erica was involved with drugs and gambling, and that's why he played hardball trying to extricate himself from the marriage and keep her away from their kid. He said she'd caused them a lot of financial problems."

"Pathological gambling?" Joe's eyebrows arched with interest.

"That's Pierre's position anyway. Which reminds me, I thought we might stop at her friend Lucia's blackjack table and see if we could get her perspective on Erica."

"I knew there had to be an ulterior motive for bringing us here. The beer is pricey and the food substandard," said Laura.

I glanced at her empty plate and rolled my eyes. "Damn if you're not hard to please."

Lucia was working the same table I'd visited with Erica and the Meditron men. She gave me a weak smile as I slid onto one of the barstools.

"These are my friends, Laura and Joe."

She nodded without making eye contact and dealt the first card around the table.

"You heard about Erica?"

Another brief nod. "Very sad. Sweet girl." Lucia's unreadable face mirrored the restrained words. She dealt a second round.

"Hit me," I said, tapping the table. "How often did she come here?"

The smile disappeared, and her shoulders tightened. Lucia flipped a card off the deck onto the place in front of me. "She came by from time to time."

"Did you know Pierre?"

"A little bit."

So far, I was getting zero, zip, and nada. "Was he a gambler, too?"

She glanced in the direction of the pit boss and frowned. "I cannot talk now. I'll lose my job."

This was not the same cheery woman Erica had bantered with two nights before. I shrugged my defeat across the gaming table to Joe.

"I'll stay," he said to Lucia. "Could we buy you a drink later at your break?" Joe's warm voice and encouraging grin could be hard to refuse. I sure hoped it worked out this time.

She frowned, then looked at her wristwatch. "I'm done here in half an hour. I'll meet you at the Beachcomber

Bar at nine-thirty?" She dealt another hand and quickly
raked in my losing chips.

"I'm not into this," I said. "And the cigarette smoke is
killing me. I'll meet you guys outside at the bar."

I bought a bottle of Bud and found an empty stool on
the boardwalk facing the amusement park. A thousand
gaudy lightbulbs flashed in the darkness: Shoot Out!
Crazy Mouse! Carousel! Taj Mahal!

"Win a big bear for your girl!" "Show her your great
arm!" hollered the workers who manned the booths. The
crowd jostled each other for position to watch the players
gun balls at a parade of dancing clowns. Did they really
think a woman would roll over for a cheesy stuffed animal?

Just beyond the ticket booth, I spotted a group of teenage girls, one with the swinging brown hair and long torso
of Aimee Joy. I banged my beer down onto the table,
hurdled the guardrail, and took off in her direction. Then
I slowed to a fast walk. I'd been a teenager, too, and not
so long ago. A direct attack rarely worked; better to surprise her with a stealthy approach. I worked my way
through the crowd until I was close enough to touch her.

"Hello, Aimee?"

The girl turned sharply. Her eyes rounded in panic and
she began to run. I followed.

"Aimee! Wait! I just want to talk." I was panting now,
and hoarse from yelling.

The girl glanced back and saw me pounding down the
boardwalk toward her. Without hesitation, she bolted into
the amusement park, ducking past the merry-go-round and
off into the darkness. I chugged along after her, still shout-
ing her name at ragged intervals. I stopped in front of the
House of Mirrors to catch my breath. Obviously, I needed
to step up my conditioning.

"Did a tall, thin teenager with long brown hair and a

bare midriff come in here?" I asked the attendant between gasps.

"Look lady, a thousand teenagers have come through here. Every one of them looks like that, only half of them blond. You want a ticket or not? If not, clear out of the way."

I left the amusement arcade and jogged the full distance to the end of the boardwalk without any further sighting of Aimee. Back at the Beachcomber, Joe and Laura waited anxiously.

"Where the hell have you been?"

"I saw the girl," I said, still breathing hard. "I tried to talk with her, but she took off. She made it clear she didn't want to chat."

"Was she with the teacher?"

"Mr. Horton? No. She was with a bunch of other girls, all dressed like ladies of the night, if you want my opinion." I looked around for my unfinished beer. "Plus, some idiot took my drink."

"I'll buy you another one," said Laura, patting me on the shoulder.

"Never mind, it's almost curfew anyway. Where the hell is Lucia?" We waited on a bench across from the bar until ten o'clock.

"Apparently, no one wants to talk to anybody about anything," I said. "Let's get the hell out of here."

Chapter 8

Ↄ **The** TV announcers had it right: a player who'd been in the winner's circle before knew she could handle it again. She knew she could belt a monster tee shot even with a river of sweat slicking the grip of her driver to patent leather. Or sink a birdie putt on the eighteenth green with her hands shaking like a jackhammer. And she would be eighty-five percent confident that the hot breath of the best golfer in the world playing in the threesome behind her would have no impact on her own game.

If like me, you hadn't won or even come close, none of the above applied. So far this season, I'd found myself to be an awesome golfer on the practice range and a hacker under tournament conditions. Which was why Joe had been summoned for an emergency appearance.

I swatted at the greenhead feasting on my leg with a Solheim Cup golf towel. "I'm so frustrated. I feel like I play well in the practice rounds, then the real thing comes, and I fall apart."

"You have all the shots," said Joe, slurping coffee from a Styrofoam cup. "You're just not allowing yourself to use them when you need them." We'd already run through woods and irons on the range. Now we stood in the practice sand trap. "I know I said it yesterday, but you seem to have an awful lot on your mind besides golf."

"Oh I have golf there, too. Things like: What the hell am I doing out here? And how can I possibly beat these amazons? Some of these girls have thighs bigger than my waist."

Joe laughed. "This winter we'll get you on a weight-lifting program. In the meantime, remember, there's nothing more demoralizing than getting skunked by a little player with a big heart."

I splashed a ball out of the trap and into the hole I'd aimed it at. "Like that?"

He laughed again. "Listen, I know you're upset about Erica. And disappointed that Lucia didn't show last night. You have to let that go for now. Work with me here, and I promise I'll help you with that stuff once today's round is over. Deal?"

I nodded.

"What the hell are you carrying in this bag anyway?" asked Laura. "You don't need water balls on this course— the only water you have to hit over is the little pond on six." She dug into the pocket with the Birdie Girl logo and tossed out several scuffed balls. Then she felt around in the small pocket that I seldom used. "Have you gone high tech on me?" She held up a Palm Pilot. "You going to be making dates during the round? Does this have to come with us now?"

"That's not mine. I wouldn't have a clue how to use it." I held my hand out to her. "I bet that's Erica's. Where'd you find it?"

"Give it here," said Joe. "I'll hold onto it until you're done." He slapped my hand away and grabbed the organizer from Laura. "We'll look at it later. Right now, we don't need distractions. We need to visualize."

"Visualize this." I stuck out my tongue. "Why don't you make yourself useful and rake that bunker?"

Joe ignored my snit. "Just remember, while you stand behind the ball looking at your target, you practice feeling the right elbow dropping close to your side. Before you swing, your only thought is balance." After hearing my experience with hooked tee shots, he'd suggested a swing thought that could carry a lot of Zen-like reverberations for life, and more important, would be hard to twist into destructive lurching motions.

At twenty to eight, the three of us walked across the road to the first tee. Laura protested that thirty-four minutes of watching the starter drink coffee and chat with the women teeing off ahead of us was too much time to spare. Time that I was likely to spend winding myself into a white-knuckled, wired-up wreck. I overruled her with a couple of horror stories about golfers who'd misread the pairings sheet by ten minutes and showed up in time to hear the announcement of their disqualification.

The last couple tournaments I played, I'd made a policy not to look ahead of time at which players I'd be paired with that day. If it was bad news, like I'd gotten stuck with a chronic whiner or someone who intimidated the FootJoys off me, I couldn't change it anyway. Worrying about it in advance just rattled my game. So I groaned when I saw Sheryl Browning and Danni Williams chatting with the starter. With these two playing partners, the round would be saturated with a plethora of self-absorbed chitchat and a big gallery of groupies following our every move.

Sheryl, a golfer turned TV commentator, had been struggling to make a move back onto the Tour. Up until now, I'd only seen her from a distance or on television. Her curve-hugging black clothing made her look a lot younger than her thirty-eight years. Even I had to admire the fashion chutzpah involved in the heavy gold necklace, midcalf black socks, and shiny patent Mr. Bojangles golf shoes.

Danni was a different story entirely. Early in the season, she nudged me out for an assignment writing a weekly rookie diary for the biggest women's golf web site. I'd spent a good month studying her entry in the *LPGA Media Guide* until I practically had her statistics memorized. What the hell did she have that I was lacking?

Joe assured me that I was better off without the assignment; the public self-evaluation would have only dragged my game down. But Danni seemed to thrive on the weekly self-congratulatory drivel she produced. I'd sworn off reading the articles after the first two: "The Cut Made Easy" and "A Surprise Visit from Mother and Daddy Makes My Day." I hadn't made any cuts, hard or easy, so it burned me good to hear a buoyant rendition of her early success.

As far as parents making one's day, my mother wouldn't be caught dead at a golf tournament. She insisted golf, golf courses, golfers—all of them reminded her that she'd been dumped by Dad. Their twenty-year-old marital trauma still clogged her emotional windpipe like a chicken bone. And my father, who ate, drank, and slept golf, hadn't bothered to watch me play since junior high school.

"I'm so glad to get to play with you, Cassandra," Sheryl said in a chirpy voice. "That's such a pretty name. It's Greek isn't it?"

"Yeah. Cassandra was the prophetess who warned people about the fall of Troy. Obviously, no one listened."

Sheryl let out an audience-pleasing tinkle of a laugh. "So your mother was a fan of Greek mythology."

"Soap operas. Cassandra was the slutty nurse screwing the docs in the supply room the day my mother's water broke."

The annoying laugh tinkled out again. I could feel my shoulders tightening. Laura cut in between us and herded me off to the side of the tee with a perfunctory smile in Sheryl's direction.

"I'm just making small talk," I said.

"Get away from her," she said. "Caddie's orders."

I fidgeted with my grip and practiced the new swing thought until the starter called our names. Both Sheryl and Danni gave a royal wave to the crowd and nailed tee shots down the center of the fairway. I tipped my hat to their fans, then yanked my drive left. As far as I could tell, it missed the stand of cedars lining the left edge of the hole but definitely settled into the naturalized sea grasses just off the fairway.

"Oopsy," said Danni. "Tough break. When you get into that rough, you can get some killer lies."

"I'll show her a killer lie," I muttered, stabbing my driver back into the bag.

"Leave the mindless twit behind you," said Laura. "Sooner or later, she'll cut herself on her own tongue."

We marched down the fairway double time. "Are you going to the party tonight?" asked Danni, trotting to keep pace.

"I doubt it," I said.

"But you have to! You know a lot of those guys from your caddie days, don't you? I was counting on you to introduce me."

I shrugged. With the PGA Tour playing a tournament just an hour away this weekend, the LPGA sponsors had arranged a big reception for the players on both Tours, along with the ShopRite Classic amateurs. I hadn't seriously considered going. The idea of running into Mike Callahan still made my stomach churn.

"I don't have anything to wear," I said. "My evening wardrobe runs mostly to cotton pajamas."

"I'd be happy to loan you something," said Sheryl. "Since I have to play dress-up for the TV commentary, I travel with trunks of stuff I never get around to. Swing by my room after the broadcast, and we'll pick you something out."

"Thanks." I glanced at her slender figure again. Anything she had to offer was liable to be high fashion and skintight. Definitely not my style.

I chopped my ball out of the rough and managed to wedge it up onto the green close enough to save par. The other two women made easy birdies. The wind had picked up off the bay when we reached the second hole. With a serious effort to keep my Zen balance, I joined the others in the fairway. My second shot left me with a fast downhill slider. I was relieved to sink the second putt and clear out with another par.

Somewhere down the third fairway, the conversation of the other two girls began to recede to a soft background buzz. I worked on Joe's mantra: visualize, visualize, and visualize some more. Pick out the cloud your approach shot will reach for, choose the exact blade of grass your putt will roll over. As I did, the birdies began to fall. Birdies on three, four, five, six, and seven. Sportswriters love to talk about the "zone." Had I finally found it? I hit another drive down the middle of the eighth fairway.

"Good shot!" said Sheryl. She adjusted the swarm of gold bracelets clanking against her forearm and swung.

"You're playing so great," said Danni as we left the tee box. "Maybe I could write about you in my column this week. Do you have a new teacher? Do you know what you're doing different?"

"No idea," I said, just smiling. I'd seen this trick before—get someone who's playing well to start thinking about her game. Pretty soon, she's so tangled up in trying to identify what her mind and body parts are doing, she forgets to swing. As mind games go, this was strictly an amateur effort. We watched Sheryl's eight-iron approach hit the green, then wander off onto the collar.

"Did you read about the murder in Atlantic City this morning?" asked Danni's caddie.

"What murder? Who got knocked off?" asked Danni, a rush of breathless excitement filling her voice.

Laura and I exchanged disgusted looks.

"It was a worker at one of the casinos. They found her on the beach this morning. Shot dead, then buried up to her neck in the sand."

I thought right away of Erica's dealer friend, Lucia.

"Someone buried her?" asked Danni. "That's so gross! Blood and sand. What a mess."

"Who was it?" I asked.

"From a distance, they thought she was a homeless person who'd spent the night under the boardwalk," Danni's caddie said. "When she didn't respond to their questions, they rolled her out of the sand and found a hole in her chest."

"Who was it?" I asked again, hearing my own voice now too loud and sharp.

Laura pulled out her orange yardage book and drew me away from the other players. "We'll find out about it after the round. What club are you thinking here?"

I plucked a handful of loose grass off the fairway and threw it up into the air to test the wind. "Right-to-left crosswind. I need to fly those traps. Nine iron?"

Truth was, I hadn't been thinking about my approach shot at all. What Danni hadn't been able to orchestrate, her caddie had. Instead of running through my preshot routine, I'd been picturing the dead body on the beach. And on the body, I'd pasted the face of Lucia. I shook those thoughts out of my head and swung the nine iron.

It came up ten feet short of the green. Laura grimaced and handed me my wedge.

"I'd suggest you chip it close."

A half-skulled chip and two putts later, I carded my first bogey of the day.

"What was that all about? Where was your zone, babe?"

Ignoring Laura's sarcasm, I waved Joe over to the ninth tee. "There was a casino employee who was murdered on the beach last night. Can you look into it? I keep thinking about Lucia, and it's not helping my focus here."

"Done. You just keep doing what you were doing." He rubbed my shoulders while the other two players teed off. "Go get 'em. I'm all over the other question."

I tried to get back my birdie mentality. Laura tried, too. But dead faces—Erica and now possibly Lucia—continued to pop up in my head at inopportune moments. And Danni's silly chitchat irked me in a way it hadn't on the first eight holes. By the time we dragged up the eighteenth hole, I was soaked with sweat, dotted with greenhead bite lesions, and irritable as hell. Still, I'd managed to hold the damage to two more bogeys.

"An eagle here would salve our wounds," Laura said as we walked in the direction my drive had bounced. We found the ball buried in the deep grass of the left rough. "On the other hand, par would be nice, too." She laughed and handed me my wedge.

After holing out for par, I headed to the scorer's tent with the other girls to check our scores and sign cards. Danni bubbled over with excitement; not only was her sixty-three a personal best, she explained several times, it tied the tournament record for the course.

In contrast, Sheryl maintained a practiced cheerfulness that did not match the seventy-nine on her scorecard. I had to hand it to her. Even though she'd played like a hacker who belonged in the second flight of a club championship, she greeted her fans as if she'd just won the tournament. Unless she came out tomorrow all guns blazing, she would miss another cut and smother her slim chance at a comeback onto the Tour.

"Ms. Williams, the press would like to interview you. We need you to go over to the press station inside the clubhouse. We're having some technical trouble with our equipment here." Danni hugged her caddie and went squealing out of the tent. The media representative glanced down a second time at our scorecards. "Ms. Burdette, would you be so kind as to come along, too?"

"Be happy to." This was a first: Cassandra Burdette interviewed by the press, even if I had been upstaged by Danni the piglet and her record-tying sixty-three. I guess they figured me shooting under par was unusual enough to merit newsprint. I found Laura waiting outside the tent and told her the news.

"Hot damn! It's about time you got some airspace. I'll go over to the lunch tent and tell Joe you'll be along shortly. Unless you want us to come with . . ."

"I can handle it. Thanks anyway." I was nervous enough going alone. Just the sight of Joe sitting in the audience would transform me into a babbling fool. "Grab me a sandwich, and I'll be over shortly." I trotted across the street before she could try to change the plan.

Chapter 9

I darted into the pro shop to avoid walking to the pressroom with Danni. With a quick wave to the assistant manager, I hurried past the locker room and up two flights of stairs to media mecca. A volunteer in a ShopRite LPGA Classic official polo shirt stopped me at the door.

"I'm Cassie Burdette. They sent me over from the scoring tent for an interview?"

The woman checked her legal pad and nodded. "It'll be a couple of minutes. You want a Coke or something?"

"No thanks." After five hours of pit stops at every courtesy cooler on the golf course, I was nothing if not well hydrated.

"You can go on in and listen to Miss Williams's interview while you wait, if you like."

"Thanks. I need to stretch my legs." No need to blurt out that five hours of nonstop chatter from Danni had been torture enough.

I wandered down the corridor toward the bar, the thick green plush of the carpet barely giving way beneath my feet. The walls were lined with photos: Sam Snead at the 1942 PGA Tournament, golf course architect Donald Ross with the club's first greenskeeper, and Julie Inkster, two-time tournament winner in the mid-eighties. Now there was a woman who had everything together: an unimaginably successful career and a Donna Reed family on the side. Hard not to feel insubstantial in comparison. I moved to an old picture of the original inn. A framed notice was posted underneath it.

"In cases where unmarried couples without proper chaperonage apply at the desk for rooms—in order to avoid any embarrassing situations, it will be requested that the lady be assigned a room on one floor and the gentleman on another. By order of the Board of Governors, Seaview Golf Club."

"Miss Burdette? They're ready for you now."

She directed me down the hallway and into the media room. The carpet was green here, too, but with pink ribbons and bows woven into the pattern. Enormous ferns flanked two wing chairs on the stage in front of a ShopRite LPGA Classic banner. Four reporters sat on folding chairs at the foot of the stage.

"Have a seat," said the volunteer, pointing to one of the wing chairs.

"I have to sit up there by myself?" I asked.

The reporters laughed.

"You're the one who shot sixty-nine," said a portly man with graying curls. The chubby man introduced himself as a writer for *Golf Northeast*. "Nice round. Five birdies on the front nine. Tell us how you did that."

"I wish I could." I shrugged and smiled. "All I can say is, once the putter got hot, it just happened."

"Sarah Sanderson from *Women's Golf World*. Things didn't go so well on the back. What was the difference?"

"Putter cooled off, I guess." I groaned inwardly. I'd waited a long time to be interview worthy, and now I'd stepped right up sounding like a first-class dork. Not that the questions were all that brilliant either: standard-issue early-round inquiries, special to me because no one had bothered to ask before today.

"How were the conditions out there?" asked the portly man.

"Beastly hot, buried lies if you got in the rough, and the flies were even worse. . . . I loved every minute of it." The reporters laughed again. Make that a first-class dizzy dork. I remembered the photos I'd seen on the walls and tried to add something sophisticated. "I love Donald Ross designs." I sure hoped they wouldn't ask me to expound on the unique character of Donald's projects; I'd be exposed as a fraudulent, dizzy dork.

"Tell us how it feels to be well on your way to making your first cut."

"I'm in trouble if I start thinking about that," I said, holding my fingers crossed in front of me. "Just one shot at a time, that's my motto."

"What's your year been like so far?"

"A roller coaster. New cities to get used to every week, new beds, too, and all the stuff we rookies have to learn. It's not so easy to concentrate on golf."

"Robert Bradley from the *Cape May Sun*. I understand you had Erica LeBoutillier in your foursome on Tuesday. The *Press* ran a story this morning about her possible drug and gambling connections. Can you comment on that?"

My mouth flapped open, then closed again. What could I say? I didn't have any hard facts, just hunches. Best not to step on your frankfurter, as Mike Callahan used to say. "I don't know anything about that, so I don't have a comment. Except I'm really sad it happened."

"Thanks for your time, and good luck tomorrow." I

shook hands with the reporters and followed the volunteer back out into the hallway.

"Take care, Cathy," she said.

I'd made quite an impression on her.

Joe and Laura were camped out at a corner table in the chow tent with the remains of a substantial lunch on a tray in front of them.

"I had a whole plate fixed for you, but it started to get cold, so we ate it," said Laura. "We saved you a sandwich and some chips anyway."

Between bites of my ham and cheese on rye, I told them about the interview. "It went okay, even though I was nervous as hell. No, I take that back. Actually, I sounded like an idiot."

"You are an idiot." Laura reached over to noogie my hair with her knuckles.

"Thanks, pal. I'll do better next time. What'd you find out about the murder on the beach?" I asked Joe. "And one of the reporters wanted to know if I had any information about Erica's drug and gambling habits. What was in the paper this morning?"

"Mostly speculation. People assume a death in a casino has to be related to gambling. They tried to get some information about Erica out of the local Gamblers Anonymous chapter, but no one's talking. Take a look at this."

Joe slid the front page of the *Press* across the table and pointed to a photo in the bottom right-hand corner. It was a head shot of Lucia. The exhilaration I'd been feeling after the interview drained away.

The article accompanying the picture was brief. Lucia Jimenez, thirty-four, had been found shot to death on the beach near the boardwalk. She had been an employee of the casino for four years. She lived on Haley Street and left two sons, ages eleven and nine. Police were involved in an ongoing investigation of the murder, and anyone with information should contact the Atlantic City Police

Department. I felt a sickening clunk in my gut, reading about the children. I fought back an image of bullet holes crusted with beach sand.

"Oh my God." I started to feel queasy with the thought that came next. "What if she was murdered because we tried to talk to her last night? I need to call Detective Rumson and fill her in."

Joe nodded.

The sick feeling got worse. "I feel awful about this. Maybe we should stop by Lucia's—"

"Just call the police; that's all you should do," said Joe. "Then go practice your putting."

He'd taken on that tone I hated: shrink/father/general superior being. I wasn't willing to let it drop. "There are now three kids who won't see their mothers again, ever, and you want me to putt?"

"You're a golfer, not a detective." He laughed.

I glared.

"I did do some research on Meditron while you were playing. Interesting stuff."

Curiosity overwhelmed my irritation. "Spill."

"They've headlined three major news stories in the last four years—not the kind their public relations department would welcome."

Joe laid out copies of three *New York Times* articles on the table. The first caption read: *"Pharmaceutical Company Gets Bad News From FDA on New Drug."* The second one was worse: *"Meditron Disputes DEA Data on Neuroxytin Fatalities."* And the third, worst of all: *"Meditron Forced to Pull Drug Linked to Deaths."*

I waved my hand across the articles. "Give us the summary version."

"Four years ago, Meditron developed Celair, a groundbreaking drug that treated asthma and hay fever. The regulatory process had been completed and the drug was poised for public launch. The potential market was huge, and so were the possible profits. Then some unexpected data came back demonstrating cardiac side effects. The FDA demanded more studies, which deferred the launch date. And this didn't only affect Meditron—the economic effects rippled through the entire industry."

"Bad news." I pointed to the second headline. "What about this one?"

"Medical examiners were recently surveyed by the Drug Enforcement Agency for autopsy data related to Meditron's new opiod painkiller, Neuroxytin. The drug's been in the news a lot. It's very addictive and people will do almost anything to get their hands on it. Anyway, the DEA study reported almost five hundred drug-related deaths. Meditron, of course, is arguing that the study's methodology was flawed and the conclusions misleading."

"Really bad news," I said. "Doesn't anybody look into these things before they sell them to us?"

"Oh sure. There's a rigorous testing process they put the new medications through. First animal studies, then clinical trials. But it's always balanced against the enormous pressure for the bottom line—profit."

"You said Meditron had three problems." I tapped my finger on the third article before Joe could launch into a philosophical discourse on the evils of capitalism.

"Have you heard of Lochol?"

"No."

"A couple years ago, it was touted as a breakthrough in the arena of cholesterol-lowering drugs. Meditron beat two other major companies getting the drug to market. Again, a lot of people connected to the business were licking their chops about getting rich in the process. Then the reports about deaths related to Lochol started coming in, and the company had to pull it off the shelves."

"Jesus," said Laura. "What did they die from?"

"Heart attacks."

"Jesus," Laura said again. "I'm surprised the company

isn't bankrupt after all that. How the hell do they have the dough to send their employees off on pricey golf outings?"

"Sounds like getting approval for the Alzheimer's drug is crucial for Meditron," I said.

"Exactly," said Joe.

"And Erica talked about hindering the approval process just before she died."

"Exactly," said Joe.

"What about the Palm Pilot?" I asked. "Maybe Erica documented something there that might help."

"We looked at it while we were waiting for you," said Laura. "Some of the files are password-protected, so we couldn't get access to all of it."

"But like you said, this doesn't resemble the datebook of someone who was planning to take her own life," said Joe. "She had appointments scheduled through next year. People planning to commit suicide generally don't pack a calendar this full of personal engagements."

"Look at this." Laura turned the instrument on and touched the screen with a stylus. A page of notes flashed onto the screen. I skimmed the words over her shoulder as she read them aloud.

"Keep the left thumb just right of center. In the backswing, upper left arm swings up against the chest. In the downswing, right arm straightens just before swinging across upper body. Be aggressive in your straightening in the forward swing."

"It's notes from a golf lesson."

Laura nodded. "And take a look at this." She touched the screen again and brought up a page of notes with the title "Lila Rose: Eleventh Birthday." The list included: call florist/dozen yellow roses, take LR to ShopRite LPGA Classic to meet a pro, dinner at Friendly's, buy Prom Barbie and junior makeup kit.

I wanted to cry. The list was a portrait of a mom trying

every tactic she could think of to connect with a daughter caught in the no-man's-land between childhood and adulthood. Not to mention caught between warring parents.

The calendar for the month flashed in front of us. "Her schedule was intense," said Laura. "I don't know how she was even going to shop for that stuff on Lila's list."

I looked at the appointments that Erica had set up for the month, most identified by initials. LR, on Wednesday nights and alternate weekends, was easy. The image of the grieving girl left me weak with sadness.

"DG is the golf pro," said Laura. "She'd been seeing a lot of him lately."

"She had that big amateur tournament next week," I said. "She didn't feel prepared. What about SA and RB?"

"No clue about SA. But there were two listings in the address book with initials RB," said Joe. "Richard Bataka in Santa Monica, California, and Dr. Rebecca Butterman, Pleasant Heights, New Jersey. Appointments every other Saturday morning at seven A.M. over the past two months. Our money's on Dr. Butterman."

"We checked her out in the Yellow Pages," said Laura. "She's a shrink."

"That makes sense, the regular sessions," I said. "Let's give her a call."

"I did," said Joe. "I made an appointment to see her at three."

I glanced at my watch. "We better get going, then. Where's her office?"

"I think it's best if I go alone," said Joe.

"I'm the one who knew Erica," I protested. "I'm going with you."

"Chances are, if Erica was her patient, she won't be willing to discuss her anyway, patient confidentiality and all that. But she's more likely to talk to me alone as another professional."

"The woman is dead, for God's sake. What can it hurt now?"

Laura patted my hand in a calming rhythm. I could tell from the looks at the next table that my voice had shot up into shrieking harpy range.

"It's the law, Cassie."

I was silent. His argument was sound, but it still pissed me off that he was going without me.

"How about I meet you at the party tonight, we'll have one drink with the tournament muckety-mucks, then go grab some dinner? I'll fill you in on everything I found out." His scolding professor tone had become conciliatory.

I shrugged and smiled. "Fine. See you around six."

"Rest up this afternoon, okay? Big day for you tomorrow." Joe came around the table to hug me. I felt a small patch of low-grade stubble on his chin and smelled a faint mixture of sweat and mint. Then he left the tent. Laura reached over to grab the last potato chip on my plate.

"You rolled over easy there, girl. I thought we were in for a big fight."

"No." I smiled again. "He doesn't think I should talk with Lucia's family or meet Dr. Butterman? That's just fine. It gives you and me time to take a field trip to Meditron headquarters. I'll go call Travis now and see if he's free. What do you say? Are you game?"

Laura was on her feet before I finished the sentence. She scooped up the Palm Pilot and stuffed it in her back pocket. "After you. . . ."

Chapter 10

Laura lurched onto the Garden State Parkway. Pine barrens stretched out for miles on both sides of the highway. Half an hour later, we found the exit and pulled into a winding driveway that curved around a small man-made lake and up to the Meditron headquarters.

"It's a lot bigger than I pictured," said Laura. "So do we have a plan here? Or shall we just step up to the receptionist and ask who killed Erica LeBoutillier? Maybe she could announce it on the company loudspeaker—"

"Nobody likes a smart-ass." I flipped the visor mirror open and combed my fingers through my hair. "Travis said we have to stop at the gate and get a pass. Tell the guard Dr. Smith is expecting us. They won't even allow you on the grounds of this outfit without an engraved invitation."

The man in the tollbooth checked his logbook, found my name, and issued us a parking permit. He directed us to a distant lot and recommended we catch the shuttle bus back to the main building.

"I reminded Travis on the phone that he invited me over for coffee and a tour," I explained to Laura as she locked the car. "He wasn't exactly pirouetting with excitement. We'll need to warm him up, then we can admit we came because we're concerned about Erica. I hope we get the chance to meet with the other guys, too. You keep your eyes peeled; you may notice something about one of these characters that I missed."

The bus delivered us to the main entrance of Meditron, and we walked the length of a sidewalk planted with ornamental grasses and muted perennials. Inside, a three-story pink granite wall with a two-story waterfall dwarfed the lobby. Enormous fig trees strung with café lights defined a sweeping staircase.

"Wow. Some big money went into this," whispered Laura.

"We're here to see Dr. Travis Smith," I told the receptionist.

"Is he expecting you?" She conveyed her serious doubt with a faint tone of incredulity.

"Yes."

The receptionist made a quick phone call. "His secretary says he can only see you for twenty minutes. He has a very tight schedule today. You can wait for him over in the gazebo." She pointed to a group of rattan seats positioned among the fig trees. Several large tropical birds in cages squawked in the nearby foliage. While Laura canvassed the parrots for the presence of salty vocabulary, I tried to plan the most fruitful approach to Travis.

"Ms. Burdette?" A middle-aged woman in a blue business suit and sensible pumps descended the last steps of the stairway. She stuck her hand out and shook mine firmly. "I'm Teresa Biacci, the department's administrative assistant. I'll show you to Dr. Smith's office."

"This is my friend, Laura Snow."

Teresa wrung her hand as well.

"Your building is lovely."

"The areas that need to be impressive impress." Whatever the hell she meant by that, she made it clear she did not welcome further conversation.

As we stepped off the elevator on the sixth floor, we ran into Hugh Gladstone. He looked like he wished he could duck back into the men's room, where he'd come from and where we couldn't follow.

"Dr. Gladstone! How are you?"

"Nice to see you again," he muttered.

I pushed Laura forward. "I'd like you to meet my caddie and old friend, Laura Snow."

They shook hands. "Today went well, I trust?" The chilly politeness I remembered from earlier in the week confirmed that his question was not meant to invite a play-by-play of the round.

"A good start, thanks. Sixty-nine, in fact." I couldn't help smiling. It still sounded amazing to me. "Dr. Gladstone was the backbone of our scramble team on Tuesday," I told Laura. "He plays what we call boring golf—he puts his drives in the fairway and leaves his putts below the hole."

Hugh smiled briefly. "It was a good team."

"Travis invited me over to see your company, and we had some free time this afternoon."

"I'm sure Ms. Biacci will show you the way to his office." He nodded to where she hovered by a desk several yards down the hall.

I dropped my voice to a near whisper. "Before we go, I had one question to ask. It bothers me a lot that they're calling Erica's death a suicide. You were one of the people who knew her well. Do you really think she killed herself?"

Hugh's face flushed a strangled purple color. He

straightened the knot of his striped club tie and cleared his throat. "We were colleagues rather than friends. I would certainly not qualify as someone who knew her well. Other than her work, of course, which was of uniformly high quality."

"Even so, you may have inadvertently gathered information about her that would help explain what happened."

"Frankly, I believe her personal problems had begun to seriously impinge on her professional judgment. I have nothing more to say." He turned to leave.

"One last thing. In your opinion, if your Alzheimer's drug was not allowed to go to market because of Erica's actions, could she have become a target for murder?"

Hugh looked horrified. Finally I had broken through his reserve. "No one here would murder her, for Christ's sake. Even if she gave us reason to feel homicidal from time to time."

He began to move down the hallway in the direction of his corner office, labeled with a prominent nameplate. "We need to conclude our conversation," he said over his shoulder. "You'll find Dr. Smith at the end of the corridor on the left. I will have Ms. Biacci call him to expect you and she will escort you there."

Teresa Biacci was already on the phone at the desk stationed outside of Hugh's preserve. "I'll take you down to Dr. Smith's office," she said, placing the phone into its cradle.

"I'm sure we can find it. Hugh pointed us in the right direction."

"It's no trouble," she said firmly.

We trailed her past a sea of workers' cubicles. "Jesus," Laura whispered. "Why didn't you just go at him with a sledgehammer?"

"I told you I wanted to shake the tree and see what dropped down. Anyway, it just popped out." I snickered. "He did look like he might blow a gasket. I bet he wishes he never made that homicidal comment. It'll give him something to think about. Travis Smith is our next victim. See if you don't catch a whiff of something more than business in his relationship with Erica."

We stopped behind Ms. Biacci, who tapped on Travis's partly open door.

"Cassie!" He leaped up from his computer and hugged me. "Thanks, Teresa. I'll take it from here. Great to see you! Hey, how did you play?" He reached a hand over to Laura. "Travis Smith."

"Laura Snow. I carried her bag, and she played awesome. Broke par, even though she missed a couple short putts along the way."

"We came for the promised tour," I said. Based on our brief phone conversation, he was friendlier than I expected. So I got right to the point. "And to talk about Erica. Do you have a couple minutes?"

Sadness flooded his eyes. "Absolutely. Can I get you a coffee?"

"No thanks." He waved at two upholstered chairs across from his desk and shut the door behind us.

"I still can't believe she's gone. I miss her already." He took his reading glasses off and wiped his damp face with a white handkerchief. "How can I help?"

I leaned forward. He seemed ready to talk. "You don't think it was suicide either."

Travis blew his nose loudly and shook his head. "I'm certain her bastard husband was behind this. The custody trial was coming up, probably early in the fall. They were about to start the depositions. He was never going to be able to block her access to her own daughter. And then there was the financial settlement. He was terrified that Erica's lawyer would take him to the cleaners."

"How did her husband get custody of Lila Rose to begin with? Don't most judges bend over backward to award custody to the mother? Unless something was really wrong . . ."

For several moments, Travis gazed out the window toward the fountain in the pond. "She had a gambling problem. And he exploited it. But over the last few months, she'd gotten it under control."

I leaned forward again. "So why did she take us to play blackjack?"

He looked down at the floor and then back up at me. "This is how she explained it. She said some people are alcoholics who can't ever drink again. Others can have a few social cocktails without bad consequences. Playing a few hands of ten-dollar blackjack, that was social gambling for her, not serious at all."

Laura looked skeptical. "Did you know Lucia Jimenez?"

"She was the dealer at our blackjack table Tuesday night," I added.

Travis shook his head.

"The cops found her shot to death on the beach this morning."

"Holy shit! Honest to God, I swear I hadn't been gambling with Erica before this week. I discouraged her from getting back into it. And as far as I knew, she wasn't going on a regular basis."

"Did you speak with Erica the night she died?"

Travis's eyes, rimmed in red, now bulged with moisture. "I called her room, but she didn't answer. I thought about leaving a message. . . ."

I patted his hand. "This is hard for you, losing a friend."

He nodded and sighed.

"She seemed concerned about the timetable for the Alzheimer's drug. Could you tell me more about that?"

He picked up the watch hanging from his belt loop, studied it, and sighed again. "Our job is to develop new drugs. Many of them are extremely helpful in treating serious medical problems. These advantages must be weighed against the risk of serious side effects, called adverse events. The FDA monitors the entire process. Phase one involves animal studies and small, closely watched studies with human subjects. A safety committee evaluates this data very carefully. If the results are satisfactory, we move into phase two, involving a wider range of clinical trials. A new drug application or NDA is submitted to the FDA to request permission to market the drug. Follow me so far?" We both nodded. "The FDA has a year to complete their evaluation of the drug. We are approaching that time limit now."

"And Hugh told all of you on Tuesday that the news looked good."

"Yes. We've played everything by the book on this one. We brought in liver experts, we went above and beyond in our data collection." He tipped forward and placed both elbows on the desk. "Our main goal is that this critical breakthrough for a terrible disease reach the public. But safely."

So far, we weren't getting much in the way of new information. I decided to push a little harder. "Supposing the drug was deemed not ready to go to market at this late point. What kinds of fallout would your team expect?"

"We would be disappointed, that's for sure. Like in every other business, time is money. And in this case, a delay would mean more suffering for the people affected by this disease. They would not be getting the help they need." He had segued into what sounded like a canned public relations pitch.

"Are you the only company working on this product?"

Pitch over, tone now cool. "I would have no way of knowing that."

My antennae shot up. Of course he knew what the competition was up to; they had to make it their business to know. And why the sudden frosty tone? We'd reached the end of the line with Travis—for the moment. "Could you arrange for us to meet with Roger for a couple minutes? We were hoping to get his assessment of Erica's mental state, too."

"You won't get anything useful out of him. First off, he and Erica didn't have much to do with each other. Second, he's a tight-assed, humorless number cruncher who doesn't know how to deal with people."

"Could we talk to him anyway?"

Travis made a phone call. "He's tied up for another half an hour, then he'll come over. You can wait at the reception area at the end of the hall."

The idea of even a few minutes under the glacial hawk eye of Teresa Biacci did not sound appealing.

"Can we wait in Erica's office? I'd like to see where she worked."

Travis shrugged. "Sorry. Company policy. Can't leave the interlopers alone."

"Aha," said Laura. "We might steal secrets from the crown."

"You got it." He laughed, shook both our hands, and thanked us for coming. I very much doubted he was glad we came, but his mother had taught him well.

"Hey!" I called down the hall after him. "Are you guys coming to the party tonight?"

"Wouldn't miss it. Erica wouldn't have missed it either." He saluted in the direction of her office and disappeared into his own space.

Ms. Biacci appeared out from the cubicle maze and assumed her guard dog position at a desk across from us in the waiting area. She gave us the shadow of a smile, then buried herself in a journal called *Physicians' Drug Watch. Visitors' Watchdog* would be more like it.

"What'd you think?" I whispered to Laura.

"If they were just coworkers, I'm a contestant for the

Miss America swimsuit contest." Standing on her tiptoes, she put her hands on her full hips and sashayed across the hallway. Ms. Biacci glared at her until she took her seat again. "Even Dr. Gladstone, who claimed he didn't know her well, had something to say about how her personal problems were affecting her work. I can't wait to meet the third Musketeer."

"Roger's different. He's more stiff than Travis, but not as unfriendly as Hugh. He won't be in a hurry to spill his guts, but I think we can get him talking if we ask about the drug mechanism and how they set up the studies."

"Travis didn't seem to want us to talk to him. What did he call him? A humorless number cruncher. That's harsh."

Just then, the beeper clipped to Ms. Biacci's waist went off. She studied the window on her pager. "Drat. He'll serve my head on a platter if I don't answer this immediately."

Laura held up her fingers in the position of the Girl Scouts' oath. "We'll stay right here. We promise." I nodded with enthusiasm.

Ms. Biacci stared at the beeper again, then squinted back at us. "I'll return in five minutes," she warned. "Don't go anywhere."

As soon as she'd moved down the hallway and out of sight, Laura pointed to a small office several paces away from the waiting area. "See the nameplate there? That's Erica's office."

"I know." Without any further discussion, I stood up and slunk down the hall and into the room.

"Cassie!" she whispered. "Get the hell out of there!"

I moved quickly around the space where Erica had spent most of the hours of her working life. Framed photographs of Lila Rose and an older couple I assumed must be her parents were displayed on the shelf above her computer. I could see Erica's smile in her mother's face, although her ski-jump nose and brown eyes had come directly from Dad. On the far wall hung a handwritten, construction paper sign whose words marched crookedly across the page. "We like to work. Work is fun. We like to work. Work is fun. We like to work. Work is fun." The paper was signed in the loopy script of a child: Erica Jorganson. In the bottom corner, "Good" had been red-penciled in an adult hand.

"She must have been one weird kid," said Laura, who had followed me into the office. "I wish we could get into her computer. I'd love to know what was in those locked files."

"Forget about it. We've got the general idea. It's not necessary to get hauled away for criminal trespassing." I walked over to peruse the titles in Erica's bookshelf: biochemistry manuals, the *Physicians' Desk Reference*, and David Leadbetter's *Positive Practice*.

"Hey—do you see what I see?" Laura pointed at the cradle for Erica's Palm Pilot, wired to the back of her computer. "Maybe there's a way into her secured files. If we HotSync it, we can look everything over back in our hotel room."

"Forget about it. . . ."

Before I could slam my foot down, she slid the organizer into the cradle and pressed the button.

Chapter 11

The computer clicked, then issued a whining noise. A sequence of HotSync progress memos flashed onto the screen. "Connecting with the desktop, identifying user, synchronizing datebook, address book, to-do list, memos . . ." the screen informed us.

"You're going to get us kicked out of here," I said in a low voice. "Or arrested."

"Almost done," said Laura. "I just want to take a look at which conduit logged a message. It'll only take a sec."

At that moment, the door to Erica's office flew open. Laura popped up and planted herself on the desk in front of the computer. I stood in front of her, hoping to block any view of the illicitly connected Palm Pilot.

I expected to see Roger. Instead, a tiny woman with curly black hair and a turquoise jumper smiled at us, creating small cracks in her thick layer of pancake makeup.

"Hi there!" she chirped in a nasal voice. "Travis said

the golfer he played with at the pro-am was here to talk about Erica. I came to say hello. I'm Christine. She was my boss." Two red spots appeared on the woman's cheeks. "And my friend."

"So sorry for your loss," I said, beginning to get a feel for just how empty that phrase could be. It also felt rude to not go over and shake her hand, but I didn't want to expose our computerized snooping.

"Travis said you had some questions about whether Erica killed herself. I thought maybe I could help."

"What do you think happened?" Laura asked.

"I don't know for sure." Christine leaned against the doorjamb. "That girl knew how to stir up excitement."

"How so?"

Christine peeked out the door and down the hallway. "Her and Travis, they had something hot going for a while." She blew on her fingers and shook her hand.

"So they were more than friends."

"Way more than friends," she repeated with raised eyebrows. "From what I saw, though, he was on the way out." She smiled. "One of those don't-let-the-door-slam-you-in-the-butt deals."

That sounded like an invitation for us to hear everything she knew. And I wanted to pump her for more gossip, but I'd started to worry about Roger Ranz catching us with the Palm Pilot. Or the formidable Teresa Biacci trapping us in forbidden territory. "Would you mind directing me to the ladies' room?"

"Down the hall and first right around the corner. But you're not supposed to go by yourself. I'll show you."

"Great." I couldn't go to the bathroom alone? Maybe they thought I was a graffiti risk, too. Just as well; our absence would give Laura the chance to get the damn Palm Pilot out of Erica's office.

"You'd better have a seat out here in the waiting area," she told Laura. "They don't like visitors loose in someone's office." Christine turned to lead me down the hall, leaving the powdery smell of an old woman in her wake. I followed, motioning behind me to Laura to pack up the Palm Pilot.

"So they had something going, but you think it was over," I said when we'd both emerged from our stalls.

She lowered her voice to a whisper. "I think she dumped him for the golf pro. That guy was a hunk." Christine washed her hands, smoothed the foundation around her lips, and plucked at her bangs. "He came by here once last week. I thought I'd die when I saw him. I can tell you this for sure—chubby little Travis didn't stand a chance compared to that beefcake. He thinks he's such a Romeo. Geez Louise, not only is the guy fat, he stinks besides."

I had to wonder why this woman was so interested in the sordid details of Erica and Travis's affairs. And why she was so eager to share her opinions with someone she'd just met. Maybe her own social life was seriously stunted.

We returned to the waiting area outside Erica's office. Laura lounged in the chair by the door. I glanced into the cubicle and saw the Palm Pilot cradle was empty.

"How do you like working here, Christine?" Laura asked.

"Shoo-ey. No one likes working here," whispered Christine. She glanced down the hallway—left, right, then left again—like it was a busy thoroughfare. "It may not look like it, but this place is a sweatshop. Every morning I wake up and say I can't go in there one more day. I lie in my bed and think: seven more years, and I'm vested in my pension. And so I get dressed and come in, just like every other morning." She gave a heavy sigh. "It was like that for Erica, too."

"What's so awful about working here?"

"My cubicle is right over here. Let's go where we can

talk." We followed her several steps into an office papered with Charlie Brown cartoons and festooned with plastic plants. Christine sank into the desk chair, her lip curled into a sneer. "I know visitors are so impressed when they see the place: the marble, the tropical trees, the fancy phony architecture."

She held out both arms. "This is what it's like for the real people; we're jammed into cubicles barely big enough for a hamster. Everything's regulated. Twenty-five minute lunch periods assigned like we were in junior high school. And privacy—ha! Most of us don't get walls or a door. The ones that do had better remember they're thin as waxed paper."

Christine raised her finger to her lips. Then she narrowed her eyes to slits and leaned closer to us. "I could tell you details of every conversation Erica had with Pierre. I could tell you the details of the separation agreement. Want to know which days she and Travis went to the Residence Inn instead of going for Subway sandwiches? I got that, too."

"Why was Erica unhappy here?"

Christine rolled her eyes. "Second-class citizen all the way. I'm sure you noticed the difference between her office and her other colleague's." She waited until we both nodded in agreement. "I was the designated transcriber in all the teleconferences her team had with the FDA reviewers." She clucked her tongue. "I saw the way they treated her in those meetings. Dr. Gladstone would go around the room—with us today are Dr. so-and-so, Dr. so-and-so, and Dr. so-and-so. He'd never even acknowledge her presence. She was just a nurse. Trust me, she did not have the right initials before or after her name. No wonder she wanted to sabotage the project."

Laura flashed a surprised look at me behind Christine's back. "You really think Erica wanted to sabotage the project?" she asked. "Did she have something against Glad-stone?"

"Let me put it this way—she wouldn't have been sorry to see him taken down." A small smirk played around her lips.

This woman had a serious chip on her shoulder. In her mind, Erica had carried one, too. Besides that, she seemed to have more intelligence on this case than everyone else combined. At the very least, she was willing to spill everything she *thought* she knew. I pressed on.

"Supposing the new drug gets put on hold. How will that affect the members of the team?" I asked.

"In my opinion, Dr. Gladstone is a relic if this thing doesn't hit the market soon. A friggin' brontosaurus. He's already got guys stepping on his heels."

"You think he'd be fired?"

"Not fired maybe. But he's been around a long time without much happening on his watch. We have new brass all through the company—new president, new vice president, new board of directors. Way I see it, the drug goes to market, he's earned a spot on the board. But these people are ruthless. The drug gets delayed and stays in development, or even trashed altogether? Someone younger, smarter, and hungrier tramples him flat and takes his place. As for the other gentlemen—"

Just then, Roger's lanky frame loomed in the doorway. Under a blue blazer, he wore a white shirt starched stiff. The initials discreetly embroidered on the pocket matched the exact shade of green of his tie. Christine appeared to shrink even smaller than her baseline size.

"Nice to meet you," she squeaked in our direction. Then she ducked past Roger and scurried down the hall.

"I see you've already met our resident vicious gossip," said Roger. "If I were you, I would discount ninety-five percent of whatever garbage she spewed out to you. Maybe ninety-eight percent."

"This is my friend and caddie, Laura Snow."

"Cassie's told me a lot about you. She said you made amazing progress in your lesson the other day."

Roger grinned.

"Laura's the real teacher," I said, grateful for her graceful intervention. "She could have taken you a lot further than I did."

"You were fine. Travis mentioned you're investigating Erica's death. Have you been deputized or something?"

I laughed. "Not really. I spent the last day she was alive with her, and then I found her body. I can't shake feeling I owe her something."

Roger said nothing.

"I know it's kind of silly."

He nodded. "I'd think the police could cover all this more effectively and leave the chip shots to you."

"Like I said, it's a personal thing. Maybe a way to say good-bye, even though I didn't know her well." I could scramble to explain my interest in Erica all afternoon, but it didn't look like Roger was buying. He led us down the hall and into a conference room.

"Cassie tells me you're working on a new Alzheimer's drug," Laura said. "My brother's father-in-law is being treated with something that helps a little—Exelon, I think it's called."

Roger nodded. "That's a cholinesterase inhibitor."

As if that meant a damn thing to us.

"It would be so great if someone found a real cure. How does your drug work?" Laura asked.

"I'll give you the abbreviated layman's lecture. The brains of patients with Alzheimer's disease are atrophied and contain plaques and tangles. These effects are correlated with degeneration in the cholinergic system, which is related to functional deficits."

"Pretty much with you so far," said Laura.

Easy for her to say; she'd spent three weeks our sophomore year of college as a biochemistry major, before the rigorous demands of pledge week kicked in.

"To be more specific, scientists have found some enzymes in the brain that seem to degrade acetylcholine, which leads to a decrease in ACh-dependent neurotransmission and then, the functional deficits. Exelon is one of the drugs which inhibits the destructive enzyme."

"Uh-huh," I said, trying not to appear stupid. Though I had only the vaguest understanding of his explanation, and I doubted Laura got much more, I wanted to keep him talking. "Your new drug is different from that one?"

"Related, but different," said Roger. "There has been ongoing debate about whether the functional problems are caused by the plaques or the tangles. Based on the work we've done, we believe the amyloid-beta deposits found in the plaques are the culprits. We hypothesized that if we could inject minute amounts of the amyloid-beta compounds into the bloodstream, antibodies would form. These would travel across the blood-brain barrier in small quantities and attack or bind the beta-amyloid in the brain. Are you following me?"

"Not really," said Laura. "But there's a bottom line here—your drug attacks the disease in a slightly different way, and I'm guessing you expect better results."

Roger grinned. "Bingo. Everyone's trying to go after the enzymes. Our drug is functionally a vaccine."

"A vaccine! That's really cool," said Laura. Roger's grin got even wider.

"But Erica was concerned that you hadn't paid enough attention to the safety of the drug. Wasn't she worried about hepatotoxicity?" I asked.

"That's just absurd," said Roger. No further explanation appeared to be forthcoming.

"You felt you'd done everything by the book," I suggested in my best soothing tone. "So her concerns must have been puzzling."

"Beyond puzzling. Idiotic and obstructive. We had already performed exhaustive studies. We went over the data in detail. We pored over the statistical analyses until our eyes gave out. The FDA reviewer approved us every step of the way. What was she thinking?" His voice trembled with frustration.

"Could she have discovered some problem that the rest of you weren't aware of yet?"

"No. We all saw the same information. No one held anything back. For Christ's sake, no one on the team wanted to botch the outcome by ignoring serious adverse events. That would be far more costly than slowing the project down to do more studies. Besides all that, she would not have been able to slow the project down unless there were data to support that. There are not."

The skin around his lips tightened as he spoke. "I'm quite sure you're following a trail with a dead end. This young woman was bright and ambitious but also psychologically flawed. As badly as I feel telling you this so bluntly, it did not surprise me to hear she took her own life. Even from my position as an outsider, it looked as though she had made a terrible mess of it."

"You mean the divorce?"

"To be quite honest, I tried not to know too much about the details. Unlike my esteemed coworker, Christine, whom one could suspect of spending her days with her ear pressed up against a glass on various walls. Work is work, and personal life is just that—personal. Erica LeBoutillier did not seem to be capable of making that distinction." He stood up and pushed his chair flush to the table. "I'm sorry to be abrupt, but I have to get back to work."

"Just one last question," I said. "Were Travis and Erica having an affair?"

Roger straightened his tie and cleared his throat. "Dr.

Smith is not known for his discretion, nor for his judgment. That's all I'll say."

"Are you coming to the party tonight?" asked Laura.

"I'm going to try," said Roger with a grimace. "I took too much time off this week already. And Erica's death left a lot of unfinished business here. If we want to maintain the project on schedule, we all have to keep our oars in the water." He looked at his watch. "I hope I've been able to clarify your conclusions about this unfortunate event."

"Appreciate you taking the time to talk with us." I said. "If you come tonight, I'll introduce you to a couple of the PGA golfers. And next time you hit the links, remember to keep your right hand strong."

Roger chuckled. "It'll be awhile before I get the opportunity to put that lesson into play."

Chapter 12

◁Ò **Laura** drove back out of the winding driveway and onto the main highway.

"There you have it," I said. "Three quarters of my little pro-am foursome, plus Christine the vicious gossip thrown in for good measure."

"My hat's off to you for winning with that team," said Laura.

"What do you think?"

Laura floored the gas and swerved around a FedEx truck. "First of all, Teresa Biacci has a corncob up her butt. If there's any way we can work it out, I'd like to pin the murder on her."

I laughed. "The only problem with that theory is she wasn't anywhere near Atlantic City on Tuesday night."

"You don't know that. She could have driven in later and killed Erica."

"Possible, not likely. Next subject: Hugh Gladstone."

"That guy definitely looked like he had something to hide."

"But the only thing he admitted is that Erica gave all of them reason to feel homicidal. And if he did have anything to do with her death, I'm certain it wasn't hands-on."

"Yeah, he'd hire some goon to do the dirty work," said Laura. "As far as those other two dudes go, I wouldn't want to spend my time socializing with Roger, but I don't see him killing anyone. He's too anal. He'd be plotting statistical analyses of which method would be most effective and never get around to following through."

"Maybe. Though he did spend a lot of time convincing us that their project is viable." I shrugged. "That leaves Travis."

"Who knows for sure? He comes across like a broken-hearted teddy bear."

"Which does not fit with the way he behaved toward Erica in the casino Tuesday night. And what's going on between him and Roger?"

"Here's a theory," said Laura. "Maybe Roger had a crush on Erica, too. And he's pissed off that she chose Travis, fat little smelly man that he is." We both laughed.

"Christine wasn't all that fresh herself," I said. "I'm thinking we should talk to Erica's golf pro and get his side of the story."

Laura shook her head and frowned. "I'd like to have a few words with that moron anyway. For the love of God, don't screw your customers! It gives the rest of us a bad name."

"You know Travis was telling a whopper when he said he didn't know if any other companies were working on the drug," I said. "They've got to have their fingers on the pulse of their competition, with a honed knife ready to cut their throats, if necessary. Did you notice how his voice changed when I asked that question?"

She nodded her agreement. "Are you buying Christine's theory that Erica was out to sabotage Meditron?"

"That sign on her office wall summed it up: she worked like a dog," I said. "It's hard to imagine her wanting to hurt her own company. Though given her personal life, it wouldn't be surprising that she was open to temptation."

"Why were you so interested in whether those bozos are going to the party tonight?"

"If one of them killed Erica, I bet we got him plenty nervous with our questions. He might show up and try to correct the bad impression he thinks he's made."

"Last I heard, you weren't going to spend much time at this shindig."

I shrugged. "Don't have anything better to do. And Joe promised we'd only stay for one drink."

"Are you up for seeing Mike?"

"I'll deal."

Laura's expression bristled with curiosity. I turned the radio up and began to hum along with Emmy Lou Harris singing something about the pain of loving. I was not ready to dissect my feelings about Mike in public, even the small and comfortable domain consisting of my best friend.

I leaned my head back against the seat, closed my eyes, and thought about my caddying days. When Mike and I first started on the PGA Tour, we'd go out after he finished his round, for dinner or drinks or just to hang out. That changed quickly though. Mike said he needed the nights away from his golf game, and with me sitting on the barstool beside him, it was hard to get that space. Even when I tried to talk about something else, my ideas about how to attack the course the next day or what I'd noticed about his swing while he practiced would come spilling out. After that, we lived parallel lives off the course, mine lonely, and his—who knew?

Later, I realized there were other reasons we quit going

out, too. Caddying for Mike was as close to a dream job as I could have imagined. No way was I going to ruin it by getting romantically involved with him. Even if he was interested. And guaranteed, judging by the glamour girls he dated, I just wasn't his type.

Even supposing he stretched his criteria to include me, there would have been big problems. Before Mom married Dave, my family scraped to get by: no-meat meals, school wardrobes courtesy of Kmart, and transportation via an old Ford station wagon with fake woody panels. Afterward, with the money pinch relieved, I didn't ask Dave for anything unless I had to. I knew I'd pay too much later on. Mike would never have understood all that. His family was loaded from a paper manufacturing business that had been around for generations. He worked hard, but he'd never had to worry about paying the rent late or waiting a season to buy a new pair of golf shoes.

Anyway, romance was fairy tale material. In real life, I'd only seen it turn sour. I didn't know how to avoid the rotten luck my mother had. My own relationships so far hadn't set standards for either longevity or success. So I figured the best policy was to stay away from trouble.

I still cringed every time I remembered the day Mike broke the logjam and suggested we take our relationship to another level. I'd given an interview to some golf columnist about the tension between golfers and their caddies. Can you be friends and coworkers, too, that sort of thing. Big mistake. The writer twisted my words out of proportion and I came out looking like a lovesick puppy dog who'd been kicked by his owner. I just about died when I saw it.

Mike found me on the driving range the next morning. "About your interview."

"That's not what—"

Mike brushed past my protest. "I had no idea you were feeling that way."

As I opened my mouth to explain, he placed his finger on my lips. "Shhh. Let me talk. I need to say this before I lose my nerve." He took a deep breath. "I'm thinking we should reconsider the terms of our relationship. I want you to continue to work for me, but maybe we should try something more, too. You think about it, and let me know." He leaned over across his golf bag and kissed me on the lips—a kiss hovering someplace between a peck from a friend and a new lover's embrace.

For the next couple months, I was too damn conflicted to say anything back. The more tense I got, the more awkward things got between us, and the worse he played. One day I got so rattled, I read the yardage backward on a sprinkler head—231 instead of the 213 it really said. Which maybe doesn't sound like a capital offense, but he airmailed the green, plugged his ball in a back bunker, and took an eight on the hole. And then he let me go.

"Sorry Cassie, this isn't working the way I'd hoped. You're making mistakes, and it's costing me money. Maybe you should look for a gig on one of the feeder tours. Build your confidence back and get a little more experience."

Now that pissed me off, because other than that one boneheaded move, I knew I handled the caddie aspect of the job just fine. I only bombed out when it came to his romantic interest. We'd barely spoken since.

Laura turned the volume on the radio back down. "What are you wearing tonight?"

"I have no idea. I may have you drop me off at Sheryl Browning's condo. She said she'd loan me something."

"I can't wait to see this," said Laura. "Cassie does Victoria's Secret. You sure you don't have designs on Mike?"

I punched her in the arm.

"Ow!"

I dialed Sheryl's number on the car phone and arranged to stop by her place. Laura pulled into the driveway of the Seaview and located the suite where Sheryl was staying.

"I'm going back to our place to unload the data from Erica's handheld onto my laptop. I'll meet you at the party in about forty-five minutes."

I approached Sheryl's door slowly and took a deep breath before knocking.

"Cassie! I'm glad to see you. Come on in and have a drink. A friend gave me this huge bottle of Maker's Mark, and I haven't made a dent yet." Before I could protest, she poured a tumbler three quarters full and dropped in a handful of ice cubes. "Be right back."

I set the drink down on the coffee table. Bourbon wasn't my favorite. Besides that, Baxter had hammered home that it was one thing to have a glass of wine with dinner and quite another to pound drinks down because you were tense and didn't know how else to handle the feelings. Besides *that*, I needed to keep my wits about me for this stupid party.

I wandered around the living area of Sheryl's suite, admiring the view over the eighteenth hole of the Pines Course and trying out the overstuffed couch. Today's paper lay on the coffee table. The picture of the murdered blackjack dealer stared up at me. Which reminded me that I needed to call the police and tell them what I knew about Lucia Jimenez. I found my cell phone in the bottom of my backpack, but I was unable to get a signal.

"Mind if I use your phone?" I called out to Sheryl. "My damn cell phone service has screwed me again."

"Go right ahead."

I dialed the Atlantic City Police Department and asked for Detective Rumson. While I waited for her to pick up, I took a tiny sip of the drink Sheryl had pressed on me. I wondered how much to tell Rumson. I decided to start with our nonconversation with Lucia last night and let the rest unfold based on her reaction.

"Hey Cassie. What's up? Staying out of trouble, I hope."

My laugh sounded phony, even to me. I bet a trained detective would see right through it. I took another small sip of the bourbon and told her about reading the paper this morning and recognizing the dead woman on the front page as the blackjack dealer who'd known Erica.

"We tried to talk with her last night," I said. "She never showed up, and then this morning they found her murdered on the beach."

"You think there's a connection."

"I don't know. The timing struck me as odd."

"Consider this," said the detective. Her voice had made a distinct shift from friendly to severe. "If there was a connection, and I doubt it, you just may have gotten her killed."

She fell silent. I drank more bourbon.

"Look. I don't know how the police function in your hometown. Here, we take murders very seriously. We are certainly investigating the shooting. But unfortunately or fortunately, your friend Erica was not murdered. The final autopsy results came back, and in addition to enough antidepressant to kill a three hundred–pound man, the lab found high levels of barbituates, opioid analgesics, and alcohol. I'm sorry. I really do appreciate your interest, but there's nothing more for you to do. Except play well. But we've already been through that, haven't we?" Underneath her pleasant words, the warning was clear.

I thanked her for her time and hung up. I drained the last of the bourbon and stretched out on the couch. No doubt about it, the physical evidence said Erica did herself in. Why was that so hard for me to believe?

"I didn't have much luck," said Sheryl as she returned to the living room. "You'd be mopping the floor with most of my dresses. But how about this?" She held up a tiny, sequined, blue silk sheath with delicate spaghetti straps where shoulders and sleeves would normally go. I frowned. I picked up my empty glass, peered into it, and swirled the ice cubes.

"Gosh, there's not much to it. I don't think I have the nerve."

"Try it on. Let's see how it looks. I dug out some heels, too—you'll need them to carry this off."

I shucked off my shorts and polo shirt and slipped into the dress. The glittering silk that would have draped gracefully on Sheryl's willowy form stuck snugly to mine. It hugged every curve, dipping too low in the front and leaving my shoulders and upper back bare. I groaned.

"It's stunning, Cassie, really. I hardly recognize you!"

"Thanks a lot!" I laughed. "I hardly recognize myself." I turned slowly in front of the mirror. Then I bent over to try on the shoes. My feet flopped around in them like a little girl's.

"Forget about it, they don't fit. And I sure don't own anything that would go with this dress."

Sheryl laughed. "You give up too easy." She grabbed a box of Kleenex and stuffed a couple in the toes. "Now try that."

I teetered a couple of steps. "I guess this will work, as long as we're not dancing."

"Let me make you up. You'll really look polished."

I shrugged. If I was going to play dress-up, why not go all the way? Sheryl led me into the bathroom and applied mascara, silver eye shadow, and a slash of copper lipstick. She loosened my braid and combed my hair to fall in soft waves around my face. Then she stood back to admire her work. "You look fabulous, babe. Really. You should dress up more often. Especially if you're gonna be a star."

"I wasn't planning on it," I said.

"Let's have another drink while I get ready. We can stumble over together." She poured both of us a second glass of bourbon and ushered me into the bedroom. "Come talk to me while I get dressed."

I lowered myself to the edge of the king-size bed, hoping the borrowed dress wouldn't split right up the seams. "What made you decide to try playing again? You seem to have a good thing going with the TV broadcasting." My curiosity about her attempted comeback had escalated since we'd played together this morning. Only now the alcohol lent me the nerve to probe.

"I never really felt like I gave it my all when I was out there the last time," she said, her voice muffled through the closet door. She pushed the door open and looked out at me. "Then there was the divorce. You've read about that, I'm sure."

I nodded. No point in pretending I didn't know. It had been the main topic of gossip on both Tours for the better part of two years: a fiery, on-again/off-again relationship between a promising rookie from each Tour. It culminated in a grisly front-page photo of Sheryl with two eyes blackened and the disappearance of her husband from the professional golf world.

Sheryl stepped back into the bedroom wearing a long, black gown. It had a deeply plunging neckline and an uneven hem that swooped well up her left thigh. No private parts actually showed, but you sure got the idea that if only you'd stick around . . . She'd swept her streaked blond hair into a sophisticated knot and added several layers of heavy gold jewelry.

"You look really nice!" She didn't look nice, she looked fantastic. And hers wasn't a phony, make-believe, dress-up-in-Mommy's-clothes job, like mine.

"Thanks." She sat down at the dressing table and began to draw a black line across her eyelid. "It's such a hard life anyway, don't you think?"

I nodded.

"I got involved in designing golf clothes, modeling for

Vogue, endorsements, you name it. I lost my footing. I had no focus. I started to wonder what the hell I was doing out there. And that maybe my success that first year was a fluke. You know what I'm talking about?"

"I can imagine," I said with a grimace. I fished out an ice cube from my drink and chewed on it. "Though I don't exactly have people banging my door down to endorse their products. And they certainly won't be calling me from *Vogue*. L.L. Bean, maybe."

Sheryl's laugh jiggled the mascara wand she was using. "Shit." She dabbed at the black dash she'd made just below her eyebrow.

"But I can relate to the fluke part," I said. "The game that got me through Q-school, who the hell knows where that went."

Her turn to nod. "So then this TV commentator offer comes along, and I think I better grab it. So I find myself watching golf and talking about these girls and how great their shots are. And all the time, I'm thinking, *That should be me. I could do that.*" She shrugged and blotted her lips with a Kleenex. "So I came back out. I'm not sure I can do it. But I'm damn well going to give myself a fighting chance."

"I hope you make it."

"Thanks." She turned away from the mirror and pointed at me with her lipstick. "That part's hard, too—getting along with the other gals. You need to make some friends out here in order to survive. And it's not always easy when you're trying to beat the bogey out of the same girls. Come on, let's go wow the party."

Wobbling from the parking lot to the hotel on the unfamiliar spike heels, I began to feel foolish and very exposed. I had gotten used to being looked at on the golf course, but not parading myself half naked in front of a group of strangers.

Why was I going to this party anyway? If detective

work had been my primary motive, the two glasses of Maker's Mark had fogged any analytical powers I might have ever had. Besides, Detective Rumson had been crystal clear. When it came to Erica LeBoutillier's death, there was nothing more to analyze. The coroner's report had told it all.

Chapter 13

Once inside the Marriott clubhouse, Sheryl was swept into the ballroom by a wave of TV types and general golf paparazzi. I hovered behind a large potted palm, searching for Laura's familiar face and yearning for my PJs, a pepperoni pizza, and an evening of *Friends* reruns. Comfort for body, mind, and stomach.

"Cassie! Wow! I hardly recognized you." Hugh Gladstone appeared next to me and skimmed a clammy hand across my bare back. One tuft of silver hair stuck up from the crown of his head like a flaccid rooster tail, and the knot of his tie hung crookedly several inches below his neck. "Let me get you a drink? Bud Light, if I remember."

He headed off in the direction of the bar. What the hell got into him? And why was he here, anyway? I knew I hadn't mentioned the party to him. Of all my pro-am partners, he was the one I'd never expected to show. Then I got annoyed at his quick offer to fetch a beer. I wanted one, sure. But his remark to Annie Strauss about my fondness for partying still stung.

He returned quickly, with the beer and Travis Smith in tow. Travis kissed me on the cheek. "You look beautiful."

"Wow," said Hugh again. He raised his eyebrows and his glass in a mock toast. Just that quick movement threw him into a precarious sway.

Travis reached over to steady him. "Don't mind him," he said to me in a stage whisper. "He's already hit the bourbon hard tonight."

I managed a thin smile. That made two of us. I tried to focus on why I'd thought it so important to show up at the party.

"Thanks for talking to me and Laura earlier today. I know you guys are under a lot of pressure at the office with Erica missing from the team."

"We'll be just fine," said Hugh. He took a swig of his drink, then sloshed some down the front of his shirt. "Shit." He brushed a fragment of lemon rind off his tie. "That woman was a pure pain in the ass." He punctuated the end of his sentence by reaching down, cupping my right buttock in his hand, and squeezing. I smacked his arm hard.

"Long time, no see, Cassandra." Synchronized perfectly with the ass grab, Mike Callahan had moved into the open space next to Travis. His eyes traveled down the length of my borrowed dress and settled on my butt, now clamped a second time in Hugh Gladstone's grip. A surge of embarrassment reddened my face, neck, and chest. With a fierce glare, I removed Hugh's hand and stepped forward to greet Mike. Should I shake his hand? Kiss his cheek? Kiss his lips? My hesitation resulted in a clumsy wrist-grasping and air buss. And then an awkward silence that I stumbled to fill.

"I'm sorry, these are two of my Tuesday pro-am partners, Dr. Hugh Gladstone and Dr. Travis Smith. This is

Mike Callahan. He plays on the PGA Tour. Plays very well lately, I must add."

"The putts drop once in a while." Mike's deep voice was gruffer than I remembered. "Joe Lancaster said you had a good day today?"

"She sure played like a champion with us," said Travis. "This girl can definitely putt."

"I'm going to get us another drink," said Hugh. He marched off in the direction of the bar.

"Sorry about that," said Travis, nodding toward my derriere. "The board of directors meeting this afternoon rattled him bad. I'd better go keep an eye on him. Nice to meet you." He shook Mike's hand, then turned back to me. "We'll see you tomorrow on the course—play well!" He followed Hugh's wobbly path toward the bar.

"So," said Mike. "How do you like being on the other side of the bag? You seem to be quite a hit with the amateurs. I see you've already taught them the squeeze play."

I chose to ignore his razzing. "It's hard. Harder than I ever even imagined. All that time when you had the yips, I kept thinking why doesn't he just get over it and put the ball in the hole. Now I know what the pressure really feels like."

"Get over it? You were thinking get over it? Bad vibes from my own caddie. No wonder I choked."

I started to protest.

Mike laughed. "I'm tugging your chain, Cassie." He looked me up and down a second time. "Overall, I'd say life on the Tour agrees with you."

A crop of goose bumps spread across my chest. "You look great yourself." He did, too. Tall, dark, and casually preppie: a well-filled-out blue blazer, khaki slacks, and a woven navy necktie.

"Gosh, Cassie, hi there." My hot flash and hotter thoughts were interrupted by Danni Williams. She wore a micro-miniskirt, a spangly spandex tube top, and eyes only for Mike. "Aren't you going to introduce me to this good-looking gentleman?" Without waiting one nanosecond for me to do so, she took both of Mike's hands in hers and began to gush about how she'd been looking forward to meeting him. "I write the *Rookie Diary* for womensgolf.com. Maybe you've seen it?"

"I haven't had the chance to do a lot of reading," said Mike. He was not making much of an effort to liberate his hands from her grip.

"I have half a mind to put you in it this week," said Danni. She finally let him go and posed with one hand on her hip and the other tapping her temple. "I bet you'd have some fabulous tips for our amateur fans."

"No one wants to read about me," Mike protested. "My rookie year was a disaster from start to finish."

Still, I could tell from the little smile that he was enjoying the idea. Or at least, her fawning attention.

Danni saw it, too. She grabbed his hands again. "Let's see, we could call it 'Rookie Gets Hot Tips from a Real Pro.' Or maybe 'Do Pros Look as Handsome in Real Life as on TV'?"

Oddly enough, Danni's transparent suck-up act did not appear to have the same nauseating effect on Mike that it did on me. If his golf game had improved over the year we'd been apart, his lousy taste in women had certainly not. Where the hell was Laura? I needed a caddie to make it through this party.

Across the room, I spotted Roger Ranz snaking his way through the crowd with a tall, thin woman in tow. I prayed Roger would not be as obnoxious as his boss.

Mike grazed my shoulder with his knuckles. "I'll catch up with you later. Danni wants me to meet her editor."

Speechless, I managed only a small squeak and a hopefully uninterpretable facial grimace. That girl was a man-eating, woman-flattening bitch.

"Hugh asked me to bring this to you." Roger exchanged my empty bottle for a very welcome cold beer.

"You made it after all," I said. "Thanks."

"How many chances will I get to hobnob with the pros? Besides, everyone else was coming. Why should I stay behind and bust my tail?" He pushed the tall woman forward. "This is my wife, Beverly."

I shook Beverly's limp hand.

"It's such a thrill to have this tournament close by," she said. "Roger so enjoyed his outing with you on Tuesday. And Roger the Third got to play in the junior clinic yesterday. You girls do such a nice job. I almost didn't mind giving up our ladies' day tournament to bring him here. Everyone in our family had a big day this week, except for me." She pursed her lips into a pout.

"I'm sure your son will remember the experience for a long time."

Beverly nodded. "Wasn't that Danni Williams who just left? She was so good with the kids. I think I'll go thank her myself."

I gritted my teeth and smiled as she rushed off. If Mrs. Ranz had had the poor judgment to marry Roger, I could understand why she hadn't seen through Danni.

I recognized that being dumped by Mike for Danni was turning my thoughts into a toxic waste pit. I needed to regain my focus. Not so easy with two tall bourbons and a beer down the hatch, and another on the way.

For several minutes, I made small talk with Roger, trying to fashion a subtle approach for my questions. I settled for direct. "Hugh seemed very upset tonight. Something to do with the board of directors meeting this afternoon?"

"I'm sure they put him on notice. The word's leaked out that there's a problem with getting our drug approved."

Beverly bustled back up as he finished his sentence.

"I'm sure everything will be fine," she said, stroking

her husband's arm. "You always worry over the smallest things."

Had they been at home, I was guessing Roger might have lashed out about how the fate of a drug that could make the company millions was hardly trivial.

Instead, he turned to me. "Hugh has a very personal investment in this drug, too."

"Oh?"

"His mother has Alzheimer's disease. She's gone downhill very quickly in the past year. As you can imagine, it would mean a great deal to him to be able to reverse that process."

"What a shame," said Beverly. "One of the ladies in my bridge group has been having trouble like that recently. Her bidding is all gone to heck."

Roger rolled his eyes. "It's way beyond bridge, dear. Mrs. Gladstone doesn't even know how to dress herself now, or whether she's eaten a meal. Hugh says she comes back to the kitchen over and over, demanding breakfast. She'd have a hundred bowls of cereal a day, if they'd allow it. But he refuses to consider placing her in an assisted living facility. This drug could be the only thing standing between his mother and a living hell for all of them."

"That's so sad," said Beverly. "At least her son is taking care of her. I hope Roger the Third will do the same for us one day." She glanced at her watch and grimaced. "I'm afraid we need to go, dear." She turned to me and offered her limp fingers a second time. "Roger just told me about this party this afternoon. Men!" She shook her head with disapproval. "I was able to get the sitter last minute, but only because I promised her we'd be back by seven."

"Good luck tomorrow," said Roger. "Nice to see you again."

I retreated to my potted palm tree and sipped the beer

I shouldn't have been drinking. I waved at Joe, who I could see was scanning the faces of the crowd from across the room. Hopefully looking for me.

"Hey Cassie," he said when he'd reached my palm tree. "This is Dr. Rebecca Butterman, the infamous Palm Pilot RB. Cassandra Burdette." Joe's hand rested comfortably on the small of the doctor's back.

Her handshake was warm and firm. "I've heard a lot about you, Cassandra."

"Cassie," I snapped. Unfair to take an immediate dislike to this woman. Too late—I already had.

"Cassie started out caddying for Mike Callahan on the men's tour," Joe explained. "Mike went through a stretch where he couldn't make a putt. Cassie had the good sense to call me."

Dr. Butterman tilted her head and smiled at me. "Now you're playing, too. How strange it must feel to be on the other side."

"Not really," I said. "They're each stressful in their own way, but more similar than different." A razor-sharp analysis if I ever gave one.

"Dr. Butterman—" Joe began.

"Rebecca, please," she interrupted, placing her hand on his forearm. Her nails were long, perfect ovals, polished to a soft sheen.

A goofy grin spread across Joe's face. "Rebecca has always been interested in sports psychology. You two would have a lot to say to each other."

I bet we would.

"I'm going to find the ladies' room," said Dr. Butterman. "Want to come along? It'll give us the excuse for a little girl talk."

Though she wasn't actually drooling, her sloppy overture reminded me of a golden retriever. Too bad I was a cat person.

"All set here," I said. In fact, I did need to go, and

badly, but I needed a chance to talk to Joe alone even more. I watched him watch her trim figure move purposefully toward the door. In spite of my guess that she had to be pushing forty, she exuded a sexy confidence whose transmittal apparently did not rely on cleavage, tight-fitting clothing, or flashy makeup. I folded my arms across my chest.

"What did she tell you about Erica?"

"Short version, she doesn't seem to believe that Erica killed herself. That's my impression. As I predicted, she can't talk about her treatment without the patient's permission."

"But the patient is dead!"

"I'm aware of that. The only way she can divulge information to us now is if Pierre LeBoutillier gives her the heads up."

I groaned. "That'll never happen. So why is she here, if she won't help?"

"It's not that she won't help; she can't help. She's an ethical psychologist, and it's the law." Joe studied my face. "I think you're jealous."

"Don't be absurd."

"She is kind of cute, though. Don't you think?"

I painted another in a series of sickly smiles on my face. "Adorable. I am going to hit the bathroom. Back in a few." I turned and headed for the door in the opposite direction from the adorable and probably brilliant Dr. Rebecca Butterman. Where the hell was Laura?

Chapter 14

I remembered the makeup only after I splashed half a sink of cold water on my face. Stripes of mascara and silver eye shadow ran down from both eyes. Damn. All I needed now was for Joe to think I'd been crying over him. Or for Mike to think the same thing. To hell with them both.

I scrubbed the blotches off my cheeks with a damp paper towel and fluffed my hair with my fingers. As soon as Laura surfaced, I was ready to blow town. I could collect my backpack from Sheryl tomorrow. As I stepped out of the bathroom, I saw a glimpse of a thin brunette at the end of the hallway. In spite of my alcohol-fogged brain, something familiar registered. Could it be Erica's mystery girl again?

"Aimee! Aimee Joy!"

The girl glanced back in my direction, then swerved quickly into a stairwell. Whoever it was, blurting out the name had scared her off. I began to chase after the girl, but the wads of Kleenex in Sheryl's high heels reduced me to a slow totter. I kicked the shoes off in the stairwell and darted down the stairs. Just ahead, I caught another small glimpse of maybe-Aimee disappearing into the basement level of the hotel. I followed her into a dim and empty hallway and pushed open swinging double doors that led to the hotel kitchen. The room hummed with noise and activity.

"Can I help you?" barked a harried-looking chef in a stained white coat.

"Have you seen a teenager with long brown hair?"

"No one's come through here." He turned back to the two men shaking frying pans over the stovetop flames. "Just lightly brown—if the butter burns, you have to start from scratch."

I backed out of the room and continued down the hallway. The next two doors I tried were locked. I was starving and getting nowhere. Time to collect Laura and put some distance between me and everyone at that stupid party. I pushed open the last door and stepped into what appeared to be an auxiliary kitchen. This room was deserted and dark, with no signs of recent food preparation other than a lingering odor of garlic and grease.

"Aimee! It's Cassie. We met the other night in the casino. If you're in some kind of trouble, maybe I can help." I padded forward cautiously in my bare feet, watching the floor for food slicks or worse, broken glass. From my days as a substitute busgirl at the restaurant where Mom worked, I knew the linoleum of even the fanciest kitchens could harbor unpleasant surprises. "I know I can help, however bad things seem. If you'll just come out and talk."

Now the place had started to give me the serious creeps. Had it really been Aimee? Considering the number of cocktails I'd consumed, I knew my reactions were not as sharp as they could have been. Still, I thought I recognized the shiny, straight hair—almost the same chestnut color as mine—plus the slim hips, and even the slight tilt of her shoulders from left to right.

Threading my way through the stovetops and counters, I noticed a walk-in cooler with the door open and the light on. I approached cautiously and poked my head around the corner.

"Hello? Anybody home? Aimee?"

From behind, a pair of strong hands grabbed my shoulders and shoved me into the cooler. I was too stunned to react until the door slammed shut. I stood literally frozen with disbelief. Then I began to bang on the inside of the door.

"Help! Let me out! It's freezing in here." No joke—especially in a cocktail dress and bare feet. I leaned all my weight on the handle. It didn't budge.

With the help of a tiny red light glowing near the door, I could see that I'd been shut into a freezer. The back shelves contained enormous hunks of some kind of meat swathed in layers of plastic wrap. Industrial-sized vats of ice cream and blocks of butter had been arranged along the left side of the cooler. The right shelves were stacked with sacks of frozen vegetables and fruits. At least I wouldn't starve to death.

My teeth began to chatter violently. As I moved closer to the door, I felt a layer of skin tear off the balls of my feet.

"Damn!" I screamed. "Ouch!" I spotted what appeared to be an emergency release latch on the door and pressed hard. Nothing happened. Then I banged and yelled until I was hoarse. No one answered.

Using small, mincing steps that I hoped would discourage the freezing of skin to metal, I toured the interior of the cooler again. In the back corner, I found a folded canvas sack that smelled of old seafood. I removed several layers of plastic from the frozen roasts and wrapped them around my feet. I draped the fishy canvas sack over my shoulders. Then I tore open three plastic bags of green beans and corn, dumped the vegetables, and pulled the bags over my head down to my eyebrows. It was far from a fashion coup, but on the only ski trip I'd ever taken, a chaperone had required that we all wear hats.

"Ninety-nine percent of your body heat can be lost from your uncovered head," she insisted.

Then I picked up what looked like a frozen pork loin and began to alternate banging on the door with the meat and singing. I started with "Ninety-nine Bottles of Beer on the Wall." That one song could take me a long ways into the night, if necessary.

At fifty-four bottles of beer, I took a break for jumping jacks and jogging. Out of breath and slightly warmer, I began to sing my father's favorites: "The Piggedy Poor Old Sliggety Slave," "Lay That Pistol Down, Babe," and "Brightly Beams Our Father's Mercy." God knows I needed some mercy, or the breakfast cook would find me frozen to a pitiful lump in the morning. The initial shock of the ambush had worn off, giving way to waves of fear. I tried not to cry. The first tears had frozen hard against my cheeks and lips. More would only make me feel colder and more sorry for myself.

Without a watch, I had no idea how long I'd been trapped in the cooler. My lips grew too stiff to form the words of the songs. I was numb with cold and fright and ready to admit I was likely to freeze to death without ever having made a tournament cut. I regretted that I hadn't talked with my older brother Charlie lately. Between his frantic legal schedule and my travels, it had been hard to make the time. He'd have a big load taking care of Mom by himself. Losing me like this was liable to knock the legs out from under her already precarious grip on sanity.

I wished I hadn't snapped at Laura. I should have told

Joe I loved him, as a friend, at least. We weren't going to get the chance to figure out what other feelings lurked beneath the surface. As for Mike, I hadn't a clue.

I sank down to the cooler floor, overtaken with exhaustion and very, very cold. Suddenly the door swung open. My frozen lips cracking, I screamed in tandem with the man who stood outside the freezer. I rose up and staggered out of the cooler.

"Shit man. You just about gave me a heart attack," he said. "You took five years off my life anyway."

"And you saved mine," I said, bursting into cold tears.

Within minutes, the sous-chef brought me a cup of coffee from the main kitchen and four blankets from the storeroom, and then located Joe, Laura, and Dr. Butterman.

"Detective Rumson's on the way," said Joe. He rubbed color into my left hand, while Laura massaged the right. My frozen feet rested in a large tub of warm water. "We called the EMTs, too."

"I'm fine," I said. "I don't need medical attention."

"They'll be the judge of that," said Joe. The cook who had rescued me hovered in the background with the hotel manager and Rebecca Butterman.

"How long was I in there?"

"We've been searching for you for about forty-five minutes," said Joe. "You said you'd be right back. We called your room and looked all over the resort and when we found your shoes, we really got worried."

"It felt like a lot longer than that."

"Lucky thing you came by," Laura told the chef.

He flashed a sheepish grin. "I forgot to take the roasts out to thaw. I would have been working at Burger King if the boss got here tomorrow and found them still in the freezer."

"Thank God for your lousy memory," I said.

"Why were you in the kitchen?" Joe asked me in a stern

voice. He was about to shift from "Just grateful you're safe," and launch into "How did you get yourself into this pickle" mode.

Just then, Detective Rumson arrived with several uniformed police officers. She clamped a firm hand on my shoulder. "So, we had another little adventure. I thought we agreed you were staying out of any further investigations."

"You don't know Cassie very well," said Laura. "Staying clear of trouble isn't in her nature."

"Do you have anything to eat around here?" I asked the sous-chef. "I'm starving." I hoped he wouldn't offer me ice cream.

He and the manager bustled off, promising to heat up the kitchen's signature vegetable beef soup. With Detective Rumson's prodding, I explained how I had followed maybe-Aimee Joy into the kitchen and been lured into the freezer.

"You're quite sure it was the girl who flagged you and Erica LeBoutillier down at the casino on Tuesday?" Her mouth had drawn into a grim line as I described chasing the girl and becoming trapped in the cooler.

"I think so. She had the same shape and the right hair."

"And she pushed you into the freezer?"

"I never saw the person who shoved me. I just peeked in, when I got pushed from behind."

"Was it a woman? A man? Did you hear anyone say anything?"

"I didn't hear anything. Only felt someone pushing. I wasn't expecting it, so I went in pretty easy." I felt my eyes starting to tear up under her brusque interrogation.

Joe stepped forward and placed his hand on my shoulder. "Let's try something here. Close your eyes and see if you can visualize the moment you were pushed."

I did what he suggested. Anything to escape Rumson's beady-eyed glare.

"Picture the hands shoving you. Were they small? Large?"

I shrugged helplessly.

"Could you feel a ring of any kind on one of the fingers? Was the skin rough or smooth?"

Nothing was coming to me. Absolutely nada. I opened my eyes. "I can't do it. Maybe medium-sized hands and strong? That's all I know."

Detective Rumson turned to the two policemen who had accompanied her. "See if you can get any prints off the door—inside and out. We'll need to print the staff in the morning—anyone who works here, whether they specifically remember opening the freezer or not. Don't over look anyone, do you understand me?" The officers nodded and hustled off in the direction of the freezer.

Detective Rumson turned her fierce look back to me. "Are you certain you were pushed? Or is it possible that you might have stumbled and pulled the door shut behind you as you fell?"

"I'm sure I was pushed." That seemed like a dumb question to me. Even if some moron chucked headfirst into the freezer, what were the chances they'd pull the door closed after them? And why the hell wouldn't they just turn the handle and step back out?

"How much have you had to drink this evening?"

"I had two beers at the party. What does that have to do with anything?" I was very aware of the audience of interested onlookers, including Joe, Dr. Butterman, Laura, and a potpourri of hotel staff. I knew I had been shoved into the freezer, not stumbled in myself in a drunken stupor. The amount of bourbon I had consumed was unrelated to the incident and absolutely none of their business.

"Even if she had fallen in, someone had to have tampered with the lock on the handle," said Joe. "Otherwise she could have just pressed the emergency release button, right?"

The detective shrugged. "We'll look into it. You'll need to come down to the station house in the morning and look over some mug shots. Maybe Ms. Joy is on record. So far, your description doesn't give us much to go on."

"Fine," I said, wishing I had another beer now to help withstand her scrutiny.

"Why do I have the idea that you are not telling me everything?"

Laura spoke up before I could protest. "I think we better hand this over." She pulled the Palm Pilot out of her pocket and held it out to Detective Rumson.

"What is this?"

"It belonged to Erica. Laura found it in my golf bag yesterday morning," I said.

"Tell me every detail," said the detective grimly. She took the handheld from Laura. "Leave nothing out, please. That means tell it all."

"I get it." I accepted a bowl of steaming vegetable soup from the cook and began to spoon it in. "You start while I eat," I told Laura. "Tell her about visiting Meditron."

Laura described our visit to the drug company and summarized our impressions. "We met a nosy coworker while we were waiting to speak with Roger Ranz. According to this Christine, Erica had been involved with Travis Smith, but she dumped him in the last couple weeks for her golf pro."

Joe snorted. "Bad judgment there. Those guys are trouble."

"Travis admitted that Erica had been a compulsive gambler, and that maybe she hadn't recovered as completely as she let on."

I watched Dr. Butterman's face while Laura talked, looking for any reactions—surprised or otherwise. How well had she known her patient? She kept her expression neutral, other than the smallest flash of pity whenever she glanced in my direction. As far as I could tell, the woman had missed her calling. Wasn't the CIA looking for a few good men who could keep their secrets? Preferably someplace foreign.

"Both Roger and Christine said Erica had trouble with boundaries at work."

"Speaking of boundaries, isn't Hugh the one who grabbed your ass?" asked Joe with a smile. "Mike told me all about that."

"Thank you so much for bringing that up." I rolled the blankets off my shoulders and dried my feet with the end of one of them. "Apparently Hugh had a run-in with the board of directors this afternoon; his status at Meditron is on the wobbly side. Tonight the guy was plastered—totally out of character from anything I'd seen before."

"You're still operating under the assumption that one of Erica's coworkers killed her," said Detective Rumson in a freezer-cold voice. "But her death has been ruled a suicide. There is no evidence of foul play."

I stood up. Even barefooted and minimally dressed, at least I could meet the detective eye to eye. "You guys don't seem to understand how big this Alzheimer's drug is going to be. I imagine there are lots of companies who would kill to get their product to the market first, and people who would kill if they saw an impediment—"

"And you don't seem to understand that we are quite capable of doing this job, and that it is dangerous for you to insert yourself in the middle of it," said the detective, her mouth and eyebrows set in matching severe lines.

"The paramedics are here," announced the manager.

"I'm fine," I said. "You can send them away. Are we finished?"

The detective nodded. "We'll see you tomorrow at the station."

I touched Laura's arm. "Let's hit the road. I've had it."

Chapter 15

○ **The** numbers on the clock radio glowed faintly: five-thirty A.M. My sheets had twisted around me into a sweaty mass. Even after the soup and a hot shower last night, I collapsed into bed shivering. So Laura agreed to sacrifice the air-conditioning. Now I felt overheated and nauseous, with a throbbing headache. I reminded myself that I knew no one who had died from a hangover. Embarrassment, maybe. Queasy stomach and a headache, not.

I rolled out of bed, flipped the air-conditioning on high, and ran through my stretches and calisthenics in the dark. Then I carried Laura's laptop into the bathroom and switched on the light. While the computer booted up, I popped two Advil and chewed half a roll of Tums. I began to search for the files that she had copied from Erica's Palm Pilot.

"What the hell are you doing?" Laura stood at the door, hair disheveled, wearing her favorite night gear: an extra-large, brown cotton T-shirt that read Will Golf Fore Food.

"I couldn't sleep. I'm trying to look at the stuff from Erica's Palm Pilot."

Laura yawned. "It's gobbledygook if you don't have the password. I looked at it yesterday afternoon, and I couldn't figure it out. What time is it anyway?"

"Early. But we've got to get busy. I want to go by the Showboat and look at their gallery of wedding pictures before we stop at the police station."

"Aren't you forgetting something?"

I looked at her blankly.

"Like practicing, so you have a shot at making your first cut?"

"Oh that, sure," I said, in a breezy tone that skated past her sarcasm. "I'll do that, but after I visit Lila Rose."

Laura crossed her arms across her chest and frowned. "Detective Rumson told you to lay off."

"It's Lila's birthday today," I said. "Nothing wrong with dropping by to give her a present. If we happen to have a conversation with Pierre while we're there, and he happens to agree that Dr. Butterman can talk to us about Erica's sessions . . ." I shrugged.

Laura's eyes bugged, and her shoulders drew up. I could see she was gearing up for a big argument.

"I'm going," I said. "If you want to come along, fine. If not, see you back at the range around ten. I told Joe I'd meet him then. We don't tee off until twelve-thirty-six."

"Give me ten minutes," she said. "I need to jump in the shower."

I could hear her muttering to herself even after she'd closed the bathroom door. I did fifty more sit-ups—the rest of my self-imposed penance—then dressed in white shorts and a light blue plaid, sleeveless polo. Tiger Woods liked to wear red on the days he planned to close his opponents out. I tried to choose something that wouldn't remind me of the recent string of missed cuts.

At Laura's insistence, we started with a forty-five-minute session on the putting green. After I'd sunk a hundred two- to three-foot putts, we swung by the chow tent for a quick breakfast. Easy to tell which of the players had the early tee times. They wore a haggard, anxious look and only nibbled at the food heaped on their plates by well-meaning caddies or boyfriends or mothers. My time would come soon enough. I was grateful for the list of chores that would help distract me from ruminating about my performance this afternoon. If I scratched just below the surface, I had to admit I desperately wanted to survive the cut by the end of the day. I gobbled a sausage biscuit, two bananas, and a quart of OJ, and declared myself ready for any and all action.

"First stop, Showboat Casino," I told Laura as she drove us down Route 9. "When Erica and I were talking to Aimee Joy the other night, a wedding party came by—complete with champagne toasts, floor-length veil, and professional photographer. If we're lucky, the casino has a place they post photos to encourage more of that kind of business. If we're really lucky, that particular wedding will be there. If we're lottery-style lucky, Aimee Joy will show up in the background somewhere."

"You're grasping at straws," said Laura. "Juice box–size straws."

We entered the casino through the back door, blasted by the familiar but startling transition from steamy heat to chilled air. With the artificial lights blazing, the slots clanging, and the drinks being guzzled by the gambling patrons, it would have been hard to swear it was early morning. We discovered a gallery of photographs near the exit to the boardwalk. The first section was devoted to the Miss America Pageant across the twentieth century. The curators seemed to have a special fondness for the swimsuit competition.

Then we moved on to the bridal displays: hundreds of brides in every outfit imaginable, with the flotsam and jetsam of the casino hovering in the background of their vows.

"This is a feminist's nightmare," said Laura. "You mean to tell me that these girls dreamed of this exact wedding all their lives? Whatever happened to church and a white gown?"

I skimmed through rows of pictures. Then pay dirt. "Here it is." I jabbed my finger at the third photo in the bottom row. "And there we are, right by the Coke machine." Half of my face was obscured by the bride's outlandish carnation and dice bouquet. But next to me was a small but clear shot of the teenager, Aimee Joy.

"What in the name of God does that chick have on?" said Laura, pointing to the bride's skintight Capri pants.

"It's probably the work of a famous designer. We're just too fashion impaired to recognize it." I yanked discreetly on the flimsy lock holding the Plexiglas over the bulletin board until it snapped open. Then I removed the tacks from the four corners of the photo and slipped it out of the case. "Let's go."

"Mike was looking for you last night," said Laura, once we were back in the car. "He seemed disappointed that you'd left."

"Last I saw, he was tied up in knots by that silly bitch, Danni."

"I wonder if you two will ever figure each other out." Laura put on her sunglasses and shrugged. "Do you know how to get to the police station?"

"Take a left on Atlantic, then right on Baltic."

"What did you think of Rebecca?"

"Rebecca who?"

Laura looked at me in disbelief. "Dr. Rebecca Butterman, shrink to Erica LeBoutillier? Geez, where is your mind today, pal? You're scaring me."

"She seemed uptight," I said, ignoring Laura's theatrics. "What could it possibly hurt to talk about Erica now? She's dead. Dr. Butterman's probably embarrassed that Erica didn't spill her guts in her sessions. I know I wouldn't have talked to her."

Laura stared at me over the top of her sunglasses. "You're mean as a snake this morning, too."

We stopped to make a photocopy of the wedding picture, then parked in front of the police station. It was a red brick building with plots of orange marigolds choked by weeds lining the front walk. A slur involving pigs and sexual activity had been spray-painted in black letters on the cement. Once inside, I approached the dispatcher seated behind a glass window and asked for Detective Rumson.

"Not in," said the woman. She cracked her gum and turned back to the papers she'd been sorting when we entered.

"Could you make sure she gets this?" I scribbled an explanatory note on the outside of the Kinko's bag, slipped the photo in, and slid the package into the space under the glass window. I was relieved that Rumson wasn't in the station to accept it personally; I didn't need another reprimand.

Finally, we made a quick stop at Wal-Mart. While Laura shopped for toiletries, I perused the toy aisles until I found a Barbie doll golf outfit, including knickers, saddle shoes, and a miniature golf bag containing a driver and putter.

Laura drove us back up Route 9 and into Edgewater Estates. "Their house is at the end of the cul-de-sac," I said. "I think it will work out better if you wait in the car."

Laura stopped in front of number 264, put the car in Park, and left the engine running. "I'm coming after you if it's more than fifteen minutes," she warned. "It's almost ten o'clock now."

"I'm worried the Barbie stuff is going to be too babyish for her."

"Take some golf balls along. Then you're covered."

Lila Rose was swinging a golf club in the front yard. She wore the same pink flowered shorts set I'd seen her in on Thursday, only now the clothes were wrinkled and stained. Her hair hung in stringy clumps. The patchy layer of makeup she had applied did nothing to disguise the dark circles under her eyes. Not that I was much of an expert on the subject, but it looked like the palette of colors I'd seen in Erica's cosmetics kit.

I handed Lila Rose the Barbie doll outfit and a dozen Slazenger golf balls. I had scribbled an autograph on the outside of the box: *"Hit 'em straight. Fondly, Cassie Burdette."*

"Happy birthday," I said. "Those are the balls I use. I hope you like them, too."

"Thank you." Without making eye contact, she set both packages on the grass and continued to swing the club. "I've decided to be either an actress or a golfer. Last year, I wanted to be Miss America, but Mommy said it was silly." She took a big cut with the wedge. She missed the ball completely, though the divot she dug out flew by my ear.

After I'd made several other attempts to chat, I concluded that Lila Rose was not much interested in either the gifts or conversation with me. Maybe the reality of her mother's death had finally set in. I flashed suddenly on the idea of showing her the photo.

"I wondered if you could take a look at a picture and tell me if you know this girl." I held the photocopy of Aimee Joy out to Lila Rose, folding the page so that only the teenager's head showed.

She nodded her head slowly. "It's Olivia."

"Who's Olivia?"

"Della's daughter. We played Monopoly once but she was on the phone and kept forgetting when it was her turn."

"Who's Della then?"

"Della works for Daddy sometimes. He and Mommy fight every time she baby-sits me," she said in a high-pitched, singsong voice.

Now I was really confused. "Your mom and dad fought about Olivia?" I felt harsh using the past tense, but those were the facts.

"Not Olivia. Della."

If Della was the babysitter, then why the hell was Olivia playing Monopoly? And why did Erica fight about Della? And if she knew Della well enough to dislike her, did she also know Olivia, aka Aimee Joy? My brain spun with confusion.

"So your mom didn't like Della."

Lila Rose nodded.

"Why not?"

The girl shrugged her shoulders. "They fought about everything."

If she knew any more about the details of this particular argument between her parents, she wasn't going to tell me. I shoved the photocopy into my pocket before Lila Rose could identify that the arm around the teenager belonged to her mother. Her eleventh birthday was already grim enough.

"Lila Rose? Who's there? Who are you talking to?"

A young woman dressed in a shortie nightie stood at the front door. She made no attempt to cover the dark patch of pubic hair revealed through the gauzy fabric of the nightgown. Her voice was husky but lacked warmth.

As she swung the screen door open, Pierre loomed behind her and yanked her back. "For Christ's sake, Claudia, go upstairs and put some goddamn clothes on." His tone shifted from critical to wheedling as he turned back to the front yard. "Come inside, Lila Rose. It's time for breakfast, baby."

Erica's daughter trudged toward the door, leaving my gifts and her golf clubs scattered on the lawn. Pierre ushered her into the hallway and stepped out onto the portico.

"What do you want now?"

"I'm hoping you'll give me permission to talk with Erica's psychologist about her treatment."

"Leave us alone." None of the charm I'd noticed yesterday was evident this morning. "Just let us get on with our lives."

From the looks of the babe in the nightie, he was doing a damned good job of that already.

"How can it hurt if we speak with her?" I asked. "If you have nothing to hide, talking to Erica's shrink can only help."

"How can it help?" he demanded. "What's she going to tell you that you don't already know? That we loved each other. Then we hated each other. Quite possibly, Erica had never even bothered with the first. And she stank at taking responsibility for her part in anything. So I'm sure you'd hear about what a bastard I am. Bullshit, all of it. Forget about it." He turned and snatched open the screen door. "Leave us the fuck alone."

"Listen, someone tried to kill me last night. Locked me in a freezer and left me to die. Please." I held out a piece of Fairview Inn stationary and a pen. On the paper, I had scribbled two lines to the effect that the undersigned gave permission to Dr. Rebecca Butterman to discuss any and all aspects of her treatment of the deceased Erica Le-Boutillier.

He walked over to me, glaring. He snatched the paper from my hand, crumpled it into a tight ball, and waved it in the direction of the house. "My daughter's going through hell dealing with her mother's death. It only makes it worse to have you skulking around stirring things up." He threw the paper to the ground. "Just get out."

I trotted back to the car where Laura waited.

"That appeared to go smashingly."

"I did get one thing," I said. "Lila Rose identified Aimee Joy as someone named Olivia. She baby-sat for her one night or at least they played Monopoly. Apparently Erica fought with Pierre more than once about the child care arrangements. She didn't like this woman named Della."

"Who the hell is Della?"

"Olivia's mother."

"So Erica knew Olivia or Aimee or whatever the heck her name was?"

"I don't think so. I think she knew Della."

"Did you show him the picture?"

"He was so mad about the release, I was afraid. What if he hired Aimee to kill Erica?"

"I hardly think he'd hire a teenage bimbo to kill his wife."

"He's a creepy guy," I said. "Did you see the chick in the doorway? His wife's not in the grave yet, and he's humping Miss Pornographic America right in front of his daughter."

"They'd been separated for a while though, hadn't they? A guy has needs, Cassandra."

"Oh please." I couldn't really explain the fierce loyalty I had developed for Erica. First of all, I hardly knew her. And the more we learned, the less angelic she looked. Though Pierre gave me the creepy-crawlies, I had to admit he had a charming side, too. He was as protective as any mother with his brokenhearted little girl. My eyes wandered to the white colonial next door.

"Eureka! I met Erica's neighbor the other day leaving the wake. She obviously had some kind of problem with Pierre. I wonder if she'd tell us the real story?"

My friends at directory assistance connected me to the number for Paul and Marilyn Porter. Marilyn answered on the first ring.

"My name is Cassie Burdette. We met the other afternoon at the LeBoutilliers' home," I explained. "I was hoping you could answer some questions about Erica."

"Who is this? Why are you calling me?" She sounded shaky.

"I could tell you were good friends with Erica," I blundered on. "You probably feel the same way I do—you can't understand how she could kill herself."

The woman's muffled sobs filled the line.

I rushed forward.

"We're looking into a few leads for the police. I thought you might be able to help us out."

Laura rolled her eyes and crossed herself. "Detective Rumson is going to kill you," she hissed. I made a face and a noiseless shushing motion.

"Where are you calling from?" Marilyn asked.

"In the car outside your house." I waved from the passenger seat, as the curtains in the front right window parted. "I tried Pierre, but he refuses to talk to me."

"That selfish bastard," said Marilyn, her voice choking with anger. "He's responsible for this."

"You think he killed her?" I asked cautiously.

"He might as well have. He drove her out and made her life miserable. Poor thing. He couldn't stand her to be successful. If he'd wanted a Stepford wife, he should have chosen one to begin with."

"Did she have a boyfriend?"

"Nothing serious." Marilyn giggled. "More than one, actually. She wouldn't tell me the names. I told her she deserved to go out and have a ball." She giggled again. "Excuse the pun. She said men were all alike in the end."

Laura tapped at the face of her watch. "Let's get out of here."

"One more thing. Lila Rose mentioned a baby-sitter named Della. Did Erica ever talk about her?"

"No, but I hadn't talked with her in a couple of weeks," said Marilyn, starting to cry again. "I miss her."

I muttered a couple words of condolence, then gave her my cell phone number and reminded her to call me if she thought of anything else. I waved to her as Laura peeled out of the cul-de-sac. "Enough of the Agatha Christie Show," she said. "Let's go make the cut."

Chapter 16

We pulled into the players' parking lot and found a space near the maintenance building. Laura sent me to the driving range to stake out a spot while she collected my clubs from the pro shop. The sun blasted down from a cloudless sky, and the air hung thick and moist. I stood in the scanty shade thrown by the volunteer tent and slapped at the greenhead flies.

"Try some of this stuff," offered one of the volunteer staff. He held out a bright blue roll-on container. "It's from Scotland. Some of the other players say it works like a charm."

"Thanks. Probably kill us all before the flies even feel sick to their stomachs." I rolled the goop generously across my arms, legs, and neck. As I returned the bug repellent, I noticed the thermometer hanging in the tent read ninety-two. I rolled my neck in slow circles, working to release the tension that would ruin my tempo. My

Slazenger cap was soggy with sweat, and I hadn't even swung a club yet. Feeling woozy and nauseous, I lay down on the bottom row of the spectator's risers to stretch my back.

Pulling my right knee tight to my chest, I pushed my thoughts away from the flies and the oppressive heat toward the next two days' work. The problem with Sunday was obvious. Everyone, even the veterans, talked about the pressure of the tournament's final round. I'd seen it plenty carrying Mike's bag. Lots of times, the golfers who played conservatively to protect their position ended up losing to some guy who held nothing back. On the other hand, a guy who hadn't checked the scoreboard to see if he really needed a birdie to pull ahead could press too hard and shock himself with a ball in the water, or worse yet, out of bounds.

But today, known in the golf world as "moving day," would be different. The players would be going all out to make the cut and scramble for a position in the hunt. Anyone in the clubhouse Saturday night within six or seven strokes of the leader had a shot at winning; coming from ten shots back wasn't unheard of. Supposing I just survived the cut, I would be an implausible champion on Sunday. But even if I moved up in the ranks a few slots, I'd go home with a small chunk of cash and some desperately needed confidence. And that would be very good news.

"Morning Cassie!" called out Annie Strauss. "We're playing together today, I hear."

"That's great. I'm looking forward to it." Other than lingering embarrassment from the party girl conversation we'd had two days before, Annie's presence in my threesome should not be a disadvantage. There'd be no head games; Harvey Penick would have frowned on that. I leaned against the bench to stretch my hamstrings.

"Who's our third?" I asked.

"So Won Lee. Do you know her?"

"A little. She hits a really long ball." I wasn't sure how it would feel to play with So Won. I hadn't had any real contact with her since the day she'd been disqualified from the Florida Q-school sectional by Kaitlin Rupert's illegal driver. But she sure hadn't let the episode ruin her future; she'd lapped the field at both the California sectional and the Q-school finals. And then she'd made every cut this season. Maybe I could learn a thing or three by watching her.

Once Laura returned to the range, we started on my pregame practice routine. It was the same one Mike used before every round, the one I helped him develop over his rookie year. It had the Joe Lancaster stamp of approval on it, too.

I knew I had to tuck my elbow, extend my forearms, and clear my hips. But what I needed most of all was enough ritual and visualization to crowd out overly-technical or negative mental chatter.

We finished our warm-up at the practice range and hopped the shuttle back to the putting green. The top scores from the morning rounds flashed on the leaderboard next to the green. A sixty-four, two sixty-fives, and a sixty-six led the pack.

"How're you feeling?" Laura asked. "You're awfully quiet."

"Good. Okay. Hot. Nervous as hell," I admitted. I wiped my forehead with my golf towel. "I don't see how I'm going to go that low."

"One shot at a time," said Laura. "You're playing the golf course, not those girls."

"Where the hell is Joe anyway? I thought he'd be here by now." He wasn't likely to produce any new insights about my round at this late date, but I sure could have used a jolt of his optimism.

After half an hour of putting and still no Joe, we

tromped across the road to the first tee. I greeted Annie again, then extended my hand to So Won Lee. She offered me a firm American handshake, accompanied by her abbreviated but formal Korean bow. She used an interpreter for press interviews, so I doubted we'd do much chatting today.

"This is the twelve-thirty-six tee time for the ShopRite LPGA Classic," said the starter.

A smattering of fans applauded the introductions and the straight drives of my playing companions. As soon as my name was announced, I stepped forward, visualized my ball sailing down the fairway, and yanked it into the trees.

"Dammit!" I said. "That's two times in two days."

"Down girl," said Laura. "We'll find it; it's only one shot."

Which was exactly why I'd make a lot of sacrifices to have her around. Besides being a cheerful roommate and all-around good friend, she knew just the caddie line to take with me. If you were on the edge of losing your Tour status already, you couldn't afford the emotional calories that breaking in a new caddie took. Earlier in the season when Laura was tied up in Connecticut, my substitute caddie sank into a hangdog sulk after each of my bogeys. I nearly quit the game on the spot.

With Laura's encouragement, I threaded my second shot out of the trees and to the right of the first green. Then I lobbed a chip shot high and soft, and walked off pleased with a tap-in par.

"Great up and down," said Annie. She seemed honestly happy about my recovery.

"Thanks." I flashed her a grateful smile. We traveled the short distance to the second hole, where the threesome ahead of us had just teed off.

"Hurry up and wait," said Annie, dropping down onto her bag. She began to clean her cleats off with a red tee.

"Man it's hot. At least in Texas we have dry heat. Did they ever find out what happened to your friend?"

"Autopsy results came back—she had loaded up on antidepressants, plus alcohol, barbituates, and pain killers. She wasn't taking any chances she'd make it through the night."

"I thought about it after we talked," she said. "Honest to Pete, I couldn't see any of those guys as a killer." She stood up and took her titanium driver from her caddie. "They'd all worked together a long time, you know. According to Dr. Gladstone, he trained everybody on that team. They were all mavericks with a lot of potential and no discipline."

"That would be Hugh's take on things," I said, still annoyed about the double butt-grabbing incident.

After checking her lineup and adjusting the placement of her hands on the grip of her driver, Annie pantomimed her swing in slow motion. "Roger's the newest on the team; he joined them a year ago. His last job was in Texas, though you'd never know it from the accent. He didn't learn a thing from us while he was down there. But he sure does love Texas barbecue." Annie giggled. "Did you see Gladstone at the party last night?"

"More of him than I wanted," I said. "Drunk as a skunk. And I still didn't care for the guy."

Annie shook her head. "He surprised me. But Travis is a sweetie. He reminds me a little of me."

Now there was a curious comparison. "How so?"

"Everyone thinks I'm so easygoing," she laughed. "But look out if I want something really bad. I think he's the same way."

"Tee's open," her caddie said. "You're up. Take dead aim."

By the time I stood over my approach shot ten minutes later, the wind had begun to swirl in unpredictable gusts. According to Joe, you can let yourself get wound up about this kind of condition. Or you can try to block it out with the routine you've practiced until your body parts know it by rote. "Let it go," I told myself. But the club stubbed the ground in front of the ball and the ball floated into the marsh grass lining the right side of the hole.

"Damn." I did a head-hang my ex-caddie would have been proud to call his own. Laura hustled the bag up ahead of me to look over the lie.

"It's not so bad," she called out in a cheery voice. "You'll just need to take a short backswing and follow through. If you clip the bank about a foot below the collar, it should trickle down to the hole."

Easier said than executed. I hit the bank where I aimed, but the ball took a harder hop than we'd anticipated. Two putts later, I carded a bogey, and we moved on to the third hole.

Here was where my birdie binge started yesterday, a circumstance I hoped to repeat. No such luck. I didn't line up my first birdie putt until the seventh hole. And that putt slid right by the cup, leaving a knee-knocking four-footer that I barely sank for par. Two over after nine; all signs pointed to adding another missed cut to my résumé. I thought about how well the day had gone yesterday. I thought about how badly I wanted to play tomorrow.

"We're just going to have to grind it out," I told Laura. "What number do you think I have to shoot?"

"Never mind the number," she said. "Let's just grind."

Walking down the tenth hole, I finally spotted Joe's head bobbing through the crowd. As he worked his way closer to the ropes lining the fairway, I could see that Rebecca Butterman was with him. She was suited up in a short khaki skirt, a sleeveless white shell, and pearls. Who the hell wore pearls on a golf course? Her face was plastered with an empathetic expression—the look shrinks get when things are not going so well with their patients, but it's too early in the relationship to start pressing them on what their contribution was to the mess in the first place. The whole thing burned me up good. She wasn't my shrink, and I didn't need her sympathy. Or her insights. I could, however, have used a little moral support from my esteemed psychological consultant and so-called friend. At times like this, I wished my relationship with Joe was all business. I'd pay, he'd provide his services, that would be that. No feelings involved.

I knew I needed to set my annoyance with Joe and the phony solicitude of Dr. Butterman aside. I squatted down to study my putt, my hands cupping either side of the visor of my cap. The tenth green had serious undulations that increased the challenge beyond what the size of the putting surface would suggest. Without waiting for Laura's read, I lagged the putt over the hill and down toward the hole on the lower shelf. It skidded to a halt four inches past the cup.

"Couldn't have done better myself." Laura grinned and slapped me on the back. "Even if you didn't ask my advice."

I glanced back over at Joe, who gave me a thumbs-up. Then he leaned over to listen to something Dr. Butterman was telling him over the noise of the crowd. Probably some stupid interpretation about which of my psychological hang-ups would keep me from breaking through. I felt more determined than ever to knock that silly empathy off her face.

With the wind blowing in from the marsh, I selected a six iron for the tee shot on the eleventh hole. I swung easy and watched the ball sail up toward the pin. It wasn't clear to me why I found Butterman's presence so grating. But who cared? This was not the time for self-analysis. I'd use my irritation to stoke my competitive fire as long as it worked. I could be a nice guy after the round. Maybe.

After making a textbook birdie putt on eleven, I drew a plugged lie in the greenside bunker on twelve, and gave the stroke back. I glanced at the leaderboard next to the green.

"Five pars and a bogey, and I play tomorrow," I said.

Laura nodded. "Cutsville, here we come."

We looked at each other and burst into a unison chorus: "But one shot at a time."

Six pars later, Joe waited in the shadow of the risers to congratulate me as I exited the eighteenth green. His elegant little sidekick was no longer with him. I felt myself relax. I wanted to enjoy his excitement without scrutinizing their interactions for possible meaning.

"Fantastic job—you were incredible. I'm so proud of you! The putt on eleven was awesome—it was in the jar all the way across the green. . . ." For a few minutes, I allowed myself to bask in his superlatives.

"I can't listen to you run on about how great I am all afternoon," I laughed finally. "I gotta go sign my scorecard. Do we have a plan for dinner?"

"I promised one of the other women I'd spend an hour with her at the range. Rebecca made a reservation for the Japanese steak house down the road at seven. That should give you time to get cleaned up and maybe even a catnap. Sound good to meet you there?"

The steak house sounded fine. Rebecca choosing the restaurant, making the reservation, and coming along, did not. "Where were you this morning, anyway? I thought you were going to meet us on the putting green."

"Sorry," said Joe. He didn't sound sorry. "Rebecca and I had an appointment at the New Jersey Psychological Association to get an opinion about the ethics of her discussing Erica's treatment with us."

"Jesus, Joe. We're not asking her to gossip. Someone else's life could be at stake here."

"It's a big deal for a therapist to break confidence," he said, bypassing my snottiness with his soothing shrink voice. "When Anne Sexton's therapist turned the tapes she made of their sessions over to a biographer, people went crazy. Every patient who'd ever complained they hated their mother worried their words would show up in the tabloids. So Rebecca went back to consult their lawyer this afternoon. We'll tell you more at dinner, okay?"

He tousled my head like I was three years old, then went off whistling, both hands in his pockets and a smile on his face.

Chapter 17

I speed-dialed Mom on the ride back to the motel. We'd had a heart-to-broken-heart a couple weeks ago, in which I'd told her she couldn't count on me calling after every round. I needed to make a clean sweep of anything that might drag my golf game down. Morose, daily tête-à-têtes with Mom made the short list. But juiced with exhilaration over making the cut, I wanted to tell everyone who might have even a passing interest. Which by definition, should include Mom. Besides, locked in that freezer last night, I swore to God I'd keep in better touch with her if only I got out alive.

I held my breath and flashed Laura my crossed fingers, hoping Mom'd pick up the phone and spare me a round with my stepfather.

"Hallo," said Dave. I grimaced and gave Laura the thumbs-down sign.

"Hey. It's Cassie. How are things going?"

"They're going," he said. "How about you?"

"Made my first cut."

"Congratulations," he grunted. "Does this mean there will be real money changing hands? We have our retirement to think about, and I haven't seen any signs yet of you becoming self-sufficient."

I was silent, just rolling my eyes and mouthing the yak, yak, yak of Dave's voice for Laura's entertainment. Conversations with Dave tended to pick up almost exactly where you'd left them off. And cut or no cut, we'd had this one so often, I knew the lines by heart. First, he would carry on as though he was bankrolling my stint on the LPGA Tour. Next I'd hear about how all this traveling worried my mother sick.

"Besides which," he went on, "your mother drives me crazy when you're on the road. It's not a normal girl's job, what you're doing. You're just asking for trouble." He banged the phone down without waiting for any rebuttal. "It's Cassandra, Winifred," he bellowed. "She made the cut."

"I'm going to get a Coke," whispered Laura as we entered the motel lobby. "I'll see you back at the room."

Then Mom came on the line. "Hi honey."

"Hi Mom! I'm in New Jersey," I said in my best cheerful voice.

"How was your drive, honey?" she asked. Her words slurred slightly, syrupy with gin, which explained why she'd asked about a fifty-mile drive I'd taken five days earlier.

"Not bad at all. Hey, it looks like your daughter's finally going to make a cut."

"That's nice dear." She sighed. "I always worry when you're on the road."

"I know, Mom. I'm careful. How are you feeling?"

She sighed again. "You know how it is. My feet hurt. And Mr. Nettor changed my hours again. I'm working all the lunches when the tips are lousy. Any young thing who comes in here and jiggles herself in front of him can pretty much get the shift she wants."

I said nothing. Lubricated with her evening cocktails, she was quite capable of swelling to fill the space on both sides of the conversation.

"Your brother called yesterday. He asked after you. He's in New York City this week doing something—a deposition, I think he said. I told him he should try to get down and see you, but he's scheduled tight."

"I know how busy he is, Mom."

"I just wish we could be together more often, that's all. And Cashbox really misses you."

Mom had stooped low on that one. She knew how much it hurt me to leave the old guy home. But it just wasn't possible to travel thirty weeks a year with a cat—an elderly, carsick fellow at that.

"I know Mom. I miss you all, too."

Reaching our room at the end of the hallway, I fumbled for the card key, inserted it into the slot, and pushed the door open. I gasped. The room had been trashed. The drawers in the desk and bureau gaped open crookedly, with our clothes hanging out of them. And the contents of every bag we owned had been emptied onto the floor. Even our pile of dirty laundry had been kicked out of the closet and scattered across the carpet.

"What? What's wrong? Is something wrong?" Mom's baseline level of tremulousness ratcheted up two notches.

"Nothing, Mom. Sorry. I stubbed my toe on the darn bed. Look, I haven't eaten supper yet, and I'm starving. I'll call you soon."

"Are you wearing sunscreen every day, Cassie? The paper had a big article on antioxidants and skin cancer yesterday. I've clipped it out and saved it for you. You're at high risk, you know. Uncle Howard died of mela-noma—"

"Gotta go, Mom. Love you." I hung up before she could chronicle the fatal diseases of every relative on our family tree. Then I called the cops and waited for Laura.

Two uniformed officers showed up twenty minutes later, accompanied by the very nervous motel manager. After questioning us about finding the room torn apart, they began to pick through the debris.

"What's missing?" asked the taller of the two cops, eyeing the trail of underwear that marched across the room.

"We didn't dare touch anything," said Laura. "But I can't think of what anyone would want. Cassie's golf clubs are at the pro shop. Oh wait! I had two hundred bucks in the buck pocket of my suitcase."

With gloved hands, the second officer, a redhead with a Woody Woodpecker–style cowlick, opened the bag she pointed to and felt around the pocket. The money was there.

"Not much of a robbery," said the tall cop. "Someone had something else in mind." He peered at us, no longer smiling with solicitude. "Got any ideas?"

"I think you should call Detective Rumson," said Laura. "We've already talked to her about a couple of incidents this week." Both cops raised their eyebrows. "Someone tried to kill Cassie last night," Laura explained. "Shut her in the freezer at the Marriott."

"Dear Lord," said the motel manager, layering several more worried creases on his forehead.

"We'll dust for prints," said the tall cop. "I doubt we find any. These kinds of perps usually wear gloves. If something turns up missing, give us a call."

Perps. I tried not to giggle. Either this fellow was new to the job, watched a lot of old TV, or wanted to impress his audience.

Laura made a run for a nearby package store while the police searched our crime scene again and looked for fingerprints. "Call us if you need anything," said the redhead when they had finished cataloging the chaos. "We'll fill in Detective Rumson as soon as she returns our page."

Laura came back as I was dressing and pulled a sweating six-pack of Budweiser out of her backpack. She cracked a can open and lay back against the pillows on her unmade bed. "We've got an hour and a half until our dinner reservation. We need to figure out what the hell's going on here."

"No joke." I was starting to feel more scared than I wanted to admit. I smoothed out the shirt I had planned to wear for tomorrow's round, then draped it on a hanger. Should I borrow the motel's iron? Mom would freak if I showed up on national TV wrinkled. I decided to take that chance.

"This is the thing," I said to Laura. "Someone was looking for something, and we need to figure out what that is. What do we have that they—whoever they are— want?"

As I shook out the khaki shorts I'd worn yesterday, a key dropped out of the back pocket.

"What the hell is that?"

"It's the key to Erica's apartment. I forgot I had it." I turned it over in my hand. "Maybe this is what they're after."

"If they wanted to get into her pad, wouldn't they just crash in? I can't see robbers breaking in here to look for a key so they don't have to break in somewhere else."

"What then? There was nothing in the cosmetics bag except makeup and that key."

"Plus the Palm Pilot we gave to Detective Rumson," said Laura. "As far as we know, no one except Joe and the cops knew we had that."

"Where's your computer?" I asked suddenly.

"I locked it in the trunk this morning."

"Let's see if we can get into those files. I'm starting to take this whole thing personally."

"Since someone's tried to kill you and now pawed through our underwear, I think a little paranoia is in order," said Laura.

I sipped on a beer and continued to straighten the room while she went to the car for her laptop.

"I put in a couple of passwords yesterday, but no luck," she said when she returned. "I tried the obvious: Lila Rose, Meditron, and Jorganson. That was her maiden name, right?" I nodded.

"Try birdie," I said. Laura typed it in.

"No go." Then she tapped out bogey, blackjack, and twenty one. Still nothing.

"She was basically an optimist," I said. "Try eagle." The computer began to hum as the locked files opened.

"She *was* an optimist," said Laura. She peered at the screen. "I see three files: Golf, Pierre's Assets, and Adverse Events. First things first." She double-clicked on golf, then skimmed through the text. "She must have taken notes after every lesson. If only my students were that serious, I could make some real progress. She's got a name and phone number listed at the bottom. Don Gulden at Sandy Pines Golf Club. Probably the golf pro hunk Christine told us about."

I had known a Don Gulden on the Tour. His wife caddied for him; she was a knockout. She looked fragile, all blond and dainty, but she slung his bag around like it was an evening purse. Don and Mike argued baseball every time they played together. Neither one had a stellar rookie year, but Don's was rumored to have been shipwrecked by his weakness for gambling and alcohol.

"I think I know this guy," I told Laura. "I haven't seen his name on the money list all year."

"So call him."

I punched in the number on my cell phone.

"Sandy Pines Golf," answered a deep voice.

"Cassie Burdette for Don Gulden, please."

"Cassie! How the hell are you? Where are you?"

"Just up the road from you, I guess. I made my first cut today at the ShopRite Classic."

"Get out! Hey, that's fantastic. So you finally took enough of Callahan's abuse."

My laugh came out weak. "Do you have a few minutes to chat? I have a big problem I hope you can help me with."

"Keep your elbow in and swing easy." He laughed the booming guffaw I remembered from the few rounds we'd played together. "Seriously, can you come over right now? I'd love to see you, but I'll be closing up at seven. Big date tonight." He laughed again, but this time it sounded forced and even a little guilty. Which gave me a pretty good idea the date was not with his wife.

"On the road again," I said to Laura. "If we leave now, we'll only be a couple minutes late to dinner. Bring the computer. We'll look at the other files with our resident shrinks."

Chapter 18

Fifteen minutes later, we pulled into the parking lot at Sandy Pines Golf Club. This was no championship lay-out: a small pro shop in serious need of a coat of paint, a practice putting green grass that had as many bare spots as grass, and a complete vacuum in the arena of attentive bag drop personnel.

We found Don behind the counter in the shop. I gave him a hug and introduced him to Laura. I tried not to be too obvious about assessing how he'd weathered the last couple of years. His shoulders, arms, and belly strained the seams of his Greg Norman golf shirt, and he'd begun combing a few long strands of blond hair over the thin spot at the top of his forehead. Even with the extra few pounds and an inch less of hairline, I could see why Christine had described him as a hunk. His energetic linebacker aura hadn't faded. All he needed was a baseball cap and a few laps around the track. Or at least a shirt in the next size up.

"How are you? How's Abby?" I asked.

"The divorce came through a couple months ago," His eyes flicked shut, then quickly back open.

"I didn't know. I'm sorry." I had a sudden urge to try to lighten the mood. "I thought you guys had a life sentence." *Ha-ha.*

"Me, too." He cleared his throat. "She wanted to settle down and have a couple of rug rats. I wanted to break into the top ten. So she finally had enough and left me." He flashed me a crooked smile. "You know how it is without the right caddie. Your game goes down the toilet. So here I am." He gave a Vanna White wave around the room. "Resident fucking golf professional and cash register clerk at Sandy Pines. Not exactly the top ten."

It did seem like he'd fallen fast and hard. But I was afraid to ask for the details. It could happen to anyone—me included.

Laura patted his arm. "I teach golf, too, when I'm not carrying my friend's bag." She nudged me with her hip. "It can be very rewarding. You meet a lot of interesting folks as a teaching pro. And you add a lot of pleasure to their lives. When someone who loses ten balls in the woods every round finally finds the fairway—it's a victory."

"I do love the teaching," Don said. "I'm not threatening Leadbetter yet, but I am starting to develop my own little cult following. And tell Mr. Callahan when you see him," he slapped his hand on the counter in front of me, "I've got season tickets to the Mets. Haven't missed a home game since I left the Tour."

"Speaking of meeting folks," I said. "We need to ask you some questions about Erica LeBoutillier." I watched his face carefully. What might he have to hide?

"She's a great gal," he said. He straightened the collar

on his golf shirt and hitched up his pants. "She could be an awesome golfer, too, if she'd only practice more."

"She's finished practicing," said Laura. "Didn't you read the newspaper this week? She's dead."

I watched his sun-bronzed face bleach white. A slight tremor started at his lips and traveled up the side of his face until his eyebrow pulsed. "No way! That's brutal. I can't believe it. What happened?"

"Cops think she killed herself," Laura said. "What's your theory?" She seemed to have copied Detective Rumson's cut-to-the-chase query style.

"I'm shocked. I have no clue—"

"We heard you two were having an affair."

The tremor rolled into a full blown grimace. "Come on into the office, and let's sit down." He flipped the sign hanging in the door from Open to Closed and ushered us into the back room. He scrambled to move piles of golf magazines, videotapes, and computer printouts off the tweed couch that sagged against the wall. Then he sank into the chair behind his desk.

"I can't believe she'd kill herself." He looked at me. "How did you know her?"

"She was on my team in the Tuesday pro-am."

"She was so excited about that," said Don. Now a sadness settled into his eyes. "Meeting a real, live woman pro. Hey, I would have canceled my lessons and come out to watch if I'd known it was you."

It was getting late, and so far he'd told us nothing. We were going to have to lean harder. "Did you leave Abby for Erica?"

He laughed. "Abby left me, Cassie. Believe me, I wouldn't have left that girl for anyone." He gazed across the room to a shelf hanging on the wall. Along with the requisite books on golf technique, he had displayed a photo from the Greater Hartford Open tournament, July 2001. Abby stood beside him with his blue leather bag posed between them. They wore the wide smiles of better days. "I'm embarrassed to tell you this, but settling down wasn't the only problem between us. The big one was gambling."

"Gambling?" asked Laura.

"You get bored on the Tour. You're probably still in the honeymoon phase where you can't believe you got so lucky."

I nodded.

"You'll see. Everyone thinks it's such a glamorous life, all that traveling. Pretty soon into it, you get tired and god-awful bored."

"I'm not there yet," I said.

He nodded. "It'll come. And you'll want some relief. I got so I'd bet on anything. Golf stuff—who's on in regulation, who's closest to the pin, whose amateurs will shoot what, even who's gonna score with a groupie that night. It got away from me after a while."

He opened the desk drawer, took out a can of snuff, and inserted a pinch between his lip and gum. He held up the container. "Started this up after Abby left, too. Erica was on me to quit. I told her I'd make her a deal—she'd help me kick the nicotine and I'd help her with the gambling."

"I thought you said your wife left you because *you* were gambling," said Laura.

"I was. Big time. When she split, I hit the proverbial rock bottom. Wife dumped me, lost my Tour card, net worth below zero. That's when I started going to Gamblers Anonymous. Twelve steps to a new life. It works, too." He spoke directly to Laura now. "When you're giving a lesson, you hear a lot about people's lives."

She bobbed her head in agreement.

"Erica told me more than you might expect about what was happening to her and Pierre. I saw she was letting off steam the same as I used to. Only she had the casinos right in her backyard. She could spend a month's salary in one night at the blackjack table."

"So you tried to help?" I asked.

He picked up a soft, blue rubber ball and began to squeeze it methodically. "I told her about the meetings—took her to a couple of them. Even offered to be her sponsor. We'd been spending a lot of time together lately. But it wasn't what you heard. Even messed up good, she was way out of my league."

"Did she seem depressed?" asked Laura.

"I'm no headshrinker. But I figure I'm the kind of guy who can read people pretty good. She was sad, mad, stressed, but I never would have thought suicide." He shook his head and set the ball carefully on his desk. "She was a firecracker. Dogged, man. She'd get on a trail, and she wasn't going to give up easy."

"Did she use drugs?" I asked.

"Not that I knew of."

"What did she tell you about the trouble with Pierre?"

"Mostly I heard about her girl. The day he told her she couldn't bring Lila Rose to the pro-am, she sat in here—right where you are now—and cried her heart out. That bastard."

Watching the fury in his face as he described Erica's meltdown, I wasn't sure I believed that they hadn't been involved. I even wondered if her gambling problems had been as bad as he described. A new twelve-step convert could be overzealous. Besides, what better entrée for him to get close to her than to play the concerned confidant.

"Did she say much about problems at work?"

"That's why she wasn't practicing the way she should have, even with the big tournament coming up next week. I told her she needed to spend at least thirty minutes a day on the putting green. I didn't want her to be thinking anything standing over a putt, besides *It's in the damn jar.*" He got up out of his chair and paced across the room,

stopping to straighten his PGA Master Teaching Professional plaque on the wall. "She was one of my best students. She took notes in her Palm Pilot after every lesson."

He shook his head in amazement. "Never had anyone
write down what I had to say, other than the interview in
Golf Weekly right after I lost my card. And most of that
wasn't printable." He laughed suddenly, a hollow snort
that echoed in the small room.

I tried to nudge him back on track. "So work interfered
with following through on the lessons."

"Whatever this latest project was, the big shots insisted
on everyone having all the pistons firing. And I think with
her being the only chick, and a goddess at that, she felt
she had to work harder than anyone else just to be taken
serious."

A goddess? I'd have said Erica was attractive, but not
in the mythological range.

"Did you ever meet the rest of her team?"

He shook his head no. "Like I said, other than her coming here for lessons, that girl outclassed me."

I glanced at Laura. Now someone was lying—either
him or Christine. I didn't know Erica's nosy coworker
from a hole in the ground, but I wouldn't have fingered
Don to shade the facts. What would be the point?

"We better get moving," said Laura. "They'll be waiting dinner for us." As she stood up, a pile of videotapes
crashed from the back of the couch down to the floor.

"That reminds me, I've got a tape of Erica in here
somewhere." He glanced at his watch. "I don't have time
to show it to you now, but you can take it with you if
you want. Just drop it off tomorrow. Maybe something in
there will help you understand her."

Don sorted through the tapes on the floor and stood up
to hand one to me. As I turned to follow Laura out to the
pro shop, he grabbed my arm and pulled me back just a
step.

"I feel a little funny about this, but they tell us in the meetings to live life like you mean it. One day at a time and all that." He grinned and blushed. "I hope you won't take offense, but could I call you sometime? Abby always suspected me of having a thing for you."

I felt myself reddening to match his color. It didn't seem like a good idea to go out with Don; between his baggage and mine, we could fill the cargo hold on a 747. "Thanks. It's a little hard to make plans, being on the road."

His smile sagged. "Well, here then. Take a Sandy Pines Golf Club hat. Maybe it'll remind you of me and the good times we had on the Tour." He held out two mustard-colored baseball caps with his new golf course's scraggly pine tree logo etched on the bill.

Saying no thanks to all of the above seemed like a good move. The hats were ugly, and Don was in no shape to start a new relationship. On the other hand, I didn't want to hurt the feelings of an old friend. I took the caps, scribbled my cell phone number on a Sandy Pines scorecard, and passed it over to him. "It's great seeing you. You haven't changed one bit." I hugged him quickly before he could read the lie in my face and followed Laura out to the car.

"I can't believe the guy tried to put the moves on you," said Laura when she'd slammed the door shut.

I tossed the hats into the backseat. "He was just being friendly."

"Friendly, my ass—" I was grateful that the buzz of my cell phone cut into her observations.

"Hello?"

"Ms. Burdette, it's Detective Rumson. I got the photo you left for me this morning. We have some officers out looking for the girl. I understand you had some trouble at your motel. Did anything turn up missing?"

"No, nothing. First I thought Laura's computer was gone, but she'd left it in her trunk."

"Let me know if you have any further incidents." She was silent for a moment. "Did I make myself perfectly clear last night that I don't want to hear about you getting involved in any other detective work?"

"All clear." I signed off and turned to Laura. "She'd really have a fit if we told her about the stuff you hot-synched onto your laptop."

"You didn't tell her about visiting Lila Rose, either."

"Let's talk to Joe over dinner and see what he thinks. I'll call her back later if he thinks I should." I leaned back into the headrest. "Tell you the truth, that woman scares the living daylights out of me."

Chapter 19

The vestibule of Ikebana Steakhouse was jammed with boisterous would-be diners. I nodded across the crowd to Meg Mallon. The sixty-three she'd rapped out today, on top of yesterday's sixty-five, positioned her in the lead for the third round. Her enthusiastic dinner entourage reflected that excitement.

Our tournament experiences tomorrow would be radically different. I'd tee off with the dewsweepers—the players who'd just scraped through into the final round and were assigned the earliest tee times. We'd have no TV cameras following us and only a handful of hardy spectators. Meg would be paired with the hottest two women on the Tour, her every waggle scrutinized by a partisan gallery and instant television replay.

"I'd like to be in her shoes one day," I told Laura.

"You will."

A petite Asian woman dressed in a red satin kimono greeted us with a deep bow.

"We're with the Butterman party," Laura said. I made a face. Since when did we become the freaking *Butterman party*? The hostess led us through a curtain of beads to the back of the restaurant, stopping at the entrance to a separate room and pointing to a row of shoes along the wall.

"Please remove," she said, bowing again and indicating that we needed to exchange our shoes for a pair of straw flip-flops. We shuffled inside and found Joe seated Indian style on a cushion behind a knee-high table.

"How's my favorite Tour rookie?" he asked, a big grin spreading across his face. "You were awesome today. It was hot enough to melt the Surlyn off your golf balls, but you stayed so cool."

"Thanks." I ducked my head modestly. "Laura deserves a lot of the credit."

"That's what they all say. But it won't be my name on that trophy." She slid in next to Joe and deposited her laptop between them. "Where's Rebecca?"

"Running a little late," he said. "Let's take a look at your files while we're waiting."

As the computer booted up, we told him about our ransacked room.

"I don't like the way this is headed." Frowning, he rubbed his temples. "What did the cops say?"

"Not a lot," said Laura. "They pretty much agreed it didn't look like a standard robbery."

"Detective Rumson wondered what else the intruder could have been after," I said. "We're guessing it's these Palm Pilot files."

Laura rotated the computer so Joe could see it. "We found three: Pierre's Assets, Adverse Events, and the golf stuff, which we've already looked at."

"Erica's golf pro was Don Gulden. Remember him from the PGA Tour?"

"Tall and blond, with a big loop in his backswing?"

I nodded. "We stopped by to visit him on our way here. He denied that he was involved with Erica, other than as her teacher and fellow problem gambler. He'd taken her to several Gamblers Anonymous meetings."

"Yeah, but I didn't get the idea she had swallowed the party line," said Laura.

"She gambled, but she didn't see it as a problem."

We both nodded our agreement of Joe's assessment.

"Yet from what you've told me about her, she fits pretty much all the descriptive diagnostic criteria."

"Such as . . ."

He ticked a list off on his fingers. "Workaholic, competitive, energetic, restless, easily bored, with depression underneath it all. In fact, twenty percent of female compulsive gamblers have tried suicide."

"So you're back to believing she killed herself," said Laura.

"Maybe," said Joe. "I'm hoping Rebecca can clear some of this up."

"Then why did the golf pro lie to us?" Laura asked. "Don flat out told us he hadn't met her coworkers. Meanwhile, Christine at Meditron tells us the opposite. He had come by the office to visit her, and Travis was jealous as hell."

"Could be Christine that's lying," I said.

Joe poured us each a small cup of green tea. "Did Don know she was dead before you came to talk to him?"

"He seemed completely shocked." I looked to Laura for confirmation. "And he was definitely sad and upset, even though he's still mourning Abby," I said.

Joe cocked his head in curiosity.

"That's his ex-wife," said Laura. "She used to caddie

for him, but she finally had enough fun and dumped his ass."

"I'm not the shrink," I said, "but I think Erica was a distraction. He saw her as smarter and more successful than he could ever be."

"Out of his league," Laura added. "You got the idea he was honored to have her pay any attention to him. He practically had an orgasm describing how she took notes during their lessons." She sipped her tea and made a face. "Who can drink this stuff? Don't they serve beer in this joint?"

"So maybe he exaggerated the problem gambling because it was a bridge he could build between them," said Joe.

A waiter appeared to take our order. He persuaded us to sample the night's special combo platter: teriyaki shrimp and sirloin steak.

"We're not scrimping tonight," said Laura. "This is a celebration. Sapporos for everyone, please."

"We have another lady joining us," Joe told the waiter. "Let's order the special for her, too."

As the waiter collected our menus, Joe clicked on the file labeled Pierre's Assets. He set the computer on the table in front of us. A spreadsheet filled the screen. Pierre's income had been recorded in excruciating detail, including a long list of stocks and mutual funds. The performance of each entry was tracked over the past six months, most of them on an upward trend.

"This guy had a lot to lose," said Joe. "It was going to be a very expensive divorce."

"Maybe he realized that having a dead wife will be a lot less costly than a living ex-wife," said Laura.

"That's a harsh way to put it," I said.

"But hard to argue. Look, he owned a big chunk of Meditron stock." Laura pointed to an item halfway down the screen. "He would have been rooting for the new drug getting to market as much as the other guys. I wonder if Erica had shared her concerns about the clinical trials with him?"

"By the way," I said. "Lila Rose recognized Aimee Joy in the photo we showed her. She calls her Olivia—says Pierre and Erica fought over whether Olivia's mother, Della, should have been allowed to baby-sit."

"When did you see Lila Rose? Where's the picture? You shouldn't be meddling in this stuff. It's dangerous."

"We took the photo to the police this morning, then dropped by the LeBoutilliers'. You could have gone with us, if you'd been around." My voice was sharp enough to shut Joe's scolding down.

He closed the finance file and double-clicked on Adverse Events. This time, a chronicle of drug company hiccups and recalls appeared on the screen. The earliest entry listed a lawsuit by the families of women killed by the Dalkon Shield. The three Meditron faux pas that Joe had mentioned yesterday were among the latest entries on the list.

"What the hell was she doing?" asked Laura.

"I'd say she was building a case," said Joe.

"A case for what?"

Just then, Dr. Butterman rushed into the room, dressed in a deep purple nubby linen sheath. The afternoon's pearls were gone, replaced by large diamond teardrop earrings and a burst of flowery perfume. Even the requisite cheap flip-flops did not blemish her elegance. I mentally downgraded my own outfit to Kmart blue light special.

"I'm sorry to be late. My engine was knocking so badly, I went back home and took a cab over. I hope you didn't wait for me to order. You all must be starving."

"We didn't wait. I chose the special combination for you, I hope that's okay." Joe smiled up at her and patted the seat beside him. "We ordered you a Sapporo, too. Would you rather have sake?"

"I'm easy."

I suppressed the urge to run with the rude comment that sprang to mind.

Dr. Butterman slid onto the empty cushion next to Joe, kissed his cheek, and then leaned in my direction.

"Cassie! Congratulations on your round today. You must be thrilled!"

"Thanks. I am." I mustered up a saccharine smile, hoping to disguise the sudden blast of teenage surliness that infused me. "Glad you could be there. And join us tonight."

If she believed that one . . .

A young Japanese man in a white coat and chef's toque arrived at our station with a rolling cart. He said something unintelligible to us in Japanese and bowed deeply. Then he picked up the tall, wooden salt and pepper shakers from his cart and began to alternately bang them on the cook top in our table and juggle them into the air. We gave him a round of perfunctory applause at the end of the performance. This was going to be a long night.

"What did you decide about the release of information on Erica's treatment?" asked Joe.

Dr. Butterman laughed. "As you can imagine, with a room full of lawyers and psychologists, nothing seems simple. They didn't even agree on whether a decedent's representative can waive the privilege to confidentiality."

"Really?" said Joe. "So it would have been a waste of time to try to twist her husband's arm."

She shrugged. "One of the attorneys insists that no one except the patient him- or herself can give permission to the therapist to talk. So if the patient dies, information about the therapy goes with him."

"A lot of good that does us," said Laura.

The chef took out a huge butcher knife and began to whack the vegetables on his tray into thin sticks. He poured a pool of oil onto the cook top, then with a grand flourish, dumped the vegetables and a container of rice into the sizzling oil. A cloud of greasy steam wafted across the table.

"There's one small caveat," said Dr. Butterman, taking a dainty sip of tea. "There is a provision similar to the Tarasoff decision, in which confidentiality may be breached if there is clear evidence that another person or personal property is endangered."

Joe nodded. "That's true in California, but doesn't each state have to ratify the decision?"

"That's just the problem. These guys don't agree on the law in New Jersey. Plus, it's not entirely clear that Erica's communications would be germane to someone else's future safety."

"They found her dead, then Lucia Jimenez was shot. It would seem like a no-brainer to me," said Joe.

Now our chef pushed the mountain of stir-fried rice to one side of the cook top and emptied a platter of steak onto the grill. Only Dr. Butterman and Joe applauded his next round of furious implement clanking and tossing.

I glanced at Laura, but she did not appear perplexed by the shrinks' exchange. Damned if I was going to be the one to ask the stupid questions. I flagged down the waiter to order another beer and opened Laura's computer, which she'd placed on the floor beside me. Scrolling through the symbols on the desktop, I noticed a fourth file which had been hidden under the icon of Pierre's Assets. I double-clicked and watched a file called Sessions load.

"Looks like the brain trust wasted its time today," I announced. "Erica kept notes about her therapy as well as her golf lessons. This could be all we need."

"Go on," said Joe. "Don't keep us in the dark."

"She dates the first entry May 3." I looked to Dr. Butterman for confirmation, but she held her face blank. " 'RB notes symptoms of depression. Strongly suggests referral to Dr. Hill for medication. Does this mean she feels she can't handle my case on her own?' "

"That's a typical reaction," said Joe, patting Dr. Butterman's manicured hand. "Taking medication means very different things to each person. Part of our job is to help the patient understand his or her resistance so the use of an antidepressant becomes a viable option. In some cases, people can't do the work of psychotherapy until their mood lifts enough to talk about their problems." He sipped his beer. "What about the other drugs in her system? Did Dr. Hill prescribe them? Did she have a pain condition?"

"No to both," said Dr. Butterman.

"What else did she say in the notes?" Laura asked.

"Here's May 17. 'Don't think Prozac helping. Talked to RB about tension with TS and HG. Looking for father figure? Ha! One father too much already.' " Again, I looked up to scan the psychologist's flushed face.

"She'd had a very difficult childhood," said Dr. Butterman softly. "She found it hard to trust men, but underneath that, she desperately wanted someone to take care of her."

"I'm guessing that in the transference, you would have been seen as the weak mother," said Joe.

Laura rolled her eyes. "Could you drop the shrink jibber-jabber and put that in plain American English for us laypersons?"

Joe laughed and turned to Dr. Butterman. "Do you feel all right about discussing the case?"

"I was just starting to say, before Cassie found the therapy files," she smiled graciously in my direction, "that I'd decided this case did fit the criteria for release of confidentiality."

"Great," said Laura. "Now we get info from both sides of the couch. So finish telling us about this transference business."

"Supposing Erica had a tyrant for a father and a mother who could not stand up to him. She would tend to bring that template to other relationships, especially in therapy, where she isn't getting many cues back. In other words, Rebecca would be seen as another weak mother. Then it becomes her job to help Erica understand that's the lens she uses to see the world."

Dr. Butterman nodded her head vigorously.

The chef pushed the sirloin strips aside and replaced them with a large pile of shrimp that sizzled as they hit the grill. He tapped and spun his implements, this time without any audience participation at all.

"What else did she write?" Joe asked.

"June 7," I read. " 'TS pissed about DG. Told RB with LR gone, life not worth living.' " I looked up from the computer. "She sounds suicidal to me. Was she suicidal?"

"It's not easy to make that judgment," said Dr. Butterman. "She was certainly depressed. And the loss of custody, even temporary, was a blow to her self-esteem. She did love her daughter, though of course, some of her attachment was narcissistic. She was grieving deeply for the loss of her little family, for herself as well as for Lola Rose."

"*Lila,*" I corrected her. "Her daughter's name is *Lila* Rose."

Butterman certainly had a smooth line of shrink's patter. But how much attention could she have paid to Erica if she didn't even have her daughter's name right? "Have you had any other patients kill themselves? It seems like you'd want to have a damned good handle on their suicidal tendencies before you allowed them out of the office and back into the world."

Now Dr. Butterman just stared at me, her green eyes wide. I noticed the fringe of black lashes framing her eyes and the fine lines that gathered around her lips as she pursed them slightly.

Just then, the chef flipped one of the shrimp into the

air in my direction. It hit me in the forehead, splashing searing hot, garlic-scented oil down my nose.

"Shit!" Before I could get to my feet, the hostess rushed over with a damp rag and began to mop my face, muttering what I assumed were apologies in Japanese.

"Easy does it, Cassie," said Laura, stroking my arm. "It's all part of his schtick. You're supposed to catch the seafood in your mouth, not take it in the nose!"

Even though my skin throbbed from a combination of embarrassment and the hot oil, I tried to join in the others' laughter.

Our chef served dinner, and after another barrage of profuse apologies, slunk away.

"Back to your question," said Dr. Butterman. From her friendly tone, it seemed she had chosen not to take offense at my grilling. "Yes, I have dealt with other suicidal patients. Most psychologists do. Erica was complicated. She was so bright and ambitious, and so tangled up in her failing marriage and the men she got involved with in various ways. It was going to take time to sort it all out. I made a few interpretations—just tossed some ideas out there to see what bubbled to the surface."

"Are there any more notes?" asked Laura.

"One more session, June 21. That's last week," I said. I read the entry. " 'RB says sex = power. Sex trophy BULLSHIT!' " I looked up again. "The *bullshit* is written in all caps."

Dr. Butterman's face reddened. "I broke the cardinal commandment there: you shall use no interpretation before its time."

I read the last sentences in the file. " 'RB thinks mother is problem. This is not news.' "

Dr. Butterman sighed. "It was difficult for her to let her guard down. Erica was very much accustomed to being on her own. Her father had abandoned the family early— from what I could tell, there was another woman involved.

Then the mother fell ill and had to be placed in a nursing home. And finally there was Pierre. I assume she chose him unconsciously trying to master the issue of an unreachable father. He was twenty years her senior and well established when she was just trying to get her career going. Unfortunately, as he grew more distant and unfaithful, it simply repeated the earlier trauma."

Joe stabbed a shrimp with his chopsticks and popped it into his mouth. "You got to know her rather well, considering the few sessions you met."

"Did she have an affair with Travis Smith?" Laura asked. "We wondered if Travis and Roger had some kind of jealous rivalry going."

"She never mentioned Roger," said the psychologist. "As for an affair with Travis? I wouldn't be surprised. Her self-esteem had been battered by Pierre's penchant for younger women. That's why I was convinced she used sex to feel powerful with other men." She smiled ruefully in my direction.

"You're saying if she screwed a guy and then dumped him, it made her feel like she had some control," said Laura.

Dr. Butterman nodded.

"That could piss a man off good. The guy's thinking he'd taken advantage of her, then he finds out it's the other way around."

"She must have been very angry about what was happening in her life," said Joe. "Angry enough to kill herself?"

"I wish I knew." Dr. Butterman set her chopsticks down beside her plate and dabbed at her mouth with the napkin.

"Did she have a gambling addiction?" I asked.

"We just hadn't gotten far enough along for me to make a judgment on that. The addictions are hard to diagnose and hard to treat. The hardest part is getting someone to acknowledge they have a problem."

"I have to get Shrimpy home to bed," said Laura, squeezing my neck gently. "We have a big day tomorrow."

"Will you be there?" I asked Joe. I tried not to sound desperate, but I was still irritated that he'd only shown up in the middle of today's round.

"Of course," he answered. "Wouldn't miss it."

"Do you think we should tell Detective Rumson that we copied Erica's files?"

"Yes to that, too. And Rebecca is going to call her tonight about the therapy. She needs to know everything, especially with strangers crashing into your motel room." A shadow flitted across his face.

"I'll take a taxi home," said Dr. Butterman. "You go with the girls."

"We'll be fine," Laura and I announced in unplanned unison.

I thought Joe looked unattractively relieved. "Dinner's on me then. See you in the morning."

Chapter 20

Ⓞ **Laura** pulled out onto Route 9. I surfed through a sequence of static-filled stations, then switched the radio off. We rode several miles in silence.

"Boy, you were just this side of rude with Rebecca," she said, as we reached the outskirts of the Marriott resort. "In fact, I'd have to say you went over the line. What's with you and Joe?"

The car rolled to a stop at the red light where we'd cross the road tomorrow on the way to the first tee. Just down the block, a noisy crowd spilled out of a bar frequented by locals, caddies, a few golfers, and lots of interested fans.

"Look who's playing at the Nineteenth Hole tonight— Andy Berlin and the Package Goods. Want to stop in for a quick beer? They have to be more entertaining than that ridiculous restaurant display."

"You're joking, right? You need to be on top of your game in nine hours."

"I'm joking."

Laura's face faded from red to green in the reflected light.

"Look, it's not about Joe," I said. "I just don't like that woman."

"Why not?"

"She's too damn perfect. Look at the way she dresses. Who can compete with that?"

"Who says it's a competition?"

As I struggled to formulate my reasons more clearly, my phone vibrated. "Hello?"

"It's Detective Rumson. I wondered if I might swing by your motel. There are several things we need to discuss."

"Now?"

"Now."

"We're on our way home. We can meet you there in ten minutes."

"She's going to be pissed that we held information back," said Laura, as she maneuvered into a narrow parking space.

"She's already pissed. She'll get over it." Reading the gruff tone of her voice on the phone, I wasn't convinced she would get over it. But I was determined to go into the conversation with a shield of bravado.

We greeted the detective at the front desk and led her down the hallway to number 119. She stopped as soon as she stepped through the door, a concerned expression on her face. "Someone's tossed your room again!"

I laughed. "My roommate's a little messy, that's all. It does get hard to tell whether the joint's been trashed or not."

Laura stuck out her tongue. "Have a seat," she said to the detective. She snatched a pair of shorts and three dirty socks off the only armchair, lobbed them toward the closet, and collapsed onto her bed.

"Thank you for dropping off the photograph this morning. We were able to use it to track down Aimee Joy, though now it seems that she's cut out of town," said Detective Rumson. "Her real name is Sally Dowling, and she was employed by a company called City Lights Entertainment."

"Some kind of escort service?" asked Laura.

"Not officially, though that's a good guess. The owner described it as an elite tour organization."

"I'd hate to see the tours they've mapped out," I said.

"Sally's mother said she didn't come home last night, which is apparently not unusual. However, she also never showed up this morning. And she hadn't checked in for work two hours ago. So we're following up on leads concerning her possible whereabouts."

"I don't get it," I said. "Why was she pretending to be a screwed-up high school girl?"

"The obvious answer is that she was setting Ms. LeBoutillier up—for something. We don't know yet why or with whom she was working. We are assuming she was not operating on her own. And we are also assuming that whoever lined her up to get involved with Ms. LeBoutillier arranged for you to be pushed into the freezer as well." She looked up from her notes and stared at me hard. "Any thoughts about that? Or ideas about why your room was trashed? Or ideas about where this girl went?"

"No to the last question. But we have lots of theories," I said, watching the grim set of her lips. "You may not like them. It sounds like you might have changed your mind about Erica killing herself?"

The detective ran her hand through her graying curls and sighed. She looked tired and even more disheveled than the other times I'd seen her.

"Suicide is still at the top of our list, even though we're

looking at all the possibilities. My guess? Whatever exchange Sally Dowling and Ms. LeBoutillier had in that hotel room was enough to put her over the edge. And she subsequently took her own life." She shrugged. "There's not another logical way to understand the variety and amount of substances she consumed. But I'd like to hear your theories."

I spilled it all out fast so I wouldn't get rattled by fierce facial expressions or more scolding. "Sally Dowling, aka Aimee Joy, had another name, too: Olivia. We talked to Erica's daughter this morning. Apparently Olivia baby-sat Lila Rose at least once. Lila Rose said Erica didn't know Olivia, but she did know Olivia's mother, Della. And Della was a bone of contention between her parents. Which makes total sense if Della worked for City Lights, too. Erica would not have wanted a call girl watching her daughter."

In slow motion, Detective Rumson stood, paced to the window, parted the curtains, and looked out. Then she wheeled around and took a turn staring each of us down. "Is there anything you don't understand when I say that I do not want you to interview any other suspects in this case?"

We both shook our heads sheepishly.

"This is not television. This is not the movies. This is a murder investigation." Rumson thumped back into the chair, as if we had exhausted her with our interference.

"We're sorry," said Laura. "We're just very interested in getting the case solved."

"We've been going over the files we pinched off of Erica's Palm Pilot, too," I confessed.

"Don't be mad," said Laura. "You had to guess we'd make copies."

I rushed on before she could rebuke us again. "And Dr. Butterman, that's Erica's shrink, she said she'll call you later to give you her impressions of the case. To make the story short, there were a lot of guys mad at her." I marked the points off on my fingers. "She used sex as a power trip with at least two men, Travis Smith and Don Gulden. She was collecting information about adverse events in drug companies for the past thirty years. We figure that was related to the Meditron Alzheimer's drug approval. Obviously, all of the Meditron employees that I played golf with would be affected if the drug was tanked. And last but far from least, Erica had grown to hate her husband. I'd say the feeling was mutual there. They were gearing up for a major financial confrontation and custody battle. And he owns a big chunk of Meditron stock, too."

"Even though our shrink friends think she was angry enough to kill herself, all the puzzle pieces don't fit," Laura added. "She had made a lot of plans for her future, which they say suicidal people don't usually do."

Detective Rumson's thin smile did little to disguise her disapproval. "You ladies have been busy. I've said this before, but I believe you can turn the case over to me at this point."

"We're leaving town tomorrow after Cassie's final round," Laura said. "Any chance you could let us know how it all turns out?"

Detective Rumson hoisted herself out of the chair. "It would be my pleasure to have a *long-distance* phone call with you ladies. I wish you a pleasant evening. I'll let myself out."

"She's mad," said Laura as soon as the door slammed shut. "She's so mad she didn't even threaten us again about staying away from the case."

"Shoot! We never told her about the golf lesson videotape."

"There's probably nothing on it anyway, but . . . want to have a look?" She rummaged through the outside pocket of her computer bag, extracted the tape, and popped it into the VCR/TV combination.

Erica appeared on the screen holding her Callaway Big Bertha driver. We could see the yardage markers at the Sandy Pines Golf Club driving range in the background. She pressed a tee into the battered turf, balanced a yellow range ball on it, and took her stance. Don approached and stood behind her, placing his hands over hers. I couldn't say for sure whether there was full body contact, but certainly no sunlight pierced the space between them. As the tape rolled forward, he reviewed the basics of her grip.

"Remember to keep the left thumb just right of center," he said, adjusting her hand beneath his. "Then close up the gap between your thumb and forefinger."

"Aren't they snuggled up cozy," said Laura. "He's asking for trouble, in my humble opinion."

"She isn't protesting."

Don guided Erica's driver into a perfect take-away position. Then she laughed and told him something we couldn't make out. A big grin stretched across his face.

"She looks older than I was picturing. He described her as a goddess, but this gal's been around the block a couple of times." Laura watched the tape another minute. The sunlight glinted off a pendant on Don's neck, mirroring the flash of his smile. Erica giggled, adjusted her grip, and waggled her butt. "At the same time, there's something very girlish about her."

"She's a lot more relaxed here than the day I played with her," I said. "She was stressed to the max by that Meditron crowd. She's got poor Don eating out of her hand." I was weirded out by seeing the dead woman leap back to life on the tape. The image of her lifeless face, which I'd almost succeeded in suppressing completely, came surging forward. I stood up and stretched. "We need to turn in. I'm bushed."

As I lay in bed in the dark, I began part one of my pregame routine for tomorrow: visualizing my way around the golf course. Each drive landed in the fairway, each approach shot hit the green, and every putt rolled into the hole. There wasn't a single lousy bounce.

"What are you thinking?" asked Laura, her voice soft and sleepy.

"I just finished the tenth hole."

"How many under?"

"Ten."

She laughed. "Awesome. Good night." Her rhythmic snores filled the room.

I lay awake, still jazzed up by the long day and thoughts of my round tomorrow. I knew I'd been hard on Dr. Butterman. And damn if she hadn't handled it with perfect grace. Maybe my rudeness had something to do with Joe, but right now my reactions felt like an impenetrable thicket. I puzzled over the psychologist's description of Erica: the father who bugged out, the weak, sick mother. It sounded uncomfortably similar to my own family. I wondered how Dr. Baxter would have described me to another shrink.

I imagined his deep voice, slightly officious, and very measured. "The patient's father left in her formative teenage years. Parents had fought for years before that. Patient struggles to be good enough to bring her father back home." *Blah!*

What had Butterman said? Erica carried a template with her, the lens she used to see the world. She'd responded to the legacy of her family in a variety of ways: looking for a man to care for her, developing a voracious ambition—even the gambling tied in there somehow. We hadn't had the time to look over her file of drug company misdemeanors in detail. If you took the shrinks' perspective, that project must relate to her sad family, too.

I wondered what was wrong with her mother. Though mine tended to drink too much and whine in direct proportion to what she imbibed, at least she wasn't confined to a nursing home.

What gnawed at me most were the drugs found in Erica's bloodstream. If you anticipated a brutal custody proceeding, you had to stay clean. Erica would know the stakes were too damn high.

Maybe she really hadn't intended to see the light of the next day.

Chapter 21

Laura fought through the traffic already starting to clog the roads around the golf course and finally found a parking space in the lot assigned to caddies and low-level volunteers. Sunday's boisterous crowds, arriving early to stake out a front-row perspective on the biggest action, had begun to choke the area around the pro shop, the putting green, and the practice range.

Everything feels different to golfers on Sunday. The TV commentators love to point out how tension tightens our relaxed grips and breeds doubt in our minds. In spite of the extra pressure, the girls lucky enough to be left in the pack have to talk themselves into playing exactly the same game that got them there: no slight shift in their grips, no untried tactics in their plans, no extra zip in their drives. Changes under pressure lead to mistakes. And even small mistakes on Sunday cost big bucks.

"She's spending a lot of money today," the TV announcers would say about a girl who carded bogeys and doubles on Sunday. For a player like me, fighting for my life on the big Tour, mistakes meant another step down the path to the minor league: the Futures Tour. Or worse: sales clerk in a run-down pro shop. Laura's job was to keep me focused in the present, confident, and loose.

I was close to being late. Even so, I took the time for a quick call to Mom. She'd left a message late last night frantic with worry. Apparently the news of Erica Le-Boutillier's death had sifted down to Myrtle Beach via Mom's sometimes slow but always reliable gossip pipeline. The phone rang twice before Dave picked it up.

"Where have you been?" he responded to my upbeat greeting. "Loretta Gates called us about that business about the amateur golfer being murdered on Tuesday. Your mother's worried sick."

Loretta, Myrtle Beach's resident vicious gossip, thrived on her reputation as bearer of timely bad news. And Mom was one of her favorite customers. So I didn't bother to remind Dave that when I'd spoken to them just yesterday, I'd been alive and well. This kind of frenetic maternal anxiety wasn't influenced by the facts.

"I'm fine. Thanks for your concern. Is she home?" Dave grunted and dropped the phone. After a pause, Mom came on the line.

"Cassie! I've been trying to reach you. Didn't you get my message? We've been worried to death down here, not knowing whether you were safe. Dave was so upset when you didn't call back."

I knew it wasn't Dave who was worried. But Mom had a hard time letting you know what she was really feeling. Put it another way. Indirect as she might be, I didn't usually have any trouble at all knowing what she was feeling. During those years alone with her after Dad left, I was enrolled in a crash course on reading her moods. And I'd carried a freight load of guilt about her unhappiness most of my life.

"Sorry, Mom. I've been real busy, with making the cut and all. And the police are doing a good job of taking care of things." I tried to change the subject. "Did you watch the tournament on TV yesterday? I doubt you'll see us today, we're going off in a few minutes. But look for Meg Mallon this afternoon. She has the locker right across from mine."

"We probably won't see it, dear. You know how Dave feels about watching golf."

I knew how *she* felt about golf. She couldn't help it. She was like one of those Pavlovian dogs from introductory psychology that were trained to salivate when a bell rang, only this association was all negative. Golf and my father, the teaching pro, were paired immutably together. Every minute she watched golf, she was stung with the memory of Dad leaving and taking "that tramp Maureen" with him to California.

"I have to go, Mom. I'm late. I'll call you later in the week from Ohio."

Laura held out the Senator, the putter my father presented me before my first junior tournament. I'd tried others, the roll-faced design, the toe-heel weighting, the forged titanium blade. In the end, like with any successful relationship, it all came down to trust. You could spend a zillion dollars on the latest technology, but if you didn't believe the ball would find the hole, you were toast.

Joe followed me around the green, tossing balls back after I'd rolled them to the flags. Like Laura, he abstained from new suggestions this morning—just offered a soothing tone of voice and a running line of positive chatter.

"I'm going over to the pro shop and make a few calls," he said. "You look perfect. I'll meet you on the tee."

I handed Laura the putter and walked to an empty bench to stretch my back. I could tell the day would be a scorcher. Much as I wanted to play in the last groups with the tournament's real contenders, I didn't envy them the conditions later this afternoon.

"Aren't you Cassie Burdette?"

I slitted my eyes open to look at a small woman wearing a backpack and carrying a notepad.

"I'm Ellen Clarke from the *Woman's Golf World*. You probably don't remember, but we met at the Hartford Open a couple years ago. I was covering the men's Tour and you were carrying Mike Callahan's bag."

"We've both moved up in the world since then," I laughed. I didn't remember meeting her at all, but her self-effacing manner and plain style of dress would not have made a big impression.

"I'd like to do a story on your round today," she said, her voice high, fast, and a little breathless. "I think there's a great Cinderella angle. You know, girl starts out as packhorse, now playing the big time. I figured I could chat with you after each hole—kind of get your impressions of how you'd see the situation from the caddie's perspective, and how it looks different as a player." She pulled a laptop out of her backpack and held it up. "I have the holes all mapped out here so we can actually track your path. I'll stay out of the way as much as possible. Then I can finish the story up in the pressroom and get it off to the magazine this afternoon. The editor's giving me one shot to come up with something big. I just know she's gonna love this one." She smiled a death-row kind of smile, a little bit hopeful, but mostly doomed.

I couldn't believe the woman thought I'd consider chatting with her throughout the round. Most golf journalists understood completely that it was one thing to talk with your caddie—you had to find a way to relax between shots. Discussing the details of your swing mechanics and course management with a stranger? Forget about it. If writing the rookie diary would have hurt my performance, this level of introspection during play would be pure suicide. But Ellen Clarke looked so eager and so desperate that I bit back the smart-ass negative that sprang directly to mind.

"I'll talk to you after the round," I said. "If you want to follow along and make notes about certain decisions, I'll try my best to tell you later what I was thinking. No way can I chat as I go. I can't afford to focus on anything but my own game. And you have to promise not to interfere with the other players."

"Oh, thank you, thank you," she said. "You won't even know I'm there."

Was that really a tear in her eye?

"I'll be praying you play really, really well."

I grunted, rolled off the bench, and trotted over to where Laura waited with the bag.

"What the hell did she want?"

"You don't want to know. I told her I'd give her an interview later. Are we all set here?"

"Ready to rock and roll." She shouldered my bag and started across the highway to the first tee. The two other players in my group, both Japanese and both Tour rookies, had the reputation for being serious and reserved. As expected, between the early hour and our low-profile names, we drew a thin crowd. I watched the other girls tee off, feeling calmer than I had earlier in the week, able to picture the day ahead of me as an exciting but manageable challenge. Finally, my turn came.

"Ladies and gentlemen, this is the third and final round of the ShopRite Classic LPGA Golf Tournament!" yelled the starter. "On the tee, from Myrtle Beach, South Carolina, Cassandra Burdette."

I stepped up between the tee markers and stared down the first hole. My club head swished through the heavy air as I whipped out a practice swing.

"Be the one," I whispered, and hammered a drive straight down the middle of the fairway.

"All right!" Laura exclaimed. "I guess you spent enough time in those scrubby pines this week."

I poked her side with the butt of the club and started off the tee box, whistling.

"Do you need a ride to the airport when this is over?" she asked on our way to the first green. "I'd like to hit the road by noon or so. Unless you end up in a play-off, of course."

That made me laugh. "My plane's not until tonight, so I'll hang here. Damn! I wanted to look at Erica's files again. I don't suppose you'd consider leaving your computer."

She chuckled. "Fat chance, pal. But I could burn you a CD. You'll just have to find some way to look at it."

I noticed my shadow, the would-be golf writer, lurking in the tall weeds along the second tee box. "That girl's going to owe me," I said. "She won't be able to say no."

I birdied the first hole, then fumbled through a bogey five on two. I settled down again after three pars and walloped another good drive on six.

"You know what I can't figure out," I told Laura as we walked down the sixth fairway. "What's wrong with Erica's mother?"

"She's old and sick." She shrugged. "What difference does it make?"

"Maybe none. It just bugs me." I removed my baseball cap and pushed my damp bangs off my forehead. My curls were already in the process of morphing to frizz under the influence of the humidity. "How old can she be? Say Erica was forty at the absolute outside. Her mom would be what—seventy-five at the most?"

Laura shrugged again. "One sixty-eight to the middle of the green. Pin's back left."

"I'll take the four. No way I get all the way back with the five."

"Put a nice, smooth swing on it."

The ball arched up toward the green, bounced just in front, and trickled down toward the pin. "I'm thinking Alzheimer's," I said. "How ironic would that be?"

"What the hell are you talking about?"

"Erica's mother. Suppose she has Alzheimer's. So Erica's desperate for the company to come up with the medication that will cure the disease. At the same time, she's terrified they'll move too fast and make a costly mistake. Maybe her judgment was clouded because she's too close to the whole issue."

"That would make two of them," said Laura. "Both her and Hugh. But we have a cloudy issue here, too—how this putt breaks."

She was right. But you couldn't concentrate on golf a hundred percent of the time out here. It was just fine to relax and let your mind wander between shots. As long as you got your focus back when you needed it—before you hit anything else. A skill that I'd heard improved with experience.

"I see the putt breaking two balls to the left," Laura suggested. "Got to hit it firm enough to hold the line."

I carded two putts for par, and we moved to the par-three seventh. With both the tee markers and the pin back, I talked myself into a three iron. At the last minute, I gave the swing an extra lurch. The ball airmailed the green and plugged into the back bunker.

I stalked off the tee box. "Nice shot, you idiot," I said, hurling the club into the marsh grass lining the cart path. I glared at Ellen Clarke, just daring her to write this move down.

"Lucky thing you spent all that time in the practice trap this week," said Laura. She fished the three iron from the weeds and propelled me toward the green. "Get back to work. You're doing great."

I chunked the ball out of the trap, sank my second putt for bogey, and trudged to the eighth hole. This fairway was wide, with a big wind pushing right to left. I started a drive out to the right with a gentle draw and let the wind carry it down the center of the fairway.

"That's more like it." I stood back to watch one of the Japanese girls tee off. She fiddled with the chain around her neck before tucking it into her polo shirt.

"The pendant!" I whispered to Laura.

"What?"

"Don's pendant—the one we saw in the videotape last night?"

Laura nodded.

"I've seen it before—on Erica, the night I found her dead."

"The plot thickens," said Laura as we walked down the fairway. "How can you be so sure?"

"Remember Renee and Bruce from college?"

Laura nodded.

"They got married in Maui because their families were such a nightmare. Her bouquet was filled with the most gorgeous tropical flowers you could imagine. I heard they're divorced now—"

"Is this going somewhere, or are you losing it?"

"I'm trying to tell you Renee and Bruce bought those necklaces when they were married. They had their names written on them in Hawaiian. That's what Don was wearing in the videotape, and Erica had one on the night I found her. I'm willing to bet it came from him. If it had his name on it, we could find out easily enough."

"So maybe we'll have another chat with Don. Because maybe he knows more than he told us."

I nodded.

After two putts on eight, the rest of my round was textbook par. Just the way I'd imagined the night before, only no miraculous one-putts. As I handed the Senator to Laura on eighteen, I felt the tension oozing from all my muscles.

"That was work," I said. "Never knew one over par could be so exhausting."

"Better than getting a real job," she said.

I shook hands with the other girls and their caddies and walked off the green arm in arm with Laura. "Thanks for coming along for the ride. It means a lot to have you here."

"My pleasure entirely. I'm going to run back to the car and get your stuff. I'll leave it all with the concierge and meet you back here with the CD." She trotted off with my leather bag slapping her calves.

I signed my scorecard, then found Joe at the leaderboard outside the tent.

"Congratulations! You're in very good company," he said, pointing to the list of names. "Dottie Pepper and Brandie Burton both came in with the same total. You'll score a couple thousand dollars for three days' work—that's not so bad. Where are we going to celebrate?"

"I have to give an interview to this reporter," I nodded in the direction of Ellen Clarke. "And I'm hoping to browbeat her into loaning me her laptop so we can look at Erica's files again. Then I have a couple leads to check out. I was hoping you'd come along." I explained how I'd recognized the Hawaiian medallion and wanted to have another talk with Don. "You game?"

"I'm all yours."

Chapter 22

I spent half an hour in the media room reviewing my round with Ellen Clarke. Without complete success, I tried to suppress the urge to pontificate.

"I really think being a caddie is the harder job of the two. You can read the wind and discuss the lie and the break and recommend the stick. But in the end, you step back and your golfer swings the club."

She nodded earnestly and typed my pearls of wisdom into her laptop.

"Michael Bamberger said that first. *The Green Road Home*—a caddie classic. Have you read it?"

She shook her head no and wrote that down, too. "What happened on the seventh hole? Give me your side of it, then your caddie's."

"It wasn't really a bad swing, I just gave it a little extra mustard there at the end to make sure it got there. So I drew a fried egg lie—I could barely see the ball in the sand. No way you're gonna blast a shot like that close to the pin. Then I got pissed because it's one of the easier holes. You want to make bird on a hole like that." I laughed. "My caddie's role? She was the one who had to fish my damn three iron out of the bulrushes."

Ellen typed more notes. "I guess that's it. Could I call you later if I think of something else?"

"Sure. Say, can I use your computer for a couple minutes?" I asked. "I have a disk I need to look at." She didn't look happy, but as I'd predicted, she didn't dare turn me down. "Be back in a few."

Laura and Joe waited outside the pro shop with my luggage. She handed me the CD and hugged me. "I saved the files in text form so any computer should be able to read them. Now listen, you two, stay out of trouble. Remember what Detective Rumson said. She can handle this case without our valuable input."

"Yeah, yeah, yeah," I said. "Thanks again, pal. I sure am going to miss you in Ohio next weekend. No telling what turkey will end up carrying my bag. And what dumb advice I might get." I knew Laura couldn't travel with me every week, but the reality of tackling the next tournament without her was hitting me hard.

"You're a hot property now," she said, patting me on the butt. "Not a rookie loser anymore. You actually made a cut, and your caddie got paid something. Or will, anyway." She raised her eyebrows. "And here's a tip on managing the new looper: if you don't like what he's telling you, stick your fingers in your ears and hum." She hugged me again. "Call me soon."

"Let's put your stuff in my trunk," said Joe. "I'd hate to see someone walk off with it. I can run you to the airport later tonight, if you like."

I rummaged through the side pocket of my golf bag until I found my wallet.

"What's that?" asked Joe, pointing to a partially crumpled photograph stuffed into the bag.

"It's the picture they took from the first pro-am day. God knows why they thought I'd want one." I held it out to him. "That's Erica, of course. Hugh's in the silver cowboy hat, Roger's the tall, yellow guy, and Travis is round and sweaty."

"A scary crew. Why don't you bring it along? Maybe studying those mug shots will jog loose some brilliant insight about the case."

"Detective Rumson came by the room last night," I told him as we walked into the clubhouse. "She said Aimee Joy works at a place called City Lights Entertainment. As far as the company's official line, they arrange specialty tours. Rumson thinks it's an escort service on the side. Anyway, now Aimee's skipped town. They think someone hired her to set Erica up—the same person who locked me in the freezer."

"The same one who trashed your room?"

"I don't know. Laura and I are pretty sure they wanted these files." I held up the CD. "Given Aimee's connection with Pierre, I'd say you have to move him to the head of the suspect line."

Back in the media room, I slipped the CD into the slot of Ellen Clarke's laptop. As the computer whirred and clicked, I told Joe about the videotape. "Those two were chummy way beyond the boundaries of a normal golf lesson. Plus, the necklace Don wore that day during Erica's lesson showed up around her neck the night I found her dead."

"Did it have his name on it?" asked Joe.

"I think so—in Hawaiian hieroglyphics. I can't see her wearing it unless they had something more than a teacher-student thing going. Bottom line? Don Gulden lied to us about their relationship. You could see it right on tape. And I want to know why."

Joe drummed his fingers on the tabletop. "Could be he was just protecting her name. She was married and going through a bad divorce. Having an affair was not going to help her cause."

"But when we talked to him, we told him she was dead. What's the point of lying then?"

Joe shrugged. "He's an old-school gentleman? I don't know."

I clicked on the Adverse Events icon and watched Erica's drug company manifesto fill the screen. She had subdivided the list into five categories: name of drug, parent company, adverse events, outcome, and litigation.

"I recognize a couple of these drugs," said Joe.

"Thirty-one people died taking this Lochol," I said, highlighting the cholesterol-lowering drug on the screen. "How could they allow that to happen?"

"The companies are eager to get the drug to market. The doctors are eager to provide their patients with new medicines that work miracles. The patients are clamoring for answers that don't involve lifestyle changes." He scrolled further down the screen. "Why was she making this list?"

"She had to be lining up data to support her concerns about the Alzheimer's drug. This is a pretty scary chart, if you work for a drug company. She's only listed stuff with serious outcomes for the businesses. Maybe she thought she could talk them into a more cautious approach by laying this out for them."

Joe shook his head slowly. "I'm not convinced. Everything here is already public information. So what's the big deal? Why would someone need to kill her off?"

I closed the file and clicked on Pierre's assets. The folder we hadn't reviewed last night was divided into phone bills, credit card bills, and finances.

"Where did she get all this stuff?"

"She was still married to him. There are ways," said

Joe. "I once had a patient who asked a friend to call the phone company and change his wife's billing address to his office. Easy as pie. He had his wife over a barrel once he got the records for long-distance calls to her boyfriend in Arizona. Then his lawyer literally subpoenaed her hard drive so she couldn't erase the E-mails talking about the X-rated things they were going to do to each other."

"Life is hell." I scrolled through credit card charges for florists, jewelers, and hotels not far enough from Pierre's home to qualify for business travel. "This is one slippery dude."

"Can you print it out?" asked Joe. "We need to get going."

I thanked Ellen for the use of her computer, and we headed to the parking lot. From the crush of spectators crossing the street, I assumed the tournament leaders were just teeing off on the first hole. We heard a cheer from distant fans—noise that matched an eagle maybe, or at least an unexpected birdie.

"Next time, it'll be you," said Joe. Eerie how that guy could sometimes read my mind. And other times, have not a clue.

"Tell me again what you noticed about Pierre," Joe said once we were on the road.

"He was very good at changing the subject," I said. "The first time I met him, I didn't even realize that he'd got me off talking about Erica and their marriage and onto my golf game. I left in this little haze of goodwill, thinking how thoughtful the guy was to ask about me. The second time was a lot less pleasant. He told me to get the hell off the property and leave him and his daughter alone."

Ten minutes later, we arrived at the Sandy Pines Golf Club. The parking lot was jammed with the Sunday crowd of public course golfers and range rats. Two foursomes of men wearing blue jeans and faded T-shirts sucked on cans of beer by the first tee.

"Man," said Joe, his eyes traveling over the shabby clubhouse and patchy practice green. "This is a long way to fall from the PGA Tour."

"He's not taking it too badly," I said. "Better than I would be. At least on the surface. Maybe you'll pick up something I missed."

Inside the pro shop, Don was practicing his putting on a long strip of fake turf that laced through racks of golf clothing. The volume of the television hanging from the ceiling was jacked up high, and a cloud of cigarette smoke choked the room. I called out a cheery greeting. Don's hands jerked up sharply, sending a Titleist screaming across the room.

"Sorry to startle you." I held out the videotape of Erica's golf lesson. "I came to drop your tape off. This is my friend, Joe Lancaster. You may have run into him when you were playing on the Tour. He's the guy who rescued Mike Callahan from the terminal yips."

"The golf doctor," said Don with a big grin. He wrung Joe's extended hand. "I thought about calling you a couple times, but it would have taken more than a Band-Aid to stop my bleeding."

"Oh I use tourniquets, acupressure, duct tape, whatever the patient requires," Joe said, laughing.

Don's eyes wandered up to the television screen. Tiger Woods sank a birdie putt and pumped his fist to the raucous crowd.

"Hey! How did you make out this morning?"

"Not too bad. I shot one over. Only one lousy swing and a couple missed putts. Can't complain."

"Good for you. Keep it up." He set the videotape on the counter. "Find what you needed here?"

I was surprised that he'd ask me that straight out. "I don't know quite how to put this."

Don's face looked puzzled.

"I don't think you told me the whole story about what went on between you and Erica."

He blushed. "Dad always said the worst thing you do to a woman is kiss and tell."

Joe's voice was gentle. "Tell us about the necklace you gave her."

Don sat down hard on the stool behind the counter and lit up a cigarette. So much for Erica's influence in the direction of clean living.

"She was so sad and so scared. I just wanted to help whatever way I could."

"Did you kill her?" I asked.

"Cassie! I can't believe you'd even ask me that. I loved her." From the pain in his voice, I had to think he thought he had. But I knew Joe Lancaster's mind would be filled with doubt—mine sure was. How was it possible to fall in love so soon after losing his wife? Transference, counter-transference, double-screwed-up-relationship-replacement syndrome, the shrinks would have some damn name for it.

"You told us you never met Erica's coworkers."

Don hung his head a little lower. "I went to the office once. Thought I'd surprise her and cheer her up. She seemed so down the last time she came in for a lesson."

"How did that go?"

"Terrible. She was pissed I came. I knew right then that she meant a lot more to me than I ever could to her. Like I told you the other day, she was way out of my league. It should have been obvious." Overlooking the cigarette butt already burning in a Sandy Pines ashtray, he lit up another and blew out a long stream of smoke.

Joe broke the grim silence. "Why do you suppose she was so mad?"

Don thought a minute. "Travis saw me, that weasely little bastard. I'm sure he gave her a hard time." He ground the cigarette out and banged his fist on the counter. "Something was seriously wrong at that outfit. She was afraid. She wouldn't tell me what it was, but she was scared of something. Or somebody. That's why I gave her the medal. I told her the spirits would look out for her when I wasn't around."

"Who was she scared of?" I asked.

"I don't know." His voice was flat and hopeless.

"Could it have been Pierre?"

"Maybe. I really don't know." He extracted another cigarette from the rumpled pack and rolled it between his fingers. "I wish I could have helped."

"You helped," I said. "She knew she had a friend. She was wearing your necklace the night I found her." I patted his arm and turned to Joe. "I guess we need to move along."

We exited from the cool, smoky air of the pro shop back into the broiling sun.

"That guy was already beaten down," said Joe. "Erica just kicked him in the teeth for good measure."

"Oh, come on. He knew what he was getting into. He was running away from dealing with what happened between him and Abby."

"Who's the shrink here, anyway?" Joe laughed. "You gotta feel a little sorry for the guy."

"I do," I said. "That could very well be me in a year or two. Sprawled on the LPGA landfill."

"Remember, positive thinking, positive thinking." Joe unlocked the door of the rental car and opened it for me. "He thinks someone at the office was scaring her. Supposing we take the pro-am photo to the City Lights Entertainment office and ask the staff if they recognize any of Erica's coworkers."

"Oh sure. I'm certain the owner will just love the workers finking on one of the escortees."

He turned the car on and set the air-conditioning to

high. "Here's a better idea. You call and make an appointment to apply for a job. While you're there, you can squeeze some information out of him."

"Get out of here!"

"I'm dead serious," said Joe. "If Aimee Joy's disappeared, he's down one employee."

"The guy would take one look at me and know I was a fraud."

"Not at all. Plenty of guys would be attracted to the wholesome, athletic type. You don't have to look like a tart to work at an escort service." Joe turned to look at me, smiling. "You could wear that dress you had on the other night at the party. You looked fantastic in that."

I blushed bright red. "I borrowed that dress—"

"I was kidding," said Joe. "I still think it's a good plan. In fact, we won't call at all. You'll just drop in and say you're looking for work. You won't act like you know it's an escort service. You can say you've always wanted to be a tour guide."

"I hate this idea."

"I'll wait right outside for you to be sure nothing happens. You just chat with the guy, show the picture, and that's it. If you're not back in fifteen minutes, I come in. I'll say I'm looking for an escort—someone petite, athletic, and sexy."

I blushed harder and slid into the passenger seat, my thighs burning inside and out as I went.

Chapter 23

I gave myself a vigorous pep talk on the way to Atlantic City. *Seize the day, Cassie, seize the day.* Even though Joe was the professional shrink and by all rights should have taken the lead, it was time to clear the air. I had no idea how the conversation might shape up. But I was damn sick of feeling the tension between us everywhere. Just as the skyline of the city came into focus, I cleared my throat and prepared to dive in.

"Listen, Joe—" Then my cell phone rang. I held one finger up. "Hang on. Hello?"

"Cassie, it's Mike. How did things go?"

I glanced over at Joe and flushed. Again. "Great. I mean not bad. Could have been worse. Made a few bucks, which makes Laura and me happy. I won't know my exact position 'til later. How about you?"

Mike launched into a diatribe about the thick rough and slippery greens and his own total lack of talent. "But that's not why I called. I was looking for you Friday night, but you disappeared. Are you going to Ohio this week?"

"I'm going. Not Laura, though."

"Want to catch some dinner one night? I'll be just up the road at the Memorial. I'd like to see you."

"Sure," I said. I knew I was smiling like an idiot. "I have no plans. Why don't you call me when you get settled?"

I could see Joe's face out of the corner of my eye as I said good-bye. Chances were, the way Mike's deep voice carried, Joe overheard the whole conversation. There was a subtle shift in his expression that mirrored the evaporation of my determination to call his bluff. I could feel myself backpedaling away from the direction of our unspoken feelings. Again.

"Date with Mike?" he asked. He kept his eyes on the road and his voice light.

"I wouldn't call it a date."

"Guy calls a girl up and asks her to dinner, usually that's referred to as a date," he said. We rode over the bridge leading into the city in silence. Then Joe turned up the radio and began to hum tunelessly and tap his fingers on the steering wheel.

Why were my relationships with men always so complicated? Laura insisted I had the same problem with drivers, not giving any one of them enough play to see if the chemistry would take off. Finally this summer, I'd solved the golf club question, settling on a high-tech titanium model designed by Porsche. No such luck in the man department.

"See if you can find the map I put in the glove compartment, would you?" Joe said. "I'm not exactly sure where Harriman Street is."

I rustled through the stack of car rental paperwork and pulled out a tourist's guide to Atlantic City. "Turn right at the third intersection and then left two blocks down."

"Thanks," he said, resuming his hum-and-tap routine. "What do you think about Rebecca Butterman?"

Here we go, I thought. *Tit for tat.* "She's all right. She's pretty enough for a middle-aged woman."

"That's low," he said. "She's only two years older than I am."

"You're right, I'm sorry." I reached over and patted his arm. "You might have to upgrade your wardrobe though, if you're planning to be seen in public together."

"She *is* a fox." He plucked at an invisible speck of dirt on his polo shirt and grinned.

Fox wasn't the animal I would have chosen to represent her. More like rat. Or skunk. "I thought you were dead set against long-distance relationships. Isn't that what did your marriage in?"

Joe made a noise that sounded like the air being let out of a tire. "My marriage had a lot of problems. My travel schedule was just a convenient peg to hang the divorce on. Anyway, I'm not talking about a relationship here," he said. "Just a dinner date. Like you and Mike." He laughed, but without enthusiasm.

"Won't it get boring just talking psychobabble all the time? Maybe you need someone in a different field to keep you grounded."

"Like a golfer?" he said, his voice bursting with sarcasm and outrage.

He glared at me, his eyes fierce and his mouth tight. I glared back. Then we both started to laugh. I laughed so hard the muscles in my stomach ached, and I began to worry I'd torn something and ruined my swing for good.

Still chuckling, Joe turned onto Harriman Street and tried to ease the car into a narrow slot between two large American cars. After several unsuccessful forays, he pulled into the small parking lot adjoining the offices of Coan, Lewenden, and Royston, Attorneys-at-Law, and turned off the ignition. Leaning across the seat, he barely touched his lips to my cheek.

"We'll figure it all out one day," he said. "We have time. Now get in there and convince the guy your specialty is ménage à trois."

"Are your patients aware that you're a disturbed man?" I asked as I slammed the car door.

A small, bronze plaque identified the front entrance of City Lights Entertainment. Inside, the office could have doubled for the Chamber of Commerce: upholstered furniture in soothing shades of mauve and blue, along with framed posters extolling the attractions of Atlantic City. Again, the Miss America swimsuit competition appeared to be a favorite. The receptionist wore the tallest platform heels I'd ever seen. How the hell did she walk on those things? Other than the shoes, her pale peach suit was conservative city government issue—until you noticed the short-cropped tank.

I pulled my eyes away from the diamond glinting in her belly button. "I'd like to speak to the manager." She gave me exactly the once over I'd predicted to Joe. A slow up-and-down that let me know my navy shirt was faded, the shorts grubby, and the Birkenstock sandals not fit to be seen in public.

"May I say who's calling?"

We hadn't really thought this through. I knew I didn't want to leave my own name on their records, so I said the first thing that popped to mind.

"Danni Williams."

"And what might this be in reference to?"

"I'd like to apply for a job."

She gave me a second look-over. This time her expression was incredulous. I blushed again. Today I'd become a regular blushing machine. Turning her back to me, Miss Belly Button made a phone call in hushed tones.

"Won't you have a seat? He'll be with you in just a

moment. You can fill out this form while you wait."

The form was one page and simple: name, address, phone, emergency contact, date of birth, height, weight, eye and hair color. I'd never seen the last three on a job application and doubted either they or the age question was legal. I scratched out the required information: 5'2", 110 pounds, hazel eyes, and brown hair. I listed Don Gulden at Sandy Pines as Danni's job reference and Joe, for personal reference. Then I wrote down her home address and her Mom as her emergency phone contact—stats I'd seen often enough to memorize while poring over the media guide. I signed her name in loopy script and handed the clipboard back to Miss Diamond Navel. I sure hoped they wouldn't call Danni's mother to check this out; she would have a heart attack on the spot. A little late to wonder whether impersonating another golfer was cause for dismissal from the LPGA Tour.

Five minutes later, a sixtyish man with an impressive shock of gray hair emerged from the back room. He wore two thirds of a soft gray three-piece suit, a crisp white shirt, and a burgundy tie. He glanced briefly at the clipboard and handed it back to his secretary.

"Miss Williams?" He ushered me into his office and gestured to another pink couch. He did not offer to shake hands. "I'm Mr. Berger, the owner of City Lights. How may I be of service?"

"I'm an acquaintance of one of your employees—Sally Dowling is her name." I dropped the line in, now waited to see if he'd bite. Nothing bled through his impassive expression. "She told me about the work she does here, and I'm interested in a position with your company."

He gave a very small frown, which he quickly wiped away. "I see. What type of work experience do you have?"

I mentally cursed Joe for not helping me think this charade out better. "I work at a golf course. I moved here two weeks ago and got a job in a golf shop. It was the only thing I could find." I wrinkled my nose in imaginary disgust. "I teach a little bit, but mostly work in the pro shop. I'm ready to get out of the golf business. I'm really not an early morning person, and I don't care for the sun. It's murder on your complexion." I sure hoped he had a preference for dizzy babes, because I knew that's just how I sounded.

"A golf pro. That's unusual." He leaned back in his chair and tented his fingers. "What did Sally tell you about our business?"

I had to be careful here.

"She said she gives adult tours of Atlantic City. That sounds so fascinating. I don't know the city very well yet, but I could learn." I tried to sound eager and pliable. "She said she's met a lot of nice people. She really likes helping the businessmen who are away from home feel welcome to the city. That's what I want—a job where I can help people." The deeper I dug this hole, the less clear it became how I was going to accomplish my mission: show someone, anyone, the pro-am photo and get the hell out. I giggled. "I don't want to sound like Pollyanna—Sally said the money's good, too."

There was a light tap on the door. Mr. Berger got up to open it and stepped outside, pulling it partway closed behind him. I could hear the squeaky whisper of his secretary. "The address checks out. She's not a cop."

He shut the door and returned to his seat. "You understand that we will have to call references—personal references, as well as work."

"Of course, no problem."

"When could you start?"

"The sooner the better!"

"About your work wardrobe . . ."

"Sorry about this—I came right from work." I swept my hand down the length of my torso.

"We do expect a high standard for our employees. Miss Ridley can provide you with some material on your way out. She will also be in charge of training. It will be several weeks before you're ready to operate tours on your own."

"I understand that," I said. I stood up and shook his hand. "A pleasure to meet you, Mr. Berger. I'm looking forward to joining your company."

"As I said, we'll need to check your references. We'll call you."

He ushered me out into the waiting area, resting his hand lower and longer on my back than seemed absolutely necessary. "I explained to Miss Williams that we will call her after we've spoken with her references," he said to the receptionist. "In the meantime, would you please tell her about the dress code and the training sessions?"

"Yes, Mr. Berger," simpered the secretary. "Have a seat, Miss Williams."

She pulled a sheaf of papers out of the file drawer nearest to me. She flipped through them, extracted one, and passed it to me. "This page describes our dress code and some of the other company guidelines. You'll need to read it and sign at the bottom. I'll give you a copy to take with you so you can refer to it at home." She looked over my clearly substandard outfit a second time. "He prefers all the girls to wear skirts and heels. He wants a uniformly professional look; face it, the customers prefer that, too, and your tips will show it."

"How are the tours arranged?" I asked, hoping to move toward an opportunity to show to pro-am picture to Miss Ridley. I'd long since ruled out the possibility of getting information from my new boss.

"Usually a business group calls Mr. Berger and asks for some staff to show their customers around town—take them to the casinos, a good restaurant, you get the idea." I nodded. "Sometimes it works out that you meet people

you think would enjoy our tours. You can refer them to
Mr. Berger. He issues the invitations."

"I understand."

"At first, you wouldn't go by yourself, of course. We'd
assign you to one of the more experienced girls to show
you the ropes. Don't take this the wrong way, but we like
to think of ourselves as the hostesses to the city. Our
customers have a happier time than they ever would have
alone. We *are* the city lights. Get it?"

"Sure, I get it, that sounds like fun."

Miss Ridley leaned forward across the desk, her diamond sparkling. "Some are more fun than others." She
glanced toward Mr. Ridley's closed door and smirked.
"We try hard not to let that show."

I nodded again.

"There's a nice shop at the Ocean County Mall where
I get my things. You might want to head over there." She
handed me a business card and stood up.

"One thing, before I go," I stammered. "I met a few
gentlemen earlier this week that I'd like to have Mr. Berger invite to use City Lights. But I wondered if you could
tell me whether they'd already been here. I'd hate to
bother them if they were already familiar with the company or working with one of the other girls." I offered
her the photograph, praying Mr. Berger would stay in his
lair.

Just then, Joe burst into the office. I gave him a tiny
negative head shake and rolled my eyes in the direction
of the photo in Miss Ridley's hands.

"Excuse me," he said. "I'm looking for Attorney Royston. Am I in the right place?"

"This is City Lights Entertainment. The lawyers are two
doors down."

"So sorry to trouble you. Good day." He stopped at the
door and turned back to look into Miss Ridley's baby
blues. "I hope you don't mind if I say you look lovely."

She stood up a little straighter and thrust her chest in his direction. "Why, thank you. And you have a nice day."

"You see what I mean," she said with a knowing smile after he'd left. "Sometimes just our presence can brighten someone's day."

I choked back the urge to laugh. "About the picture . . ."

"I don't recognize them," she said, after glancing at the photograph. "If you like, I could ask the other girls and let you know tonight."

"You have my cell phone number," I reminded her.

"Did you say you were a friend of Sally Dowling's?"

"Not a friend—an acquaintance."

"Just as well," she whispered. "She didn't show up yesterday for work, and the cops were looking for her today. If there's one thing Mr. Berger hates, it's trouble from his girls."

"Hardly know her at all. I'll look forward to hearing from you. Gosh, I hope the references check out okay."

"I'm sure everything will be fine. Remember to read your materials before you come back. And Mr. Berger likes us to be prompt. None of his customers are to be left waiting." She winked. "Or wanting."

Chapter 24

"**Holy** shit," I said to Joe as I slid back into the car. "Next time you get to be the hooker."

He laughed. "You did just fine. What do you have there?" He reached for my training instructions and skimmed the top page. "I've never heard of an escort service with a mission statement. Dress code, maybe."

I grabbed the papers back. "Speaking of dress code, you certainly seemed to enjoy the receptionist's outfit."

"Strictly professional curiosity."

"In case anyone asks, I masqueraded as Danni Williams."

"You devil!" Joe turned up the air-conditioning and backed out of the parking lot. "I guess that was our last hurrah. How about some lunch?"

"Lunch sounds great, but we need to make one more stop—Shady Acres Convalescent Home."

"You want to talk with Erica's mother."

I nodded. "I have the sneaking suspicion she's got Alzheimer's disease." I studied the map and gave Joe directions. "Do you think we should bring something for her?"

"Like what?"

"I don't know, a plant, a box of candy, anything."

Joe stopped the car at a Jiffy Mart and waited outside while I canvassed the aisles for a gift that wouldn't look like it had been snatched last minute off a dusty shelf at a convenience store. Fifteen minutes later, with a box of undoubtedly stale chocolate-covered cherries in hand, we pulled into the circular driveway in front of Shady Acres Convalescent Home. The building was weathered red brick, accented by white trim that needed a paint job and scraggly bushes that needed water. If there had been shady acres when the place was built, the trees were long gone. We rang the bell and waited.

"What's our story here?" I asked.

"Just say we're friends of Erica's and wanted to pay a visit to her mother, right?"

"Right." Having lied myself into a corner at the escort service, I doubted it would be that easy.

A harried-looking woman in a white nurse's uniform answered the door and waved us into a small reception area. "Sorry for the wait. We're very short-staffed today. Please have a seat, and someone will be with you as soon as possible."

I sat in a wicker love seat, leaving Joe the more spacious, though threadbare, wing chair. Dog-eared copies of *Modern Maturity*, *Yachting Magazine*, and *Reader's Digest* lay fanned on the coffee table in front of us. I leafed through the boating periodical.

"I don't think the inmates here have too much yachting in their future." I tossed the magazine back on the table. My nostrils had begun to twitch as they filled with a mixture of decaying flowers and Pine Sol, a peculiar smell I remembered well from visiting my great-aunt as a child.

"My Aunt Alice lived in one of these places for years," I told Joe. "Charlie and I used to fight over who had to go with my father to see her. Not only was she stone deaf, her mind was gone, too, poor woman. She insisted that a Negro family dressed in yellow robes slept on mattresses in her closet. They only came out at night to dance."

"Old age is not for sissies," said Joe. He cocked his head and studied me. "You don't talk much about your father."

"Not going to start now either, Doctor."

I got up and paced across the room to read the notices pinned to the bulletin board. There were sign-up sheets for wheelchair yoga, a nature writer reading poetry about the Everglades, and visiting therapy dogs. An Australian shepherd named Poco seemed to be most in demand.

"Oh my god! Here's a picture of the blackjack dealer, Lucia Jimenez," I said. "There was a memorial service for her yesterday."

Joe strode across the room and stood beside me. "That's odd. I can't imagine what the connection would be—unless she had relatives living here."

The nurse who had let us into the building returned to the lobby. "Sorry to keep you waiting. What can I do for you?"

"So terrible about Lucia," I said, pointing to the notice. "Did she have family at Shady Acres?"

"Oh no. She worked weekends. She was one of our best aides. The patients loved her. She had a very soothing manner, especially helpful when someone forgot where they were and why."

"We're here to visit Mrs. Jorganson," said Joe. He squinted at the plastic name tag pinned to her chest. "Nurse Silver, I'm Dr. Joe Lancaster, this is Cassie Burdette. We were friends of Erica's."

The nurse shook her head. "That's a sad story, too. It's

been a hard week here. Have you been to visit before? I can't place you."

"No," I said. "First time. Is it a problem to see her?"

"Not at all. I just want to warn you what to expect. She doesn't appear to realize that Erica is dead, though we've told her several times. Maybe she seems more melancholy, but not in a conscious way. And it hasn't helped that Lucia is gone now, too. She had a magic touch with Mrs. J."

We followed Nurse Silver's squeaking shoes down a linoleum-tiled hallway. The smell of decay began to overwhelm the Pine Sol as we approached the patient rooms.

"Here she is," said the nurse as she rounded the second door on the left. Her tone vibrated with cheeriness. "Mrs. Jorganson. You have visitors today, Mrs. J."

The woman slumped over and belted into her wheelchair did not look as if she had any interest in visitors. Her mouth hung slightly open, with a thin rope of drool tying lip to chin to chest. She patted her hand across her thin gray hair and looked past us with rheumy, vacant eyes. I had difficulty connecting this hunched figure with the photograph I'd seen in Erica's office. I doubted we were going to get anything out of her. Let Joe handle this one; he was the trained professional.

"Good afternoon, Mrs. Jorganson. We were friends of your daughter. Cassie played golf with her this week. Did she tell you about that?" Joe pulled a chair up next to the wheelchair and gestured for me to sit. Erica's mother did not respond.

"She's a wonderful golfer," I said. "She really held her own out there." If Mrs. J had any curiosity about Erica's golf game, it was carefully contained. "I think Lila Rose could be a good golfer, too, one day; she's starting early enough so she won't pick up any terrible habits." Did her eyes flicker at the mention of her granddaughter's name?

My cell phone rang, jarring a new rope of drool from

Mrs. Jorganson's lips. Joe reached for her hand and stroked it gently.

"Excuse me, I'll take this out into the hall."

Right away I recognized the shrill voice of Miss Ridley from City Lights. "Miss Williams? I'm sorry to have to tell you that Mr. Berger changed his mind about bringing you on board," said Miss Ridley, her tone turned stiff and formal. "Nothing personal, it's just he looked at the budget and decided he can't use a new girl right now."

"Nothing personal?" I asked. It seemed stupid because I surely didn't want the job anyway, but this news bruised my feelings. I had a silly urge to clarify why I'd fallen short. "I knew I should have gone home to change before I came in."

"No really. I have to be honest with you—the golf course reference you gave us said they'd never heard of you. Next time you look for a position, I'd really recommend that you state the true facts, even if your job history is on the spotty side."

Now I had the receptionist at an escort service scolding me.

"Damn, I really blew my chances, huh?"

Miss Ridley was silent.

"What about the photo? Did you get the chance to show it to the other girls?"

"Marianne said she thought Sally had been working with one of the gentlemen."

"Which gentleman?"

"That's the problem—she only saw them together the one time. Maybe the man in the middle."

"With the silver hair?" In the amateur lineup, Hugh Gladstone had taken the middle position.

"She thinks so. I hope that helps. Well, good luck. And do have a good day."

I hung up, feeling only the faintest guilt about leaving Danni's vital statistics on file at City Lights. When I returned to the room, Joe was holding a straw to Mrs. Jorganson's parched lips and watching her suck up breathless sips of ginger ale. He arched his eyebrows.

"City Lights won't be requiring my services after all. Get this, one of their girls recognized Hugh as Sally Dowling's client."

Joe set the glass of soda down on a bedside table. "We need to leave now, Mrs. Jorganson. It was very nice chatting with you."

Erica's mother blinked.

"Take care," I added and stepped out ahead of Joe into the mint-green hallway. I took a deep breath to clear out the odor of lily of the valley toilet water and unwashed old woman. We stopped at the front desk where Nurse Silver was scribbling notes in the charts of her patients.

"Did you have a nice visit?"

Joe nodded. "I feel sad for her. Did anyone besides Erica ever come by?"

"No." The nurse sighed. "Erica was so devoted to her mother. I know she was very busy at work, but she never missed a week. Even over the last month, as stressed out as she was, she came regular as a cuckoo clock. And she was the one who arranged for special care with Lucia Jimenez. Lucia had the touch with her . . . but I already told you that."

"So Erica hired Lucia to work with her mother?"

Nurse Silver nodded. "Mrs. J becomes agitated for periods of time. It would help if we could assign an aide one-on-one, but we're so short-staffed. Erica saw that and provided the extra support. I don't know what will become of her now. I hate to see them left all alone."

"It looks like you do the best you can," I said. "Alzheimer's is a terrible disease."

"She doesn't have Alzheimer's," said the nurse.

"What's wrong with her then?" Joe asked.

Nurse Silver glanced up, then closed the chart she had

been writing in and got to her feet. "I'm sorry. I seem to be talking out of turn here. I really can't disclose any more about her condition—unless you're related to her, of course."

"No," said Joe. "Just concerned friends. One last question, if I may. Was she like this when she came to you?"

"Very little change over the years," said the nurse. She set her lips in tight lines. The faucet had been shut off. We thanked her and moved back out into the bright afternoon sun.

"If she doesn't have Alzheimer's, what the hell is wrong with her? The answer seems key."

"Another key," said Joe, "is the Lucia connection. Could she have known something about Erica from working with the family that made the killer uncomfortable? That would explain why she seemed so afraid the night we spoke."

I sighed. "We're nowhere, really. I guess we should go back over all that stuff on the computer and see what we missed."

"I can't figure out whether Nurse Silver was adhering to a normal standard of confidentiality when she quit talking to us, or if there's something really unusual about Erica's mother's illness," said Joe as he unlocked the car door.

I slid across the hot surface of the passenger seat. "Erica probably kept copies of her mother's medical records at her place."

"And you're such great pals with Pierre, we'll just show up and tell him we'd like to look around again?"

"I'm not talking about Pierre's house. I'm talking about Erica's apartment." I pulled the key from my shorts pocket and held it up.

Chapter 25

◁
Ⓞ **After** Joe and I argued for half the drive to Erica's apartment, he agreed to at least cruise through her neighborhood. I stonewalled his suggestion that we call Detective Rumson first and ask her to meet us there. I knew we'd never set one foot in that apartment with Rumson on the scene. I figured I could talk him out of that and into the pseudo-breaking-and-entering part once we'd arrived.

"Would you dial up 489-2256?" Joe asked. "Maybe Rebecca's got something in her intake notes about the Jorganson family history. Then we wouldn't have to go in at all."

I punched in the numbers. "You have her telephone number memorized already?"

He blushed. "I have a very good short-term memory. I took a class to help with study techniques during graduate school, and the stuff still works."

I gave him a look to let him know he was protesting way too much. His return look acknowledged he stood guilty as charged. I handed him the Nokia when it started to ring.

"Rebecca? It's Joe Lancaster. Cassie and I just paid a visit to Erica LeBoutillier's mother at Shady Acres. We're planning to look for her medical records in Erica's apartment. I wondered if you could check your intake notes and see if you have any information about her."

"She doesn't remember anything, but she's looking again," he told me. We'd pulled into an older neighborhood north of Edgewater Estates. Most of the houses were wooden three-story Victorians badly in need of maintenance. Older folks in lawn chairs inhabited many of the porches—the kind of neighborhood that made block watch arrangements redundant. Joe parked across the street from Erica's address in the shade of a large maple tree. I could hear the girlish cadence of Dr. Butterman's voice when she returned to the phone. She spoke for several minutes.

"How about seven-thirty? I'll pick you up at your place?" Joe turned sideways to stare out of the window and up to the third floor of the house where Erica had lived. I watched spots of blotchy red spread high across his cheeks as he said good-bye.

My turn to keep a light voice. "Date with Rebecca?" I asked once he'd signed off.

"I wouldn't call it a date."

"Guy calls a girl up and says he'll pick her up at her place at seven-thirty, usually that's referred to as a date."

Joe laughed. "Touché. Don't you want to hear what she had to say?"

"Fire away."

"First of all, she doesn't like the idea of us lurking around the apartment."

"We won't lurk. We'll check for Mrs. Jorganson's papers and then clear out. If I thought the police would be helpful, I'd be the first one to call them. But they still don't believe this was anything other than a case of plain, old-fashioned suicide."

Joe puffed out an exasperated breath. "She said Erica's mother had been depressed for years. Obviously, there's more than that going on with her now. Erica told her she blamed her mother's dependency on her father for what happened—though she didn't want to talk about the details in her sessions. She said she'd never allow herself to be that needy. Rebecca has the idea that was partly why Erica moved out on her marriage."

"I'm not following."

"I can't say I understand it completely either. But let's say Erica started feeling depressed and overly dependent on Pierre. This could raise fears that she was too much like her mother and could meet the same end. I'm not suggesting this was conscious, mind you. We all have historical patterns that hover just under our awareness, waiting to be reactivated by the right circumstances."

"What a fatalist. I believe my choices are under my control."

Joe shrugged. "Good luck with that. Better get back into treatment with Dr. Baxter so you at least know what forces you're up against."

I ignored that last comment and waggled the key. "Let's go take a quick look. Then we turn this over to the cops."

"What about fingerprints? Or maybe you brought gloves. . . ."

I ignored the sarcasm, too. "I don't see why we would pretend we weren't there. Just say Erica left me the key, and we stopped by to pick something up. It's not a crime scene. Yet."

Joe sighed and opened his door. "This is a really dumb idea. I can't believe I'm going along with it." He held up his hand before I could answer. "And don't even bother telling me you'll go in by yourself. Let's get this over with."

The boards of the porch steps creaked as we made our way to the front door. A small piece of masking tape was stuck next to the third-floor apartment's doorbell. E. Jorganson was written in blue ink, block letters.

"That's her maiden name," I said, reaching for the screen door.

"Don't you want to knock first?"

"Joe. She's dead. There's no one home. Let's go. Sooner we get in, sooner we get out."

Just then the door across the vestibule burst open. "Who are you?" demanded a small, elderly woman in a quavery voice.

"We're friends of Erica's," I stammered, then waited for Joe to manufacture the rest of the story.

"I'm Dr. Lancaster," he said, taking her frail hand in his. He glanced at the name above her doorbell. "And you must be Mrs. Trowbridge. Erica spoke so fondly of you."

Mrs. Trowbridge stared at us, then extracted her fingers from Joe's grasp. It didn't look like she was buying his line of baloney. "There's been an awful racket here, ever since that girl moved in. Not a minute of peace since she died, either."

"A lot of people coming through," murmured Joe sympathetically.

The old woman leaned forward until we could smell the stale coffee and apple danish on her breath. "First the husband. He banged around up there like he was playing a drum solo. Young people have no idea the rest of us are even alive." We bobbed our heads in understanding. "Then the police with their questions. I told them what do I know about this woman's affairs? I keep my mind on my own business."

This I doubted, but I certainly wasn't going to contradict her.

"The police were here, too," repeated Joe in his most soothing tones. "Well, we came by to get some of Lila's things. We won't keep you any longer."

Mrs. Trowbridge watched as I led the way up two flights of stairs covered with stained industrial carpet. I inserted the key into the lock. The door opened easily.

"What do you suppose Pierre was looking for?" I asked.

Joe shrugged. "If both he and the cops have already been here, we're not likely to find anything new."

The apartment was stifling hot and musty smelling. A galley kitchen, located just inside the entrance hallway, would barely hold one cook. A computer and printer covered the small kitchen table. A full coffee cup sat next to the computer monitor, with water lilies of mold floating on the surface.

Joe had to duck to avoid knocking his head on the slanted ceiling as he followed me down the hallway to a combination bedroom and sitting area. This room was furnished with a single bed, an armchair, and two short file cabinets. One bookcase was crammed with Nancy Drew mysteries and the complete Harry Potter series. Entertainment for Lila Rose? A long string hung from the old-fashioned glass light fixture on the ceiling. Empty picture hooks dotted the walls. I knelt on the bed and looked out the window and through the bars of a fire escape to a small backyard overgrown with dandelions.

"You should see the house she left to move here," I said to Joe. "You wouldn't believe the contrast. She had to be desperate to get away from that man."

"Material things can seem really unimportant when you're in an unhappy relationship."

Which made me intensely curious about the life he'd left. I'd never succeeded in getting him to say much about his marriage. Maybe one day I'd offer to trade the story of my father's desertion for juicy details about his ex-wife. On the other hand, maybe I could squeeze that dirt out of him and offer nothing back in return. It wasn't a good idea to let shrinks know too much about you; they had the edge anyway, even without that kind of inside information.

"Why don't you rifle through the file cabinets, and I'll take a quick peek at her computer," Joe suggested.

I squatted down on the floor and opened the first drawer. Several files were stuffed with old bills, canceled checks, and insurance papers. Toward the back of the drawer, I found a fat folder labeled "Mom" and wrestled it out of the file cabinet.

"This looks like a lot of Mrs. J's records," I called down the hall to Joe. "What are you finding?"

"Nothing yet," he said. "She had copies of the same material you found on the Palm Pilot. I'm looking through Adverse Events again. Funny thing, most of the problems Erica catalogued occurred after the drugs were already on the market."

I began to leaf through the thick folder, finding page after page of medical bills and insurance claims. Cat scans, MRIs, chest X rays, ultrasounds, the list went on and on. Every five or six pages, I found a letter from Erica haranguing her mother's insurance company regarding charges that had not been paid or covered.

"She had a full-time job just staying on top of these bills," I said. I flipped through pages detailing Mrs. Jorganson's extensive medications.

"Dilantan, Lipitor, Phenobarbitol, Vasotec, Prozac . . . this woman is a pharmaceutical company's dream and a naturopath's nightmare," I said to Joe. "Tell me the truth. What did happen to your marriage?" I hadn't really planned to blurt the question out, but now it hung naked between us.

He looked up from the computer and down the hall. "Where the hell did that come from?"

"Just curious. You don't have to tell me if you don't want to."

Joe turned his eyes back to the computer screen. "It was a two-career-couple problem. She was on the fast track for partner in her law firm. She needed me to be available for going out with clients, and I wasn't around."

"She wanted you for window dressing?"

"Not exactly. Let's just say we both needed support, and when I didn't come through in the way she wanted, she found it somewhere else."

"Oh. Sorry about that." I'd imagined a lot of things about Joe's wife, but her stepping out on him hadn't crossed my mind. How could a problem that hackneyed happen to a shrink? Now I wanted to know more. Did she marry the guy she had a fling with? How did Joe find out about it? Were they still in touch? Did he still love her? I decided I'd pushed hard enough already today.

"Let's think about the possibilities," said Joe. "It sounds like Erica's mother has some kind of seizure disorder, obviously along with a cholesterol and blood pressure problem."

"Don't forget the Prozac," I added. "What would cause her to be in that uncommunicative drooling state?"

"What comes to my mind is brain damage from a grand mal seizure," said Joe. "Suppose Mrs. J was taking one of the early versions of antidepressant medications—the kind that caused seizures if you overdosed. This could explain everything; she overdosed, she had a massive cardiac reaction, anoxia, seizures, brain damage. The problem is, what does that have to do with Meditron?"

"And Hugh Gladstone," I added.

"Maybe we need to research his job history—see what he actually stood to gain if his drug hits the big time."

"It could be just this simple," I said. "He's shaded the data in some way so the Alzheimer's vaccine can get approved quickly. And then he goes berserk when Erica starts asking questions."

"It's not that easy to pull something over on the FDA. Other people would have picked that up," said Joe. "Unless the whole crowd of them was in on this together. I'll surf around and see what I turn up on Hugh."

I continued to sort through the file folder, setting aside any pages that provided information that might possibly explain Mrs. J's condition. Most of it was either in medical terminology so convoluted, only a trained professional would understand, or else summarized in numerical code.

"If Meditron pays their bonus in stock options," said Joe, "all of them stood to gain a lot if the Alzheimer's drug was a big success. And ditto for the loss."

As he spoke, the door to Erica's apartment opened slowly. I saw only the gleaming metal of the butt of a gun. Without thinking, I plunged into the bedroom closet and pulled the door closed.

Chapter 26

I crouched in the closet. A thin line of light leaked under the door, highlighting the tangle of shoes on Erica's floor. Hiding here had been strictly impulse; I had no idea who was in the apartment. But I'd gotten spooked by the abrupt freeze in Joe's voice. If it turned out to be Rumson after all, I'd step right out and confess to trespassing, all in the name of finding Erica's killer. If it was the killer . . . Much as I hated the idea of leaving Joe out there alone, having two of us in danger would do neither any good. I held my breath and listened.

"Are you here by yourself?" a man demanded.

"Yes." Joe's answer rang out firm and clear.

"Then who were you talking to?"

Joe gave a harsh bark that bore little resemblance to his usual laugh. "I talk myself through things when I'm think-ing. It's the hazard of a profession where you listen to other people most of the time. I don't think well unless—"

"Shut up," said the man.

The voice was extremely familiar, but I couldn't quite place it.

"Why are you here?" I heard him ask.

I felt for my cell phone and pressed the power button in the dark, muffling the cheery "hello" beeps by stuffing the phone in my armpit. Then I held it down to the weak beam of light at the bottom of the door.

Looking for service . . .

Damn, damn, damn. Why in the name of God hadn't I changed that stupid phone carrier? The intruder told Joe to lead the way to the bedroom. They stopped just outside the door. My cell phone beeped again, announcing that a signal had now been located.

"Sounds like you brought a friend." The man strode across the room and flung open the closet door.

"Roger!"

"Get out of there. Both of you—over on the bed." He waved a gun in the air and finally settled on pointing it at Joe.

Meeting Joe's eyes briefly, I scrambled off the floor and onto the bed next to him. He flashed me a small smile of encouragement. Still aiming the gun at Joe's heart, Roger leaned around me and yanked the window shade down. Then he perched on the file cabinet and swung his leg nervously.

"Now what shall I do with the two of you?"

"Let's work something out together here. . . ." Joe spoke with a conciliatory cadence that he must have practiced with his more disturbed clientele.

"Be quiet," Roger snapped.

Lacking the nerve to stare down Roger and his gun, I focused on the second hand of my watch. It marched around the clock face five times while no one said a word. The faint hum of a neighbor's lawnmower broke the silence outside.

"Here's the deal," Roger said with a grin. "It went so well with Erica."

"What went well?" I asked. "She's dead."

"Shut up. I want you both to get undressed and get into bed."

Now I stared at him.

"You're joking," I said.

"Not at all."

"But this is absurd. . . ."

Roger strode across the room and lifted my chin with the butt of his gun until I thought my head might snap off at the base of my neck. "I'm quite serious. After all, you did make an application to an escort service this morning, did you not? I should think stripping would be in your repertoire." I opened my mouth to protest.

"Do what he says," said Joe in a quiet voice. "I'll turn the other way."

"What a gentleman." Roger snickered. He lowered the gun and stepped away.

"What's your connection with City Lights?" I asked, massaging my overstretched neck.

Roger smiled. "Aimee Joy, of course. Didn't they tell you she's my special girl?"

"But the receptionist said it was the middle guy in the picture. We thought it was Hugh. . . ."

"Hugh drops in sometimes, but his taste runs more exotic." His smile evaporated. "Get moving!" He jabbed me hard in the ribs.

I turned away from both of the men and slowly drew my polo shirt over my head. Then I unbuckled my belt and dropped my shorts to the floor. The change and keys in Joe's pockets jingled as his pants fell, too.

"Everything off," said Roger. "And then get in bed."

I shucked off my bra and underpants, leaped into the bed, and pulled the sheet up to my neck. The stale aroma of Erica's perfume wafted up from the bedclothes. Then

Joe slid in beside me, bringing his own scent of sweat and mint. The totally bizarre thought crossed my mind that I had not shaved my legs this morning. And in the sharp terror of the moment, all the hair follicles on my body bristled like angry dog hackles. I inched toward the wall, attempting to avoid skin-to-skin contact with Joe—difficult in these cramped quarters.

I recognized that it wasn't just terror making me squirm for space. It was damn disconcerting to be abruptly in bed naked with a man I'd had an underground crush on for months—hard not to feel both curious and aroused.

"Let's talk about a compromise here," Joe said. "I'm sure you don't want anyone to get hurt."

From his calm tone of voice, I assumed that his thought processes were miles away from mine. But then a noticeable tenting of the sheet in his midsection area told me different.

"Yes, yes," Roger grinned. "Too many people dead already and so on. Weren't the antidepressants perfect? I knew Erica was taking them—everyone on the team was well aware of just how close she was to flipping out. With the exception of Hugh, who has his head too far up his ass to observe anything."

"Why not just shoot her?"

Roger grimaced. "The cops would have been crawling up all our butts. This was a flawless way to kill her—deadly, yet at the same time, it would appear to be death by her own hand."

"One thing I don't get," I squeaked, stalling for time. "What did Aimee Joy have to do with it?"

"Her job was to make sure Erica came back to the room alone," said Roger.

"What if she didn't fall for Aimee's routine?"

"She was a sap," Roger sneered. "I knew she'd go for it. You, on the other hand," he pointed the gun at me, "are not one to get involved."

"What do you mean? I gave you a golf lesson on my own time . . ."

"How did you get Aimee to go along with it?" Joe asked, patting my hand under the sheet.

Roger's grin grew wider. "Neuroxytin, of course. Once she was hooked, she'd do anything for it. *Anything.*"

The guy made me sick. Sick enough to almost upchuck right there in bed with Joe.

"Neuroxytin," said Joe. "You had access to it?"

"There are ways," said Roger, his voice smug. "I do work for Meditron."

"Opiate pain killers showed up in Erica's autopsy results," Joe said. "Did she have some kind of a pain disorder in addition to the depression?"

"The only pain she had was in her head and my ass. I thought it was a nice touch to have her swallow some Neuroxytin too. Crazy bitch."

"How did you make her do it?" Joe asked.

He waved the gun and smiled. "I held this on her while she swallowed the Valium, the Neuroxytin, and the antidepressants. Then the scotch went down easy. Look at it this way; at least she finished her life happy. She certainly made herself and everyone else miserable the last year she was alive."

"I still don't understand why she agreed to take the pills," I said.

"I mentioned Lila Rose."

"Well I wouldn't go along with it. I'd die first." That was pure bravado and all three of us knew it.

Roger came over to the bed and forced my neck into a second painful stretch with the butt of the gun. "We'll see about that." He stepped toward the small bathroom connected to the bedroom, then turned back and brandished the gun. "Stay where you are. I would hate to have to shoot one of you for doing something stupid."

We saw him begin to root through Erica's medicine cabinet, humming softly.

Joe gripped my hand and squeezed it. "We'll be okay."

I didn't see how we'd be okay. We were buck naked and trapped by a crazy but very smart killer who seemed to relish planning our bizarre deaths in great detail.

"Get out!" I whispered to Joe, shoving him hard. We leaped from the bed, clutching the sheet between us, and bolted toward the door.

Roger rushed back into the bedroom. "What the hell? I told you to stay where you were! Get the hell back over there."

I wrenched the sheet away from Joe and crawled into Erica's bed again.

"This is ridiculous," said Joe. He slid in next to me and pulled a corner of the sheet over his lower body. "You could get away with this looking like suicide once, but not two times."

Roger laughed. "I have a nice variation planned for you. The two lovers so carried away by getting high and getting laid that they forget to turn off the stove and blow themselves sky high to the heavens. Like it?"

"I won't cooperate—" Joe began.

"Then I'll shoot your girlfriend."

From the look of his shaking white lips, we both knew he meant it.

"As I was starting to say," Roger continued, "Erica had a very full stock of Ambien and Valium. Do you have a preference, Dr. Lancaster?" He cocked his head and winked at me. "Professional courtesy," he said in a stage whisper.

"Why did you kill her?" I asked.

"Your doctor friend came close to guessing," he said, gesturing at Joe with the gun. "She'd already ruined my financial future once. It was not going to happen a second time." He tapped a handful of small white pills out into his palm.

Just then someone knocked on the apartment door. "Hello! Anyone here?" called a muffled female voice.

Roger cursed. "I'm going to stand behind the closet door, ready to shoot. You get rid of your guest, or all three of you die. Understand?"

We understood.

We heard the front door creak open and the light tapping of footsteps in the vestibule.

"Hello?" Rebecca Butterman called out. Not her again. I didn't know whether I felt more embarrassed or disappointed. Detective Rumson fully armed and trained, with backup, would definitely have been my first choice. If only I'd allowed Joe to phone her. . . .

"Answer her," Roger whispered from the closet. "Tell her she's got you at a bad time. You'll call her later."

"It's kind of a bad time for me," Joe called. "Listen, I'll give you a buzz later and explain everything." His voice veered into an anguished crack.

The tip-tap of Dr. Butterman's high heels proceeded down the hallway until she stopped at the bedroom door. As soon as she saw us, her mouth began to work open and shut like a bewildered goldfish.

"I'll be able to explain everything," Joe stammered.

"It's not what you think," I said at the same time.

Her eyes traveled across the wood floor where our clothes lay scattered: Joe's chinos, polo shirt, and boxers with dancing golf balls on them. And then my underwear, crowning the top of the heap. She looked back up at the two of us huddled in the bed, her face a mask of disappointment and betrayal. I pulled Erica's sheet higher around my chin. If this was how it felt to be caught cheating, I'd learned a preemptive lesson.

"I can explain—" Joe began a second time.

"You don't owe me an explanation," Rebecca said

primly. "You are certainly free to sleep with whomever you choose. I think it's inappropriate, here in a deceased woman's bed. But to each his own. Please don't bother to show me to the door. I'm sorry to have disturbed you." She looked directly into Joe's troubled eyes. "And you needn't bother about picking me up this evening either. Have a pleasant afternoon. It looks like you have every intention of it." She turned sharply and strode down the hall. The door slammed behind her.

Roger eased out from behind the closet door, smirking, still pointing the gun at my head. "Sorry to have ruined your dinner plans," he said to Joe. "Both of you—hold out your hands." He emptied the contents of two large plastic pharmaceutical vials into our palms. He moved several of the pills from my hand to Joe's.

"He's bigger than you," Roger explained. "He'll need a few more to do the job."

"Could I have a glass of water?" I asked. "I'm sorry. I can't take pills dry. I get this choking thing. . . ." I tried to make my voice sound terrified and apologetic. The terrified part was easy.

Roger hesitated, then frowned. "And I suppose you'll just lie there nice and obedient while I get you a drink? No way. Do the best you can." His mood had definitely taken a turn toward sour. "Get busy."

As Roger paced back and forth across the small room, I managed to dump all of the pills except two into the bed between me and Joe. I could imagine worse deaths than Valium overdose while snuggled up to an attractive naked man. On the other hand, I did not want to die at all. I hoped we could con Roger into believing we'd taken the drugs and then think up some way out.

Clutching the sheet around my chest, I made a great show of dumping the handful of pills into my mouth and swallowing. I diverted one of them to the side of my mouth; the other slid down my throat. As I lay back down,

I thought I noticed a flash of movement on the fire escape in the gap Roger had left between the windowsill and the shade. I looked again. A large black crow flapped away from the metal railing.

"Tell us what happened to Mrs. Jorganson," said Joe.

"You want a bedtime story? This is a good one," said Roger. "I need to stay anyway until I'm sure you two are quite comfortable. Then I turn on the gas stove and say bye-bye."

"Two lovers lose their lives together," Joe repeated.

Roger nodded. "A tragic drug-related accident. The gas seals the job tight."

This seemed like an elaborate plan for killing people when he had a gun right in his hand, but I certainly wasn't going to point that out. He'd settled back into Erica's armchair, with the gun pointed at Joe's chest. I could feel the small lumps of our discarded pills under my left buttock and hear a lawnmower sputtering and clanking in the yard down the street.

"I worked for the Panther Corporation in Houston twenty years ago," said Roger. "A good friend was a bench scientist at Daytonix. He'd developed a new antidepressant with excellent action and fewer side effects than what had been available. Dr. Lancaster, you would be familiar with the difficulties we had with those early iterations."

Joe nodded. "Weight gain, risk of overdose, dry mouth, sexual dysfunction . . . the list was long."

"Exactly. My friend asked me to help with analyzing the data," Roger continued. "Once he showed me the numbers, I invested everything I had in the company's stock options."

"You would stand to make a lot of money on that investment," said Joe. "Coming in on the ground floor. What went wrong?"

Roger's voice hardened. "Erica's mother was one of the

patients in the first wave of clinical trials. A fucking loo-
ney tune. They never should have allowed her into the
study. That stupid bitch swallowed her entire stock of the
new drug. This wasn't the only time she'd tried to kill
herself, but on this occasion she took enough of the drug
to cause seizures and brain damage. What a loser. She
couldn't even kill herself successfully."

"Did you know Erica then?"

"No. I'd never heard of her. Naturally, her complaint
to the FDA was in confidence. And she dogged them until
she'd torpedoed the entire project." He scowled. "I lost
everything, filed for bankruptcy, left Texas."

"How did you both end up at Meditron?" asked Joe.

The Valium I'd swallowed accidentally had begun to
take effect. I snuggled closer to Joe, feeling sleepy, relaxed, and a little bit high.

"Unhappy coincidence," Roger growled. "It was only
recently that I realized who she was and what she'd done.
We were never assigned to the same project until we came
together on Gladstone's team. She told me about her
mother when we were waiting for a teleconference a couple weeks ago."

"You must have been stunned," said Joe, "realizing she
was the whistle-blower."

Roger's face twisted with rage. "I couldn't fucking believe it when she started making noise about our vaccine."

"You couldn't allow her to ruin things for you a second
time."

"We weren't allowed to cash in our stock options for
another year. Once we got the damn drug on the market,
I was certain the data would hold up at least that long
before problems surfaced. You met my wife," he said to
me. "Do you think for one moment she would understand
that we had to sell our home and cancel our vacations and
the country club membership and pull the kid out of private school? Not to mention seven years of work down

the toilet. Plus my promotion. Plus the bonus." Every visible muscle in Roger's body tightened as he spelled out his predicted losses.

My lips felt thick and fuzzy, and the Valium had dulled the edge of fear. Even so, I knew we needed to keep him talking. "I see your point. Beverly spends a lot of time at the country club. And your son, too."

Roger smiled. "Erica carried on as though she was the only parent in the world who had a child that mattered. Lila Rose this, Lila Rose that . . . did she think for one moment what she might be doing to someone else's child?"

"What was wrong with the vaccine?"

"Nothing, goddammit! That's what I've been trying to tell her for months. The whole team told her that. There is no short-term problem with the drug." As he stood up and shouted this last sentence, I glimpsed another flash of movement on the fire escape. Then came the blast of a gunshot. I screamed and pulled the sheet over my head. Had Roger shot Joe? I didn't feel a thing.

I peeked out from under the cover. Roger clutched his right arm, moaning, a flood of red spreading across the front of his white shirt. From the window and the door, the room filled with armed figures, some in police uniform, others in black SWAT clothing. Three of them wrestled Roger to the floor, handcuffed him, and dragged him down the hallway.

Then Detective Rumson appeared at the side of Erica's bed and stood looking at us in silence.

"I'm practically speechless," she said. "Suppose you two get dressed, and then we'll have a long chat."

"I could use a cup of coffee while you're waiting," I said. "I'm feeling a little woozy from the Valium I swallowed."

Detective Rumson's jaw worked furiously. She turned and marched out of the room.

Chapter 27

Rebecca Butterman joined us for the forty-five minutes we spent around Erica's kitchen table answering the detective's questions. She explained that she had called the cops after finding us in bed. Her effort had been duplicated by Erica's nosy and crotchety downstairs neighbor.

"Something seemed really wrong," Rebecca said. "I couldn't quite put my finger on it."

Joe placed his hand over hers and smiled. "You expected us to behave with a little more dignity than what you thought you saw here."

I nudged the conversation away from our humiliation à deux. "We suspected a lot of people of murdering Erica," I told the two women, "but in the end, we were pretty sure Hugh was the killer."

"The girl at City Lights identified him in the pro-am

photograph," Joe explained. "We didn't realize Roger frequented the place, too."

"You don't think Hugh was in on this with Roger?" I asked.

Detective Rumson set her mug down hard, splashing some coffee over the rim. "We've brought them all into the station for questioning this afternoon. Right now, it seems pretty clear that he was working alone."

"The strangest thing of all," said Rebecca, "is that there doesn't seem to be a real problem with the Meditron vaccine. I believe Erica was overreacting based on her past history with her mother."

"We talked to Mr. LeBoutillier this morning, too," said Detective Rumson. "After Mrs. Jorganson overdosed, he says Erica decided to find a job in the drug industry where she could watch for similar kinds of problems and cut them off before other people got hurt."

"In this case, her fervor blinded her to the truth," said Rebecca. "I wish I'd had longer to work with her. Maybe we could have sorted some of this out before it turned tragic."

And I wished she'd spilled her brilliant hypotheses about Erica earlier. She could have saved us all a lot of embarrassment.

"So if there wasn't a real problem, the Meditron men had reason to be furious with her," said Joe.

"But not to kill her." After two cups of Detective Rumson's strong, black coffee, I had begun to feel more like myself. "Roger was concerned that his stock options couldn't be cashed in for a year. Why?"

"There's still work to do," said the detective. "For us!" she added quickly, frowning at me. "It's possible that both Erica and Roger saw something in the numbers that suggested problems with the drug would surface when it was used over a longer period of time. Sometimes side effects don't appear until long after the FDA approves use in the general population."

"Which would explain the focus of her adverse events file," I said.

"Who trapped Cassie in the freezer?" Joe asked.

"I suspect Roger Ranz will be confessing to that incident as well," said Detective Rumson. "Again, there is the obvious connection to the City Lights girl."

"So Aimee was lurking out in the hallway at the party to act as a decoy for me?" It seemed like a ridiculous plan. "What if I hadn't gone to the ladies' room? What if I hadn't gone alone?"

The detective shrugged. "He would have found you alone another time."

"But why did he want to kill Cassie?" asked Rebecca.

I stifled a laugh. I was willing to bet she'd had some homicidal feelings when she caught me in bed with Joe.

"I'm not sure Roger meant to kill her," answered Detective Rumson. "Just scare her away from snooping." She flashed me a thin smile.

"What about Lucia Jimenez?" Joe asked.

The detective nodded. "That's Roger, too."

"Why go to all that trouble to make Erica's death look like a suicide, then just shoot Lucia?" I asked.

"Maybe he figured no one would pay much attention to the shooting of a Hispanic casino worker," said Rebecca.

"Why kill her at all?" I asked, looking at the detective. I wanted to hear from the professional, not more of Butterman's bogus theories.

"Roger was afraid Lucia had all the puzzle pieces. She took care of Erica's mother and she had heard her story. She'd seen Roger and Aimee Joy together in the elevator at Caesar's the night Erica died. Sooner or later, she would put all the pieces together."

She looked hard at me. "I'm not blaming you for the

murder, but he knew you were nosing around, pressing Lucia for information."

I could tell she hadn't forgiven me for meddling. And I felt ill about the possibility of being responsible for Lucia's death.

"He would have been worried about her, whether you were in the picture or not," said Rebecca.

Suddenly, hearing her theories didn't seem so bad.

While I waited to board my flight, I called Laura on my cell phone.

"How'd we end up?" she asked.

"Not bad. Tied for fifty-third and pocketed three bills and change. I'll cut you a check tomorrow."

"Hot damn!"

Then I filled her in on the rest of the day's events. "Erica's husband, Pierre, introduced her coworkers to the pleasures of his favorite escort service. And Roger introduced Aimee Joy to Neuroxytin. After that, she was willing to do whatever he told her." I described what had unfolded in Erica's apartment.

"So let me get this straight: you're lying in this bed in your underwear with Joe Lancaster when Rebecca Butterman bursts in?"

I would have been incredulous, too. "Not in my underwear," I corrected. "Stark bare naked. Both of us."

Several of the passengers seated around me turned to listen.

"So how does he look in the buff?"

"He's got a nice butt," I admitted. More heads swiveled.

"Is the other equipment up to standard?"

I laughed, a little smug. "All the parts appear to be in good working order."

"What the hell did Butterman say when she caught you?"

I lowered my voice to a whisper. "She walked off in a huff. Something about how inappropriate it was to boink in a dead woman's bed." We collapsed with laughter. "Later she told us she called Detective Rumson because something in our expressions didn't look right. Besides, she said she couldn't picture the two of us in bed together. The chemistry's all wrong."

"And she calls herself a shrink?" The incredulous voice was back. "You two have been dancing around the two-headed beast since the moment you first complained to him about Mike's putting."

"You're exaggerating, as usual," I said. "They have a dinner date tonight, as a matter of fact."

"And you're just going to let her snatch him away?"

"I have other plans. Mike asked me to go out with him this weekend in Ohio. I said sure."

After a long pause: "I'm speechless."

I laughed. "There's quite a bit of that going around."